FULL CIRCLE

A DEACON / HYTHE ACTION THRILLER

MIKE BOSHIER

This novel is a work of fiction. Names, characters, places and incidents either are the product of the author's imagination or are used fictitiously. Any resemblance to actual events, locales, organisations, or persons living or dead is entirely coincidental.

ISBN: 978-1-99-118111-4 Softcover POD
ISBN: 978-1-99-118110-7 Kindle

www.mikeboshier.com

Author's Other Books

High Seas Hijack - Short Story

The Jaws of Revenge

Terror of the Innocent

Crossing a Line

The Price of Deceit

Red Ice

The Project

Acknowledgements

To my wife and daughters who support me in my dreams, and thank you to Sandra for her continuing support.

If you liked reading this book, please leave feedback.

Check out the rear pages of this book for details of other releases, information and free stuff.

EUROPE

1

New Forest, UK.

BUILT in the 1820s by a wealthy Southampton shipping magnate, Rocklands Country House contained over thirty bedrooms, multiple reception rooms, and the privacy that comes from being set in 135 acres of a walled and gated garden near the edge of the sparsely-populated New Forest National Park. It wasn't the first time the house had been used as a party venue, and it wouldn't be the last. It was perfect.

The New Forest National Park lies within the county of Hampshire, on the south-central coast of England. Covering approximately 150 square miles in size, it was once a royal hunting ground for King William I and his noblemen in the 12th century AD. It is a sparsely populated, peaceful area where animals, including the famous New Forest ponies, roam freely.

With a mile-long winding driveway from the cast-iron gates and protected by abundant trees and bushes, the house and grounds offer isolation and seclusion. Now owned by a Cayman Islands investment company, anyone with a large enough wallet could rent it for weddings, the weekend, or longer. With guards patrolling the grounds and screening arrivals, today's long weekend rental was for a private party - a very private party.

BMWs, Mercedes, Audis, Daimlers and Bentleys, various sports cars, and at least two Rollers adorned the parking area. Many had chauffeurs sitting waiting, but a few were owner-driven.

The house itself had been updated and modernized. Most bedrooms were now ensuite and centrally-heated, windows were double-glazed, and the walls of each room were thick enough to offer a high level of sound deadening except in exceptional circumstances. The décor and furniture were in keeping with the property's age and style, and the patterned wallpaper and heavy curtains had easily hidden miniature cameras.

All invited guests were wearing facemasks. Not the medical type for protection from viruses or germs, but Venetian style to maintain anonymity. The female drinks servers wore simple eye masks, small black dresses, and high heels. The vast majority of the guests were males in their thirties or older. Various stunning young women in the 18 to 25 age range were lounging around drinking. These were working girls mainly from Eastern Europe, and their attendance was in part payment of the enormous debts they had incurred in illegally getting to the UK. Any male guest could choose any woman for sex and head to one of the many bedrooms on the first floor. Larger groups together were optional.

The second floor was even more extreme for those enjoying sadistic pleasures with younger partners. The invited guests could visit either level according to their preferences.

Then the one thing the organizers had not allowed for happened. One elderly male on the second floor had taken a hallucinogen along with Viagra for a performance boost. With his blood pressure raised to a dangerous level and already suffering from high cholesterol, his physical exertions caused a large lump of plaque to come loose from deep inside an artery. Within seconds it had traveled partway around his body before coming lodged, blocking the return flow of blood to his heart. With a crushing pain in his chest and shoulders, he cried out as he reared backward and fell from the bed. Luckily for him, the person in the basement watching and recording the multiple video feeds recognized his emergency and raised the alarm. A petite woman, attractive with mousy brown hair, seemed to be in charge. Cursing in a foreign language, she confirmed the patient had suffered a massive heart attack after a quick initial inspection. The emergency services were called, and an ambulance was dispatched.

First responder paramedics Peter Newman and Ranvir Khan were expecting a busy night. Nowadays, most Saturday evenings are busy, especially at bar closing time in town centers. Young people drinking too much and passing out were common, along with drink-induced fights, but it was still too early tonight, so they responded when the call came in. The address of the heart attack patient was a good fifteen minutes' drive away, across parts of the New Forest with its narrow roads, but Peter was an experienced driver, and with the blue light flashing, they made quick time.

The fifteen-minute delay gave the party organizers enough time to make some rapid changes. Certain things had been tidied away, and the masked male guests and available women moved away from the entrance hall and stairway into a couple of reception rooms. The gate guards were also alerted, quickly waving the ambulance through as it arrived. A male organizer wearing a tuxedo, his face illuminated by the pulsing blue light, directed the two first responders up the main staircase to the second floor.

Weighed down with bags, rucksacks of medical gear, and a portable defibrillator, the two hurried up the stairs. The patient, a male appearing to be in his mid-seventies, was lying on the carpet on the second-floor balcony. The mousy-haired woman was standing nearby. When asked how long ago the patient had collapsed, she muttered a mumbled reply of 'Not long' before moving away. Slightly surprised, Ranvir carried on and checked for vital signs, listening to his weak pulse while checking for any bleeding. At the same time, Peter unbuttoned the patient's shirt and connected the electrodes. After an injection of Perindopril, an ACE inhibitor to stabilize the patient and improve blood flow by opening the arteries, the two carefully moved the victim onto the stretcher. A door swung partly open as they began to carry the patient toward the stairs. Ranvir glanced inside the room before the door was slammed shut. Peter saw the surprised expression on his face, but before he could say anything, his colleague looked straight into his eyes and shook his head slightly. Neither saw the guy in the tuxedo watching them closely. Neither saw him speak briefly with the woman nor pull a cell phone from his pocket as he walked away.

As soon as the stretcher was secured within the ambulance, Ranvir shut the rear door and shouted to get going. Slightly slower now, Peter drove back down the long drive before reaching the gate. The cast-iron gates were swung open as they approached and were waved through.

With Peter driving to Salisbury District Hospital and Ranvir in the back looking after the patient, Peter had to shout through the sliding opening to the rear.

'What the fuck was all that about?' he said. 'Despatch said it was a party and there were loads of cars, but where was everyone? There was no music. Nothing. Just those two who were acting strange.'

'We need to make a police report when we get to A&E,' Ranvir shouted before telling Peter what he'd seen.

Although he'd been given medication and was connected to an automatic defibrillator, the patient's condition quickly worsened.

Giving him an additional injection, Ranvir shouted, 'Pete, as quick as we can. He's coding.'

Already exceeding the regulatory 40 mph New Forest speed limit, Peter accelerated, and they hurtled along at close to 70 mph. As they rounded one sharp corner by a junction, a large, heavily built SUV came out of the side road and slammed into their rear side. The impact spun the ambulance off the main track and toward a ditch. Struggling to maintain control and braking hard helped a little, but the banks were wet mud following three days of rain, and the tires wouldn't grip. At fifty-five miles an hour, the ambulance crashed headfirst into a four-foot-wide solid trunk of an ancient English oak.

Peter Newman suffered severe leg damage, six broken ribs, a collapsed lung, a broken wrist, and multiple cuts and bruises. But he survived. In the rear, the unrestrained patient and paramedic were catapulted into the metal wall separating the driving cab and the medical area. Both died on impact.

The mousy brown-haired woman's phone bleeped as it received a message. Smiling as she read the text, she dialed a number and spoke briefly.

2

Six days later.

THE Solent Times, a local newspaper for the south coast of Britain, reported the body of a dark-skinned young boy aged about eight years old, hauled up in the nets of fishermen trawling just off the Needles of the Isle of Wight. Within hours the national media had picked up on it, and for two days, the story became the third or fourth headline item. Eventually, the government announced it believed it to be the body of an African immigrant fallen overboard from an illegal crossing between Calais and Dover. They confirmed the Hampshire Constabulary would continue to attempt to identify the body. There had been no reports of a missing child, and until that occurred, it would be cataloged as an accidental drowning at sea. However, anybody with information should contact Hampshire Constabulary or their nearest police station.

The following morning the Home Secretary called in Sir Rupert Wainwright, a senior member of the UK Civil Service.

'Sir Rupert, the PM's getting a lot of flak from the media over this young boy's body, as am I. He, in turn, is putting extra pressure on me. I need you to do something about it.'

'What would you have me do, Home Secretary? Ask the immigrants to stop crossing?'

'Don't be flippant, Wainwright; it doesn't become you.'

'Be that as it may, Home Secretary, but more boat people arrive daily, particularly from the Middle Eastern war zones - Syria, Iraq, Afghanistan, Yemen. The public is very anti-immigration of illegals, and they don't trust this government to get anything done about it. There's lots of flak about it in the newspapers weekly, with channel crossing numbers rising almost daily. They expected Brexit to curb this, but it has been worse than ever this last year.'

'You don't have to tell me, Wainwright; I already bloody know. Everything I try gets shot down by lawyers or damned do-gooders. Since Brexit, I can't even send them back to France because the EU's 'Dublin' arrangement is no longer valid.'

'I understand and sympathize Home Secretary, I really do, but this government did sell Brexit to the masses on the idea it would restore sovereignty and independence to the United Kingdom, didn't it?'

'Hmmph. You were obviously a remainer. Anyway, that's water under the bridge. The Prime Minister needs some wins; I need some wins. I need something tangible done quickly, something we can sell to the media. God help us all if we get another terrorist attack, and it can be attributed to an illegal or bunch of them.'

'The way I see it, Home Secretary, is there are two issues here. One, the movement of immigrants wanting to come here is being organized and managed on a commercial scale. These *people traffickers,* for want of a better expression, are doing everything they can to land illegals here on the beaches of Kent, knowing they can then claim asylum and, even if rejected, rarely, if ever, get sent back. And they're making a lot of money in doing this.'

Seeing the HS nod impatiently, Wainwright continued, 'And two, we are only intercepting a small proportion of them. Those we do stop initially get questioned before being moved elsewhere for processing, but how many of them bid us harm, we don't know. And then there are those that slip past us and those we don't even know about. And we could be talking hundreds or even possibly thousands.'

'Yes, yes, I know all this. Get on with it,' she hissed.

'I believe we need to identify and stop the traffickers first, which will reduce the overall number of immigrants trying and succeeding to cross. At the same time, we should heavily strengthen Border Force to intercept and detain anyone crossing into the UK.'

'I'm not a fool. I know all this. I've been trying to do this, but the lawyers keep interfering. You are just wasting my time.'

'Forgive me, Home Secretary, if I may continue? We need to reconsider how we stop these traffickers. Instead of waiting until the immigrants are in Calais waiting to cross and expecting France to assist, we need to discover and arrest those organizing their transport across Europe. As these will be based somewhere in Europe, we should send a team to investigate and liaise with Europol. At the end of the day, Home Secretary, it will be up to Europol to arrest these traffickers. Since Brexit, we have no jurisdiction over there now. But remove the traffickers, and the number trying to cross at Calais will drop drastically.'

After thinking for a couple of moments, the Home Secretary instructed, 'Alright, arrange it.'

3

Two months later.
ADAM Paisley was almost thirty years old, average looking, and being a Walter Mitty type of person, considered himself a player. He was also a bully. In 2013, aged nineteen and having failed the entrance exam to join the Metropolitan Police Force, he chose to join as a police community support officer or PCSO.

PCSOs are not attested constables and therefore do not have the same powers of arrest. However, their limited powers do allow them to make a citizen's arrest. This means they are able to arrest anyone without a warrant providing there are reasonable grounds to suspect they are committing or have committed a crime.

The uniform, equipment, and title allowed him to strut around bullying people and demanding a level of respect for the role required. Unfortunately, the general public soon realized that PCSOs had little real power and quickly lost confidence in many of them, often nicknaming them *little Hitlers.*

As his influence and ability to impress diminished, and he became the butt of locals' jokes, Paisley again tried the entrance exam to become a full police constable. Failing again, he chose instead to join Her Majesty's Customs and Excise as an investigation officer. This role suited him perfectly, and he progressed well, allowing him to exert semi-bullying tactics on individuals and small companies to ensure the full customs and excise duties were paid.

He felt he had finally made it when the opportunity had been presented to him. *'Head over to France with a full expense account. Find and follow some of the trucks and vans used for smuggling. Follow them back to their operating base, wherever it may be, and report back on the smuggling ring. Don't put yourself in danger; just keep a low profile, monitor, and report back.'* HMCE saw him as an investigation officer. Sadly, Adam Paisley now saw himself as his film hero, James Bond. Instead of blending in by renting a European non-descript dark-colored saloon car in France, he drove his UK-registered vivid-red Mazda MX-5 Miata - a soft-top two-seater with a powerful two-liter engine. Initially basing himself in Calais, he toured around the area, watching and photographing arriving vehicles large enough to carry would-be immigrants. Over three weeks, he'd found at least a dozen regular vans and trucks, some with German license plates or even some with Turkish registration. In his best James Bond manner, he'd also visited a couple of the immigrant camps on the outskirts of Calais and tried to obtain information as to where they had boarded.

Unfortunately, he'd soon discovered that real life didn't emulate his film hero. The first time he sought information, he was chased off the site. The second time, at a different camp, he was threatened with a knife, beaten, and robbed of his watch and cash, narrowly escaping being stabbed.

Unperturbed, he changed tactics and decided to follow one of the identified vehicles to its base the next time it arrived at Calais. Not wanting to get too close, he followed at a distance, losing the first one in heavy traffic before reaching Reims. Trying a second time the following afternoon with a different van, he succeeded as far as Metz, but a traffic accident closed the road, and he lost sight of the target vehicle when all traffic was diverted. The twelfth attempt three weeks later was more successful. Keeping just four car lengths behind the small van, he managed to keep it constantly in sight. Outside the amusingly named village of Boucheporn were a service rest area and a self-service restaurant. Parking just a hundred yards away from his target, Adam Paisley watched the driver climb out and head toward the restrooms. When the driver reappeared, ordered a coffee and food, and sat down at an empty table, Paisley grabbed a drink, sat at the same table, and tried to make small talk.

'You follow me,' the driver said in broken English. 'You drive girlie car. Red girlie car. You girlie boy?' he continued before turning slightly on his chair and staring Paisley down.

Realizing yet again he was out of his depth, Paisley stuttered, 'What? No. No, I'm not a girlie boy.'

'You wanna fucky fuck me, girlie boy?'

'Look! No, I'm not a girlie boy, and I don't want to fuc--. Look, I was just making conversation.'

'You drive red girlie car. You follow me.'

Getting more and more exasperated, Paisley grabbed a wad of money out of his jacket, put it down on the table, and said, 'I want information,' trying to keep his voice low.

'Information, huh? No fuck fuck?'

'Correct. Just information. My name's Adam. What's your name?'

'Why you want to know?'

'You are smuggling people to Calais to get to the UK. I've seen you. What you are doing is illegal.'

Pulling out a small flick knife, Petr pressed the button opening the blade, and said, 'Fuck off, girlie boy,' before picking up his plate and drink and moving to another table.

Adam moved closer but kept far enough away to be outside the blade's reach. 'I'm a reporter working on a story.'

'You police?'

'No, I said I'm a reporter. I'm from the UK, and I'm writing a story about illegal people smuggling.'

'No, not illegal. I bring people in Europe. Not smuggle. Not illegal. Me just driver,' he said, nervously looking around.

'Look, my people will pay you lots of money. Many euros, yes? You tell me everything, yes? Here is €100. You tell me everything, and I will give you €5,000,' he said, slipping two 50 Euro notes across the table.

Taking a mouthful of food, he thought for a moment or two before whispering. 'You not police?'

'No, I not police!'

'You not police, you not girlie boy, you not want fucky me?'

'No, I not police. I not girlie boy, and I don't want fucky you. My name is Adam, and I'm a reporter. If you don't want my money, I'll find someone else who does. There's enough of you drivers smuggling ...' Adam said, trying not to get angry and taking a swig from his drink and waiting.

The driver carried on eating his lunch slowly, deep in thought. Finally, just when Adam was about to stand and leave, he answered in barely a whisper, 'Ten thousand. I tell for ten thousand. For ten thousand, I go home. But not tell here. In Munich. Give me phone number.'

'What's your name?'

Almost reluctantly, he answered, 'Petr Doležal.'

After receiving Adam's cell number Petr continued more urgently, 'I call two weeks. You bring money, I talk. OK? Now you go.'

'I'll give you another €200 now if you give me something I can use,' Adam said, slipping another four notes onto the table.

'Like what?'

'The name of the person running this.'

'No. That for ten thousand. But I give you address,' he said and quickly scribbled something down on a scrap of paper before picking up the cash. 'Now go.'

Smiling, Adam stood and clasped him on the shoulder before heading back out to his red girlie car. Heading back to his hotel in Calais, he typed up a brief report and emailed it to London. The following morning he checked out. He arrived in Munich, located a suitable 4-star hotel, and booked an executive room for three weeks.

Assuming his work was almost completed, Adam spent the next days as a tourist enjoying the sights and sounds of the surrounding area. On the eighth day, he was driving back from Neuschwanstein Castle, often known as Bavaria's 'Cinderella castle,' when his phone rang. He answered to a frantic Petr Doležal on the line.

'I am found out. They after me. I run. Deal off,' he shouted down the line in broken English.

'What? Who found out? Where are you going?'

But all Paisley had in return was the silence of a disconnected call.

Cursing and realizing he would have to start entirely again, he drove the rest of the way back to Munich in silence.

4

PETR Doležal cursed as he over-revved the engine. At fifty-eight, he'd been working for Major Govorov for four years, driving vans and trucks between Turkey and the Channel ports. He knew the cargo was illegal immigrants wanting to reach Britain. It was their choice, and he was fine with that. He'd been paid well, but everything had changed in the last few months.

First, the Albanians and the Serbians had muscled in, wanting a piece of the action. Waiting at Calais, they had started intimidating him and his fellow drivers. One had been stabbed to death when he argued back.

Then Petr had been promoted to drive container trucks to Zeebrugge. Some trips were ok, containing men willing to pay more for a direct service to get to the UK. Others held women aged fourteen to thirty who were already heavily in debt. The worst had been lone children, some as young as four. Petr had been instructed to give them drinks laced with ketamine to make them sleep the entire trip. No one would tell him what happened to the kids when they arrived in the UK, and he wasn't happy.

Married for almost thirty-seven years to the love of his life, Marena was one of the prettiest girls he'd ever met and could still turn an eye as she walked down the street. They had two grown-up children, a son, and a daughter, with the daughter soon to be married and already hinting at the possibility of grandchildren in the near future. Marena and his children still lived in Prague, his hometown, but Petr rented a single room near Munich. He was a private man and never discussed his family even though he missed them terribly.

At a recent medical, he'd had a chest x-ray. Tumors. On his lungs. A year - eighteen months at the most he'd been given. He'd been a heavy smoker since childhood, so it wasn't much of a surprise. He hadn't built up the courage to tell Marena the truth, only he'd had enough living away and wanted to spend their retirement together. But that was easier said than done. Govorov had told him when he joined it was a job for life. One of the guards at Govorov's headquarters in Austria had chosen to leave to get married. His body was found days later, naked and tied to a tree. His mouth was gagged, and his stomach had been slashed open. Not enough to kill him outright, but the smell of blood had attracted either wolves or wild boars. All the soft organs of his stomach had been eaten, with many of his ribs gnawed.

Petr had no proof, but the strong rumor was a certain mousy brown-haired woman who answered to the name of Svetlana had been involved. Even the mention of her name among his colleagues and fellow drivers brought shivers to their spines. It was clear what Govorov had meant when he called it a job for life.

Excited at the thought of his move back to Prague, Marena had arranged a new job for him. It would be lower pay, but tips, a 5-day working week, and home every evening. He also wouldn't need to rent a room in Munich. He would be driving a tourist bus around the city.

Then his luck had changed for the better. This Englishman, Adam Paisley, had approached him at a restaurant in a small village. Initially nervous in case it was a trap and someone merely trying to muscle into the organization, Petr couldn't believe his luck. Had the approach been made by an Albanian or Serb, he would likely be dead by now. But Paisley was the epitome of an Englishman portrayed on television. He seemed to think he was like James Bond; in practice, Petr thought, he was more like Johnny English, especially with his bright red sports car.

After checking that this Englishman was serious, Petr decided on a payment that would help him disappear. For €10,000, he could arrange to 'die' in an accident and escape Govorov's clutches. Marena would be overjoyed to have him home again, and the money would certainly help toward the cost of the forthcoming wedding.

A week later, everything changed. A friend in headquarters called him, telling him he was no longer on the following month's work schedule and asking why. The friend continued, saying he'd overheard Govorov and Svetlana talking about him, with Govorov instructing her to get rid of him and her replying that it was all in hand.

Realizing the game was up, Petr grabbed what clothes he could, leaped into his car, and raced away while calling Paisley.

5

THE ice-cold beer chilled his throat. Germany was famous for its strong brews, particularly Munich for its two-week annual Oktoberfest. Although it was only February, the beer was good whenever. He was on his second or third - he'd lost track of which - when the good-looking blonde smiled at him. Slim and shapely, she was his sort of woman. A few more drinks, and Paisley was hooked. His imagination of James Bond played in his mind, and he acted as the player he wished he was. He was more than excited when she suggested they return to his hotel. Although over the limit, he insisted on driving his Mazda parked outside. They walked hand in hand to the elevators at the hotel, kissing passionately as the doors closed.

Highly aroused, he couldn't wait to get her to his room. Inside they kissed again as soon as he had shut and locked the door, his hands immediately exploring under her blouse. She moaned appreciatively as his hands gently caressed her breasts, her nipples hardening to his touch. Pushing him back toward the bed, she asked if he wanted to try something different as she unbuttoned his shirt.

Eagerly answering, 'Yes, yes, whatever,' she told him to wait while she went to the bathroom.

Returning moments later with two towels, she undid his slacks and let them fall to the floor as he slipped his hands up the back of her blouse and unclasped her bra. As the rest of his clothes fell to the floor, she pushed him back onto the large king-size bed and instructed him to stretch his arms above his head.

Rolling each towel into a makeshift rope, she tied his wrists to the two bedposts before leaning down and kissing him. Slipping off her remaining clothes, she kicked them away as she climbed on top of him, straddling his hips

He was firmly erect, so it was easy to slip him inside her. Gently riding him up and down, she asked, 'So what do you do for a living?'

He murmured, sighing with pleasure, 'I work for the UK Government.'

'Doing what?'

'Customs,' he groaned.

'Who have you been talking to?'

'Hmmm? What? Nobody special. Why do you ask?' he said, another groan escaping from his throat.

Pushing down hard on her hips to receive an extra sigh of pleasure from him, she said, 'I know you have been speaking with someone. Who is it?'

'What? Nobody. Nobody,' he said, slightly alarmed.

Slipping off him, she turned and bent lower, gently caressing him between the legs, ready to take him in her mouth. She tried once more. 'His name?'

'Oh yeah, baby, please!' he groaned, anticipating what she was about to do and ignoring her question.

The sudden sharp pain in his groin was agonizing. He tried to scream, but she clutched a pillow and jammed her free hand over his mouth. Although small, she was noticeably strong and gripped onto him, giggling madly. Laying on him as she was, he could hardly move, but he struggled, thrusting and kicking as best he could, his arms and hands tied and useless. Something warm and wet was splashing all over his thighs and lower stomach.

It lasted for less than a minute before he felt himself getting weaker.

As the room seemed to darken, she relaxed her grip and rolled off him, turning back to face him with his severed penis and testicles gripped firmly in her hand. She pushed her face close to his and said, 'Say sorry, and I'll make the pain stop.'

By now, he was too far gone to fully comprehend.

Smiling, she stared at him as he weakened further until using her spare hand, she forced his mouth open wide and jammed in his genitalia.

Sighing, she climbed off the twitching body. Blood was everywhere. Over the body. The bedding. Her. The pressure of his erection had greatly speeded up his exsanguination. She slipped the blonde wig off and dropped it in the shower. Peeling the remaining tape from the small of her back that had held the small razor-sharp flick knife, she rolled the tape into a ball and flushed it down the toilet. She spent fifteen minutes leisurely soaping herself and the wig under the steaming shower until the waters ran clear. Eventually, dried and redressed, she meticulously searched his room, slipping his laptop into her handbag before carefully wiping every surface she had touched clean of fingerprints and DNA.

The hotel room was similar to a million others throughout the world. Once inside, you could hardly tell which country you were in, let alone which city. The entrance door opened onto a small hallway with sliding door wardrobes on one side and the bathroom entrance on the other. The hallway opened up to a large open area with a king-size bed against one wall and a bureau desk against the wall opposite. Two easy chairs were against the picture window, and a couple of non-descript copies of paintings were hanging on the walls, painted in two light brown shades.

Any cameras in the hotel would have recorded a blonde woman wearing a light-colored jacket walking to the room hand-in-hand with Adam Paisley. After sending a text message, she walked out of his room, closed the door behind her, hung a 'Do Not Disturb' sign on the handle, and headed downstairs. Hotel cameras would show the same blonde woman exiting the main doorway and turning left.

6

SVETLANA Petrovich climbed into the Mercedes, parked waiting around the corner for her after she walked out of the hotel. Easing herself into the soft grey leather, she took out her cellphone, made a brief call, and slipped off the still-damp wig behind the darkened rear windows as the car pulled away.

She was just thirteen when she killed her first person. The number now was somewhere between fifty and sixty, but she'd lost count. The only surviving child - her two elder brothers had both been conscripted into the Russian Army and sent to Chechnya in 2000. As a child, Sveta, as she preferred to be called, had been doted on, but the sudden death of both brothers when she was six had severely affected her parents. Her father had always been a heavy grain spirit drinker, but now he drank almost constantly. His job was loadmaster at Novosibirsk Central Station, a major stopping point of the Trans-Siberian Railway. Money was tight, but they had always just managed to get by. One day, suffering a severe hangover from the previous evening, he swallowed half a bottle before heading in to work. Unstable on his feet, he was standing too close to the platform edge when a through train whistled past. The train's wind caused his coat to flap open, and the material caught on a door handle. Smashed against the side of the train, he was unconscious as his clothes tightened and he was dragged along the platform. By the time the driver was alerted and stopped the train, he had asphyxiated and was dead.

An autopsy showed he had been drinking and was at fault. The company didn't even pay for that day's work. With little savings and a daughter to raise, Sveta's mother became more and more depressed. She found employment as a shop assistant but also turned to the bottle for comfort.

His family rallied around and tried to help, but unemployment was high, and no one had spare money. Needing the extra monetary support a man could bring, her mother eventually accepted her brother-in-law's offer to remarry. Not used to children and especially not experienced in raising a nine-year-old girl, Viktor admonished Sveta the same way he'd reprimanded his dog. When he believed she was disobedient, he raised a hand to her.

He was employed as a laborer, but work was patchy. He earned a good wage when paid, but too often, he would be passed over for younger, fitter men and would sink into bouts of depression. Her mother tried to work, making him angrier still - it was a man's duty to feed his family, not a wife's. She tried anyway, often receiving a slap or punch as his depression bit. But working as a shop assistant with heavy bruising to her face and bruised lips didn't impress her boss. Each day Svetlana became more and more used to seeing her mother crying, covered in bruises, and shying away whenever her stepfather raised his hand.

Then their luck changed. A new factory was being built, and Viktor applied to be the foreman. Elated to be hired, he changed completely. Everything seemed good for almost three years. He kept off alcohol and worked hard, earning a reasonable salary. Then the recession hit, and the company folded. Older and unemployed again, his depression came back tenfold. The call of grain vodka became too much. He became hooked on the cheapest, gut-rot black-market stuff he could find. His habit of slapping and punching those around him returned. Her mother also started drinking again - anything to try to forget and lessen the pain of his attacks on her.

Svetlana was now almost twelve, and her body was rapidly changing shape. Like all teenagers-to-be of that age, she would often answer her stepfather back, usually resulting in a slap across her face. Then one day, as her mother returned home from work and hurried through the kitchen, her handbag accidentally knocked a cup and plate from the table onto the floor. Viktor had stumbled out from their lounge when he heard the crockery smash. Sveta began helping her mother pick the pieces up, but Viktor had gone berserk and punched his wife harder than normal. She had fallen and cracked her skull against the heavy cast iron cooker, causing a brain bleed. The police were called. Viktor claimed she had been drunk and fallen. Her blood-alcohol level matched his story, quickly classifying it as an accident. Had he been sober enough, or even if he had cared enough, he might have called an ambulance quicker and saved her, but her injuries had claimed her life within the hour.

Now it was just Svetlana and him.

For eighteen months, they shared a house. She attended school each day while doing the cooking and cleaning in the evenings; him asleep on the sofa all day between watching tv and drinking.

Then one evening, he snapped. She was reaching puberty and already had the body of a young woman. Her shapely legs and pert backside as she washed up the dishes had teased him enough. He had already noticed the boys in town would look and stare.

Grabbing a handful of her shoulder-length mousy brown hair, he spun her around and slapped her hard across the face. She fell, dazed and with a bleeding lip.

She felt his hands roughly rubbing her body and breasts as he mashed his mouth against hers, as she recovered her senses.

She tried to fight him off, his foul breath making her gag as he ripped her skirt up. As he released her slightly so he could undo his belt, she scrabbled her hands around, trying to find anything to use.

Her outstretched fingers touched the hilt of a knife she had dropped when he grabbed her. Gripping it, she tried to stab him in the side, but it wasn't sharp - it was usually used for spreading jam, and it merely made him grunt.

He exposed himself, firm and erect, and moved over her. Desperate and not knowing what else to do, she stabbed hard at his face. The blade was dull but sharp enough to penetrate his left eyeball, through its soft tissue, through the superior orbital fissure, break through the sphenoid bone, and end up deep within his brain tissue.

His body spasmed, and the last few grunts left his throat as he died almost instantly. With a mixture of vitreous fluid and blood running from his damaged eye socket into her face and the overall stench as his bowels relaxed, she did what most victims her age would do.

She screamed and screamed.

<><><>

The neighbor in the adjoining apartment was alerted to Svetlana's screams and rushed to help. Used to the previous cries of both women, nothing Viktor did surprised her. She had seen him watching Sveta before and had been half-expecting him to make a move on her sometime.

Aghast at the image in front of her in the kitchen, she gagged, trying hard not to vomit. Realizing the all-male police would likely take the dead stepfather's side and arrest Svetlana for murder, she quickly came up with a plan. She pushed and heaved the dead body away from the still screaming Svetlana and slapped her twice until her screams turned to sobs.

'Sveta, lovely Sveta. You must do as I say, or you will be arrested and spend your life in prison. Do you understand?'

After eventually receiving a tearful nod in reply, she then helped her have a quick shower and gather some belongings into a holdall. Searching Viktor, they found his wallet containing a few hundred Rubles, but that wouldn't even purchase a decent meal. Adding a few hundred more to the pile, she told Svetlana to leave and never return. Live rough on the streets or anywhere she could, but she would be arrested for murder and locked up for life if she ever came back.

<><><>

Her second and third killings, just moments apart, occurred just a few weeks later. Sleeping rough in cardboard boxes and makeshift tents in Russia was not for the faint-hearted. Theft was expected, and rape of both sexes was commonplace, sometimes even by the police. Olga, an older woman in her fifties, took Sveta partly under her wing and helped her where she could. One piece of advice she gave her was to always carry a sharp knife and never be afraid to use it. One night two males decided they wanted her. Almost out of their minds from drinking alcoholic cleaner, they pulled the cardboard sheeting aside as they started unfastening their clothing. Sveta awoke, terrified, and saw the two men about to attack her. Scrambling to the side, she lashed out with her knife feeling it snag as it bit deep into one of her attacker's legs. Pulling her hand back, she immediately thrust it forward and upward and felt warm blood wash over her hand as the blade sliced deeply through his stomach.

The second attacker saw what was happening and grabbed her hair. Yanking her head back forced her face to look up, and she could see he was about to head-butt her as he shouted, '*Grebanaya suka*', meaning *fucking bitch*.

She slammed her fist, still holding the knife, straight into the side of his neck; its blade almost protruded out the other side. Her attacker's grip relaxed with a gasp, and he fell backward.

Out of the darkness, other street people appeared. The bodies were looted of anything of value, stripped of boots and coats, and pushed into the gutter. Sveta moved to a different part of the underpass.

Over the next few years, Sveta did whatever she had to to survive. She stole, mugged others, turned prostitute, and turned to drugs. By the time she turned sixteen, her body count was over seventeen, and she had been arrested twice. The first time she was charged with prostitution resulted in three months in prison. Her current savior came along the second time she was accused of murder, which would have resulted in ten years imprisonment if found guilty. It was a good match. She was classified as a psychopath with sadistic tendencies; he could make use of her abilities and her lack of compassion. A clever lawyer, a bribe, and her life changed completely.

However, she never turned to drink in all the unsavory things she had done both before and after meeting him.

7

Syrian border with Turkey

ADNAN Hussam kept silent. He had arrived at al-Salameh's Syrian -- Turkish border crossing three days previously. He had been smuggled into Aleppo, Syria, from Jordan within the small contingent of British soldiers stationed there.

From Aleppo, he'd joined a refugee group heading north, walking some of the ways and hiding in open-backed trucks for the remainder. The main flow of refugees had reduced to just a significant trickle since the major battles between the various Syrian warring factions had ended. However, people were still leaving and seeking safety and shelter. It took him ten days to reach the border, melting in with the slow-moving crowds and walking with them. Food was scarce, but some of the group would share their meager rations. The weather was sunny in the daytime and warm but almost freezing at night, causing many of them just to lay there shivering. Although there were other crossing points to Turkey, the American news channel CNN reported that al-Salameh was where most Syrians escaping Aleppo or Damascus seemed to be heading.

Further East was the homeland of the Kurds or Kurdish people. Turkey hated the Kurds, and any caught crossing were rounded up and deposited back across the Syrian border to await their fate. The Turkish government was gradually closing the few remaining open border crossing points due to the number of refugees trying to escape war-torn Syria and head to the West. In the last eighteen months, Turkey had already taken in over 4 million asylum-seeking individuals and was demanding compensation from richer western countries to help house and feed them. However, President Edvan had left this one crossing open so far.

He'd already been sleeping rough for a few weeks, so he blended in thoroughly, hiding amongst al-Salameh's backstreets and dirt alleyways. A British Government representative in Jordan had given him Syrian money, both paper and coins, and made sure his clothes and few possessions were either non-identifiable or were clearly from Syria. He wore a damaged cheap Seiko watch with a scratched face, carried a tattered Syrian passport, a small but razor-sharp knife, and a slim money belt containing a mixture of US dollars, Euros, and Sterling. He also wore a marked and faded leather belt holding his trousers up.

The following morning, as the gates were opened and the first wave of over five hundred refugees pushed forward into the relative safety of Turkey, Adnan moved from the safety of the alley. He positioned himself in the leading throng of the crowd. Moved along en masse, he was shoved and pushed by the Turkish Police until the entire group was herded into a fenced area to await questioning and buses to take them to one of the many refugee camps.

Provided with bread and water, he waited almost six hours before being questioned. Anyone with young children was questioned sooner, and injured people were treated by medical staff, but being a young man who claimed he was aged fifteen, he had to wait.

Finally, he was taken into a tent and seated at one of four desks. A Turkish Police sergeant sitting behind a dusty computer screen grunted, shuffled some paper, and looked up. The tent was already unbearably hot. Large sweat patches extended down the sides of the sergeant's creased uniform, and his dark black hair was sticking to the skin of his head. Smoke from a cigarette was slowly teasing upwards. Looking around, Adnan saw the scene replicated at the other desks.

'ID!'

Slipping the passport over, Adnan watched the officer check every page.

'Name and age!'

The questioning continued for his date-of-birth, home address, family members, occupation, and whether he was traveling alone. Adnan answered each question a little slowly. A senior officer had fully briefed him at the British Embassy that the police would often check any paperwork first, including access to a Syrian database, then ask their questions, ensuring your answers matched.

He'd memorized his legend well. The British had gone over it repeatedly and forced him to remember every detail. The name he gave the sergeant was *Mohammed Yusef, aged fifteen, of Az-Zahabijja, Aleppo. His father was a doctor at Aleppo University Hospital. His mother was a secretary for a national firm of architects. He had a sister of seventeen, Yasmin, and a brother of six, Karim. All were dead. His brother and sister had been murdered by Syrian government forces when tanks blasted their building, completely wrecking it. His mother was shot for daring to answer back. His father died when a Russian bomber aircraft attacking rebel forces misjudged and hit the corner of the hospital. He was claiming refugee and orphan status as he had no other living relatives, nowhere to live, and no possessions apart from what he was currently wearing. He traveled to Turkey to get to the West as he wanted to get to Britain or maybe America.*

The legend was genuine. As Adnan described, all the other members of the Yusef family had been killed.

However, the body of the boy Mohammed he claimed to be was still buried deep under a missile-collapsed building in Aleppo.

The police sergeant accessed what records he had of deaths in Syria. The legend held up to scrutiny. With nothing to prove otherwise, he categorized and inputted details of Adnan/Mohammed as an orphan refugee into the computer before handing him a piece of yellow paper with his claimed name, today's date, and a reference number printed on it.

'You will be taken to a camp,' the sergeant said before waving Adnan away through the tent's left exit. The right exit was to a secure area for deportation back across the border to Syria for those who failed this initial examination.

Adnan stood and walked in the direction indicated as relief flooded over him. The first part of his mission was complete.

8

Four weeks later, London, UK

SOON-TO-BE ex-SAS Major Patrick Hythe was sitting comfortably in a brown, antique Chesterfield chair. Although the leather had lost its luster and was worn thin in places from its heavy use over the years, it was still the comfiest chair Patrick knew of in the Special Forces Club in Knightsbridge, London.

He always enjoyed relaxing here. The heavy-duty fabric of the curtains, the dense carpet, and the heavy leather furniture all played their part in keeping this history alive. Although smoking was now banned, the rich walnut-paneled walls still emitted the faint smokey smells of rich cigars, hinting back to times gone by when officers in full uniform would be enjoying one of Cuba's best with a glass or two of brandy.

A keen bourbon drinker, he was idly sipping from his glass of William Heavenhill 5th Edition Bourbon, often recognized as the best in the world, when the 20:00 hour Westminster Chimes of the grandfather clock began to play. As he listened to the gentle notes, he looked around the room. Everybody was in suits or blazers, but not a single uniform nowadays. The worry of home-grown terrorist attacks had made everyone warier. Another difference from the old days, he mused, remembering what had happened just a fortnight before.

<><><>

Patrick had pulled his X5 into the rear parking area and switched off the ignition. It was just after noon. *The Ferryman's Crossing* was a public house selling food and drink. Well off the beaten track, it had originally been built to meet the needs of the shore men and traders using the Norfolk Broads waterways - a series of manmade navigable rivers and canals.

Centuries before, the need for fuel for burning had initially necessitated the digging of peat back in the 12th century - peat often being the first step in the geological formation of fossil fuels such as coal, particularly low-grade coal such as lignite. Lying on the surface or close to it, it was relatively easy to extract in large quantities. This method continued through to the 14th century before nature finally overcame man's efforts, and the massive ditches and canals began to fill with water as sea levels rose. By the 15th century, the flooding became too commonplace for peat extraction to continue, and the extraction was abandoned.

Traders trying to move their goods of wool and agricultural products from Norwich to the port of Great Yarmouth came upon the idea of expanding these waterways called the Broads - an ancient local name meaning wide expanses of water. Access points were dug, and many of the existing ditches and canals were joined together. The trading routes became busy and smaller businesses, including The Ferryman's Crossing, soon filled a growing need. By the 16th century, over 130 miles of navigable rivers and canals allowed the entire area of Norwich and what is now known as the county of Norfolk to flourish.

Looking at the building, Hythe wondered if the owners might also rent rooms, perched as it was on the very banks of the River Yare. He'd visited it one evening almost two months previously, along with a female friend, Gina, for a few beers and a plate of wholesome food. They had been traveling the Norfolk Broads in a twin-cabin canal boat when they came upon the pub. Hythe had invited Gina to join him to help her come to terms with her daughter's recent death at a New York party. She had overdosed on ecstasy laced with fentanyl.

They'd tied up their craft just yards away from the entrance close to other boat owners and enjoyed an evening of excellent fare. The only slight uneasiness Hythe had felt was when he'd noticed the barman staring at him at times. Even Gina had mentioned it to him. The woman server from the kitchen had also seemed to take an interest in Hythe, and not wanting trouble in front of Gina, he'd ignored it. Nothing else had occurred during the remainder of the evening, and they'd left a couple of hours later after enjoying homemade steak and kidney pies with mashed potato and peas, washed down with a couple of pints of locally brewed beer. Back on the boat, he had slept with one eye open, but they weren't disturbed, and the following morning after a hearty breakfast, they had continued their travels. However, the experience still niggled at him.

Soldiers, even ex-soldiers, are often said to walk and move in a particular way. Some people claim to be able to recognize them, whether it is because of being used to marching or maybe just pride in their abilities and the way they hold themselves. Back in the 80s and 90s, when the troubles in Northern Ireland were rife, MI5 discovered the IRA had placed English sympathizers to their cause near some of the UK's largest Army barracks, such as Catterick and Aldershot, to photograph soldiers and civilians suspected of being military. The IRA would then use the photographs to try and identify any of them operating undercover in Northern Ireland.

This technique was also used in and around Hereford, the home of the British SAS, which also operated in NI. Although Hythe joined the military in the mid-eighties, all servicemen were warned and instructed to report anyone acting suspiciously or taking photographs of them. With the current increase in tension in NI due to Brexit, some parties there are threatening renewed violence. Hythe wanted to double-check this wasn't starting again, and he hadn't been identified.

Walking in, he glanced upwards as all public houses in Britain have the registered landlord's name printed above the door. It read *Ian and Brenda Jenkins - Proprietors.* He walked directly up to the bar and saw the same barman as before. It was quieter inside than when he'd visited with Gina, there was just one older couple sitting at a table in the corner waiting for food. The barman looked up at him, ready to say *'Welcome'* when he did a double-take. Hythe extended his hand in a handshake, and the barman responded out of habit.

Gripping it tightly enough so it couldn't be released, Hythe said gruffly, 'Do we have a problem, pal?'

9

SLIGHTLY startled, the barman stuttered, 'What? Uh, no. Why? What?'

'It's just you seem taken aback to see me. But as long as there isn't a problem, that's OK then, isn't it?' Hythe said, just as the woman server he'd seen before walked out of the kitchen carrying a cup of coffee. Startled, her eyes widened in surprise at seeing Hythe refusing to release the barman's hand.

'Ian, is anything wrong?' she said, her voice trembling.

'You both look surprised to see me. Why?' Hythe said to the woman.

Ian started to reply, 'You look famil—' as the woman gasped, 'The photo!'

Still firmly gripping Ian's hand in his, Hythe said, 'What photo?'

'Look, I'm sorry. It's very rude of us. It's just you are the exact likeness of someone we have in a photo on the wall back there,' he said, pointing to the far side wall with his free hand. 'Does the name Hythe, Captain George Hythe, mean anything to you by chance?'

It was Patrick's turn to be surprised, and he inadvertently let go of Ian as he said, 'What? How the … George Hythe was my grandfather. What photo?'

Indicating Patrick to follow him, Ian moved out from the bar and headed to the wall. As they approached. Hythe could see it was full of photos and regimental memorabilia not visible from the bar itself or from where he and Gina had sat previously.

The wall was crowded with both color and black-and-white photos, some so old they were turning sepia. In the upper left area was a ten by eight black-and-white print of two men wearing service uniforms standing with the Eiffel Tower in the background behind them. The man on the left looked exactly like Hythe.

In faded pencil, written along the bottom of the photo was *The Jedburg Giants, Paris, 1945.*

'That's my grandfather Captain George Hythe,' Hythe gasped.

'Well, the likeness is so close you can see why we thought we recognized you.'

Looking closely, even Patrick had to admit to the similarities. The only noticeable difference, and even that was very small, was Patrick had a small scar on his chin from falling out of a tree as a child. However, without a close examination, to anyone looking, the portrait taken seventy-six years ago was of the person standing in the bar today.

Ian turned to him and said, 'The other face in the photo is of my grandfather, Sergeant Thomas Jenkins. He was the radio op and your grandfather, Captain George Hythe, was the officer-in-charge. They worked together as part of the Jedburghs.'

'Whoa! Start at the beginning. Who are you, and what's this all about?'

'You're right. Sorry. You look like you could do with a drink. Come and sit down, and I'll explain.'

Ian began after handing over a tumbler of whiskey. 'I am Ian Jenkins, and my wife, Brenda, who you've already met, and I now own *The Ferryman's Crossing*. After WWII, my grandfather, Sergeant Thomas Jenkins, married my grandmother. They had a son, my father, who also joined up. He was in one of the first groups to land in the Falklands back in '82. During the conflict, he was pretty seriously injured and pensioned out. Partly disabled, he invested his pay-out in *The Ferryman.* It was pretty well run down, so Grandad Thomas also put his savings into it, and they worked together and made it a success. Loads of their friends from the services visited, hence all the photos and memorabilia, although we've now removed a lot as it became too much. One of the visitors was your grandad, Captain Hythe. He was old and fairly ill by then, but the two of them had remained in contact after the war and relived their old stories of being Jedburghs during '44 and '45. I think both of them finally died in their late 80s. My father kept *Ferryman's* going, and I joined the Paras in '05, but he slowly went downhill with dementia. I did two tours in Iraq, then got out in 2016. Brenda and I were already married, and we took over this place a few months later.'

'Is your father still alive?'

'Yeah, but he's in a nursing home now over in Wickhampton. We visit each week, but his dementia has worsened, and he doesn't recognize anyone anymore. So did you know your grandfather was a member of the Jedburghs?'

Pondering a moment, not sure how much to disclose, Hythe finally said, 'No, not at all. My father was in the Army, and I'm in the service myself. Rank of Major. In the blood, I guess. But no, it was never mentioned. All I knew was he was in the Army and his rank. I was still a kid when he died. But I have heard about the Jedburghs. Weren't they a clandestine offshoot of the British Special Operations Executive, or SOE, and the American Office of Strategic Service – their forerunner to the CIA? I believe the Jedburgh teams were to assist allied forces who invaded France on 6 June 1944 with sabotage, guerrilla warfare, and leading local resistance forces in actions against the Germans. Is that right?'

'Correct. Teams normally consisted of three men: a commander, a local-country executive officer, and a non-commissioned officer radio operator. In this case, your grandfather, Captain Hythe, was the commanding officer, with my grandfather as his radio operator. The CO and radio op always stayed paired, but the executive officer would vary depending on where the mission was based. London felt that having a local exec officer as an arbitrator would make for better relationships with the local resistance members and stop any feeling of the British or Americans ordering everything. Our grandfathers' team was officially called *Geoffrey,* but the two of them named themselves as the *Jedburgh Giants* because of all their successful missions - over fourteen of them in total.'

'So, how do you know so much about them?' Hythe asked after a swig of whiskey.

'We were lucky. Old Tom had Eidetic or photographic memory. That's the ability to recall an image or action from memory with incredible precision. He couldn't do anything during the war, obviously due to secrecy and active missions, but immediately after the war, he recalled in great detail each of the missions they'd been on and wrote it all down in a number of journals. He passed those on to my father, and now I have them. They are all written freehand, with corrections and spelling mistakes, but they make for great reading. It's almost a day-by-day account of what they did in the Jedburghs.'

Their conversations carried on during the afternoon and evening, with Hythe staying the night in one of the rooms for rent. The following morning, with friendships now permanently bonded, Hythe headed back to London with the first four of over a dozen journals.

10

THE flashing of the Reuters news feed on one of the wall monitors highlighting *Breaking News* brought Patrick back to the present. He idly scanned the text on something or other about the Queen's forthcoming celebrations and then something about Russia building up its forces on the eastern border of Ukraine for military exercises. The fifth item shown was that four refrigerated truck trailers had been stolen from a manufacturing plant near Wiesbaden, Germany. It seemed to be a coordinated break-in as the night watchman guard was left unconscious, requiring hospitalization for severe head injuries.

That afternoon, Patrick had only arrived back from the Falkland Islands at the end of a six-day public relations event. It had been organized almost a year previously in preparation for the 40th-anniversary commemorations due later in the year in June. The Falkland Islands, South Georgia, and the South Sandwich Islands are British overseas territories that rely on the UK for their security. Forces of the British Army, Royal Navy, and Royal Air Force make up this permanent contingent, named the British Forces South Atlantic Islands, or BFSAI, and headed by a brigadier-equivalent commander. Opened in 1985, after the Argentinian invasion and their subsequent surrender in 1982, the islands' remoteness, harsh terrain, low population, and a subantarctic oceanic and tundra climate make the entire area a perfect military training ground.

The anniversary event consisted of mock battles, weapons displays, simulated aerial attacks, beach landings, and parachute drops before culminating in a simulated attack on Port Stanley. The islanders had eagerly received it, with many of them watching and joining in.

Now back in London, Patrick took another sip of his drink and thought of his godson, Peter Newman. Peter was the son of a close friend he'd known from his early school days who'd succumbed to leukemia in his early thirties. Patrick had been the best man at their wedding and had celebrated with them at the birth of their only child, Peter. A gentle, helpful person, Peter entered the care profession and found the medic role suited him perfectly. Living close to Southampton, Peter was a first responder paramedic for the Hampshire Ambulance Service. Still in contact these years on, Patrick had been Peter's first call after the accident in the New Forest, the strange goings-on at the party, and the death of his colleague, Ranvir.

Patrick visited him in hospital and promised to look into what had happened, but the trip to the Falklands had delayed it. So far, he hadn't been able to accomplish much while he was overseas, although he had managed some phone calls but had been snubbed at every turn. However, with his time in the 21 SAS due to expire and three weeks of leave planned, he would use that time to investigate further before returning to duty with the Royal Fusiliers in Wiltshire.

The buzz of an incoming SMS text message interrupted his thoughts. His attendance was requested the following morning at 08:30 at Albany Street barracks. He pondered for a few moments before catching the eye of a roving waiter and ordering a second drink.

<><><>

Traffic congestion was heavy this morning, and his journey had been stop-start almost the entire way. The heavy rain didn't help either as fewer people were walking, preferring to use public transport or their own vehicles instead.

Annoyed and frustrated, he stopped his X5 at the security markings at 08:15 as cameras scanned the bottom of his car and sniffer systems 'sniffed' the air surrounding the vehicle. He always looked but could never see the two soldiers who'd had his head firmly sighted through their Leupold telescopic sights while waiting for the order to open fire if need be as his car was checked. After being given clearance that no bombs were attached, he received a green light and motored on into the inner sanctum of 21 SAS Regent's Park Barracks, commonly known as Albany St Barracks.

After showing his ID, he headed through the main doors and up to the first floor. Major General Malcolm Ronaldson - the Director of Special Forces, along with two men wearing business suits, were waiting.

With a smile and a friendly handshake, the DSF said, 'Patrick, these two gentlemen, Sir Rupert Wainwright and Cecil Lockwood, are from the Home Office. They have a delicate matter to discuss with you,' he finished, gesturing they follow him to a private room.

As the four of them took seats around a circular table complete with glasses and carafes of chilled water, Patrick extended his hand, greeting the two newcomers, and introduced himself formally. However, Wainwright and Lockwood declined to answer what positions they held at the Home Office, merely responding they were civil servants. Having met people like this before, Hythe mentally labeled Wainwright as Laurel and Lockwood as Hardy due to their physical appearances.

'Major Hythe, as the Director has just mentioned, our matter is rather delicate, and what we discuss today must not leave this room. Understood?' Lockwood, the older appearing one of the two and the one Hythe mentally thought of as Hardy, said.

After receiving a nod from Hythe, Lockwood continued, 'Since Brexit, when the UK finally left the EU, there has been an increase in smuggling into the UK. In particular, in tobacco and people. Tobacco falls under Customs and Excise, which you may know, is part of HMRC. In order to try and trace where the tobacco is coming from and how it is entering Britain, HMRC took the initiative to place one of its officers undercover in Europe. Unfortunately, his butchered body was discovered last week in his hotel room in Munich. He was naked, and his genitals had been removed and stuffed in his mouth. We don't know if he'd been discovered asking too many questions or if it was more of a personal sexual liaison gone wrong. CCTV from the hotel doesn't show much, just him arriving with a blonde on his arm and no record of her leaving. His wallet and watch were not taken, so robbery doesn't appear to be the motive. However, some of his colleagues say he always thought of himself as a bit of a ladies' man. I'm waiting to get a copy of his last report. When I do, I'll send it on to you. But the Germans don't appreciate having a dead Englishman in their hotels, and as I'm sure you can imagine, all hell's broken loose.'

Nodding agreement but waiting for them to continue, Hythe remained silent.

'There is an investigation into how well suited this person was for this role and whether he should have even been sent in the first place,' Lockwood continued.

After a brief pause, Wainwright said, 'You will have seen in the press and media the number of migrants making the crossing of the Channel has almost tripled over the last two years. Even increasing the patrol craft of the Border Force covering the immediate area between the southeast coast of the UK and the Pas de Calais region of France has had little impact. A few months ago, the Home Secretary announced an increase in funds of over £30 million from the UK to the French maritime police who patrol and guard the waters on their side of the Channel. However, most unfortunately, this has not seen the expected decline in the number of migrants making the trip across. Several migrants have died making the crossing when their crafts have sunk or experienced difficulties in recent weeks. It's received plenty of attention from the media and has had two noticeable effects on the British public. Some say we should open our borders and make it easier for migrants to enter the UK, while a growing number, albeit currently a minority, seem to be baying for blood. Those are claiming it is only when the Border Force starts deliberately sinking the craft the migrants are using and the bodies build up on French shores that the tide will turn, and their number will reduce. Some of the more vocal amongst them are even suggesting our Navy and the Border Force machine gun and sink the boats crossing mid-channel to act as a deterrent.'

11

'SINCE when does the UK government listen to the public or even care about what the public thinks?' Hythe said, receiving a smirking nod from the DSF.

'That's beside the point,' Wainwright replied. 'The current government's manifesto clearly stated a significant reduction in illegal immigrants entering Britain each year. In fact, it was one of the driving forces behind Brexit. However, Brexit is not running as smoothly as planned, but luckily the pandemic has taken center stage. Many of the mistakes and shortcomings of Brexit are being masked by Covid. Unfortunately, the Home Secretary is receiving a lot of flak from the media, particularly over the increase in these migrant numbers. The media have nicknamed Border Force as Border Farce, and they have lost all respect from the public. It's all being put at the feet of the Prime Minister, who, in turn, is putting pressure on the Home Secretary to get results. The public is losing faith in the government, and that's where we come in.'

Stopping to take a breath and a sip of water, he motioned to include Lockwood, saying, 'To be clear, our efforts are heavily focussed on the immigrant problem. Customs and Excise are rightly concerned about the illicit trade in alcohol and tobacco, but they have agreed that we take the lead due to their last failed attempt. We know where many migrants come from, with some making their way through Europe to northern France. But we believe there are also several large smuggling operations transporting them, organizing crossings and even some onward travel within the UK, all for a nice fat fee. By their very nature, these organizations are a secretive lot, and even after fifteen months of trying, we know little, if anything, about them. At least the people that are stopped by us coming across the Channel become known to us. Many are immediately put on a watch list by our colleagues in Five. But we are most concerned about the ones that slip past. A high percentage are young males of prime fighting age. Many are ex or current Al-Qaeda or ISIS-trained and immediately go deep underground. The government cannot afford another terrorist-driven catastrophe happening on the mainland and then having to admit the assailants were migrants unknown to us.'

Coughing to clear his throat, Hythe said, 'How big is the tobacco smuggling? I assume that somebody didn't kill the HMRC contact over two packs of Marlboro's?'

'Uhh, no. One or two full container loads a week. We are talking of between fifteen and twenty million cigarettes entering the UK weekly.'

'So where is the tie-up with the tobacco smuggling? These people you are talking about come across the Channel in dinghies, but the tobacco comes in containers.'

'I was just coming to that. As you say, we are getting a lot of flak about the ones crossing by dinghy, but we believe some are still coming in hidden in trucks like the tobacco. Whether they are in the same trucks as the tobacco or different, we are missing them. We don't even know if it's the same organization arranging the people smuggling and the contraband or different. The point is we're very much in the dark. Luckily for the Home Secretary, so are the press. But we need to stop that entry route urgently.'

'And we come into this how exactly?' Hythe said, indicating himself and the Director.

'Glad you asked, Major. Glad you asked. The mission you will undertake is two-fold. First, understand and identify the routes these gangs take to get their illegal cargo into the UK; second, identify the ringleaders. A couple of months ago, we received information that the main thrust of these gangs seems to start in the refugee camps in southern Turkey, close to the Syrian border. We have placed a young man in northern Syria. He has traveled across the border along with others making the same journey and was accepted by the Turkish border guards as a legitimate orphan and refugee. He was moved to a camp outside Gaziantep, where he has been for the last few weeks. He's already been putting out feelers about getting to the UK. We believe he has been contacted and checked out. If previous history is anything to go by, he will be on his way maybe in a small group or maybe larger en route to the UK within the next two or three days.'

'How do you know all this?' Hythe asked.

'The Red Crescent is operating in the camps there, and a couple of the staff are on our payroll. But as soon as he leaves, he will be on his own. This young man, our imposter, has been fully briefed on the dangers and must remain undetected throughout being smuggled into the UK. He will have passed rigorous questioning by gang leaders and knows he cannot relax his role for a moment. He must also manage to liaise with you on a daily or second daily basis. Ronaldson here will be your liaison. The young lad's name is Adnan Hussam, and he is traveling under a full iron-clad legend we prepared for him. He grew up in Homs, Syria, and escaped with his parents to Jordan three years ago and is keen to do this.'

Waiting a few moments for everything to sink in, Hythe poured himself some more water and said, 'OK, give me the rest.'

'The largest gangs operating the long-range smuggling rings would appear to start in Gaziantep, just inside the Turkish border nearest the northern edge of Syria. Overall, Turkey accommodates over four million refugees, with over 3.7 million of them from Syria. Almost 40% of them are housed in 22 government-run camps near the Syrian border. The two largest are Nizip I and Nizip II. These were planned to be initial camps before refugees were processed and moved on, but, in practice, some people have been there for years. Although these are classed as government-run, they are, in fact, heavily infiltrated and run by ISIS. Adnan is currently in Nizip I. After contact with the smugglers, we understand that they interrogate and check the would-be traveler, but it all comes down to money.

'After any monies are paid or commitments made, the illegals are transported mostly by road through Adana and on toward Ankara and Istanbul. The route then seems to be direct to Zagreb via Sofia before splitting. Some head from Slovenia to Salzburg and take a southern route to Calais via Munich and Strasbourg. The other route is more northerly via Nuremberg and Frankfurt, through Belgium, or even further north via Bremerhaven. The problem is we don't know much about their exact routes and what support structure they have in place. However, what we do know is that for every person crossing the Channel by dinghy, only sixty-three percent get intercepted and detained before being put into the system. Almost forty percent get by us completely. By 'us,' I mean Border Force.'

Hythe nodded and thought for a couple of moments before saying, 'Go on.'

'Most of the dinghy smuggling rings are operating from Calais or very close to, getting migrants across the Channel to the beaches on the south coast. Although Border Force has stepped up operations and is working alongside the Navy, the smugglers have also stepped up. We believe they are now offering three types of service across the Channel, bronze, silver, and gold. The bronze service is the cheapest at around €400 to €500 per person, but the boats are small and heavily overcrowded. They also only have smallish and sometimes unreliable engines. Often the immigrants get to wear completely unsuitable life jackets. These are the boats that usually get intercepted by Border Force as they are the slowest and most easily intercepted. They are typically awash with water, and it is these that are photographed by the press being helped ashore in Dover or Newhaven. A few of these have capsized mid-channel, and bodies have been washed up along the South Coast beaches. These are cannon fodder but bear in mind that some get through and tie up resources enormously.

'When a Border Force craft intercepts them, often directed in by helicopter, they take the people aboard, provide them with blankets and a hot drink, take their craft in tow, and head into the closest UK port after alerting police and immigration. It's very time-consuming. One simple pick-up can easily take a BF craft out of service for five or six hours before they can get back on station. In that time, the silver service, which is better organized - bigger, faster inflatables with powerful engines, can make two or three runs back and forth across the Channel. Silver service seems to be typically €4k - €5k per person, with a limited number of people on board, thereby keeping the weight low and speed high, and improved drop-off points on the South Coast, often with pick-ups waiting to take them onward. Damned awkward to intercept.

'Finally, there is the gold service. Upwards of £20k each, it's almost guaranteed undetected delivery into the UK. It really is big money. The boats used are fast and powerful, usually enclosed, and some are built out of Kevlar for reduced weight and, if detected, can easily outrun BF launches. They don't drop at the publicized beaches such as Dover. They travel further West toward Weymouth or North into Essex and East Anglia. Contacts await with onward vehicles to transport their passengers directly into cities, mostly London, Birmingham, and Manchester. Again, these craft can easily make two or more trips while Border Force is tied up, especially if as soon as they get back on station a report comes in of another overloaded dinghy getting swamped. Virtually impossible to intercept. In fact, we've only ever managed to catch one group.'

'I didn't realize it is so organized. Like most people, I assumed that it is just a few random inflatables,' Hythe said while pouring them both water.

'The Home Office's hands are tied. Under international law, as soon as a craft is within UK waters, it is the UK's responsibility to save the passengers if the craft gets into trouble. The Channel is not wide enough to have international waters – it's either UK or French waters. Yes, the French have been known to tow a disabled boat closer to UK waters and demand the UK respond instead of rescuing the people and taking them back to Calais. Unfortunately, that is for the politicians to sort out. But the smugglers the Home Office are currently most interested in are the long-range ones working from Turkey. Your mission is to keep close to Adnan and track his route so we can close it down. If it also includes the tobacco, so much the better.'

'So is the government concerned about the number of illegal immigrants per se, or the amount of money some businesses are making and not paying tax on?'

'Major, you are becoming quite cynical in your old age,' Ronaldson laughed.

'Who, me, sir?' he said, smiling, before addressing Wainwright again, 'OK, how do I follow and track this Adnan character?'

'Not quite 'Q' from James Bond, but he's wearing a specially designed belt. It does two things. Undetectable by normal scanners, he depresses the prong or tongue every couple of hours. Normally insulated from the remaining metal of the buckle, it's switched off. When pressed, it momentarily makes contact and takes just a millisecond to record its GPS location. Approximately five seconds later, an extremely short burst radio transmission is made containing that GPS data, but it's low power with a range of only fifteen or so miles. Here's your receiver,' he said, handing over a small unit looking like a cell phone. 'You just need to be within range to receive.'

'And this belt gizmo isn't detectable?'

'No, not easily. It looks and feels like a normal leather belt. A metal detector will just sense the metal in the buckle. There's no battery - heat from the body supplies electricity from two forms of metalized stitching used throughout the belt. Transmission is just a few milliseconds long, so pretty unlucky if detected at that exact time. The transmission itself is encoded to sound like static to a listener, and if the prong is pressed and held down, the unit simply switches itself off, likewise, if the belt is unfastened and removed from the body. Finally, suppose the prong is depressed three times in quick succession. In that case, the belt sends an emergency signal at random, roughly every fifteen to twenty minutes. So if Adnan is compromised or in trouble, he can let us know.'

'What about backup and weapons?'

'Unfortunately, none. The powers-that-be have been quite adamant about that. After the fiasco with HMRC and the German police, you are to do this alone, and they specifically stated you are not authorized to be armed.'

Hythe sat there for a few moments digesting the information.

Finally, to break the silence, Ronaldson said, 'You said the belt does two things. It does three!'

'It sends position updates and has an emergency mode,' Wainwright answered, looking confused, 'What's the third?'

'It holds Adnan's trousers up,' Ronaldson said, laughing.

Thirty minutes later, Hythe headed back to his BMW. He had a business class flight ticket from Gatwick to Ankara in his pocket. Early the following morning at 07:35, he boarded the five-and-a-quarter-hour non-stop flight.

12

London

THE following morning at 06:30, Patrick was sitting in the British Airways Business Lounge, drinking black coffee and eating a fresh croissant while waiting to board his flight. After Wainwright and Lockwood had left yesterday and they were alone again, Ronaldson had said, 'Sorry to have sprung this on you with no warning, Patrick. I only got wind of them arriving just before I paged you yesterday. It seems the powers-that-be had already chosen you.'

'So why me?'

'As you know, your time with us is up. I've kept you here as long as I could and broken countless regulations in doing so, but the rules are clear. Officers transferring into the SAS can only serve a three-year term before returning to their regiment. In cases where a particularly good impression was made, and the officer holds the rank of Major or higher, an officer may be asked back for a second three-year term. That was the case with yourself, and you have an exemplary record of heading the training squadrons. For the last eight months, I managed to get you assigned to special VIP personal protection to augment SO14, but even those duties must now come to an end. Unfortunately, my hands are tied.'

'Is this really the best way you and the Service can put me to use, sir? Tracking down some two-bit smuggler when we have a potential war brewing between Russia and Ukraine that will drag us into it?' Hythe said.

'Patrick, I understand how you feel. I'm not happy about this setup either. However, as we don't know how long this mission will last, your transfer back to the Fusiliers has been put on hold until it completes. As to why you personally were chosen for this mission, I don't know. However, I have it on good authority that this decision was made at the highest level.'

<><><>

The aircraft was less than half-full, and Patrick had row three to himself. His passport and Executive Club Oneworld card showed the name Terry Johnson. As always, he was using government-issued fake documents for security when traveling on government business. After the flight attendant had brought him breakfast and coffee, Patrick reclined the seat and dozed for the remainder of the flight, waking in a sweat a couple of hours later.

He'd had the nightmare again. The same one he'd been having on and off for almost thirty years. Initially, it had woken him up each night, crying and terrified, but its frequency had reduced, although not its intensity as the years went by. It was still as clear today as when the event triggered it, but it was never complete. Just random thoughts and images. Shadows of people but never their faces but always in the same order. Now, though, it just left him feeling depressed, sweating, and breathing hard.

The pilot announced they were about to start their approach to Ankara Airport. The undercarriage squealed as the tires' rubber touched the tarmac ten minutes later.

As he walked through the terminal, he didn't notice the person in the black leather coat drop his newspaper in the bin and start following him. After clearing Customs, Hythe picked up a black BMW X5 rental and headed onto the D140 south toward Ankara city before switching onto the O-20 ring road. The person following him spent fewer than five minutes at the car rental company before taking his cell out and making a call.

Having skirted Ankara's small but crowded city, Hythe merged onto the O-21 highway to drive the seven-plus hours to Gaziantep. Annoyingly, although seemingly completed, the new excellent six-lane O-21 was only open in short sections, meaning the older, slower roads still had to be used.

Stopping for fuel and an evening meal just outside the small town of Aksaray, he enjoyed a glass of Efes Pilsen beer while eating a local delicacy - spicy meatballs with yogurt and flatbread. Turkish people are friendly to visitors and guests, and his host was keen to show off his English language skills. Finally, after two small cups of excellent strong coffee, he paid a ridiculously small amount, left a sizeable tip, and continued on his way.

The remainder of the journey was as uneventful as the start, and he arrived in Gaziantep by 21:30 pm. The foyer of the Grand Hotel was marbled in white and dark gray stonework. Although in the city, its height meant the upper floors allowed excellent views across the city. Hythe had the top floor corner suite. Before arriving, he found a modern fuel station, refueled the car, and purchased two bottles of water, some chocolate and high-energy bars, a torch, and some road maps.

Leaving all these items under the luggage tray in the rear, he tipped the parking attendant an additional 200 lira over the parking cost to have his vehicle near the front and available to exit at all times.

Showered and refreshed, he placed the belt receiver on the window sill to gain the best reception after checking it worked. He'd already decided his next course of action.

Picking up his cellphone, he pulled up an encrypted app and dialed.

13

IT was still early afternoon when John Deacon's cell began vibrating seven time zones away. Glancing at the screen, he smiled before thumbing the green button. 'Hiya pal, to what do I owe this honor?'

Aware that even encrypted end-to-end phone apps may be monitored and most countries' intelligence services have cracked the software, Hythe immediately got to the point. 'When we spoke last week while I was in the South Atlantic, you said you were heading to Dubai this week but stopping off in London on the way.'

'Correct, pal. But I take it you are no longer in London?'

'See, you yanks aren't all dumb schmucks,' Hythe laughed, 'I'm currently in Turkey doing a job looking after someone for my bosses. He's traveling across Europe. It would be interesting to meet and have a chat. Are your plans flexible? Can't say much more than that, really.'

Although neither had definitive proof, they believed that all international calls would likely be logged and recorded, so they kept their conversation short. Both understood that Turkey's National Intelligence Organization, headquartered in Ankara, works closely with both the CIA in the USA and the various intelligence agencies in Russia. The current Turkish leader, President Edvan, is rumored to be the most corrupt President in over 100 years of Turkish history. Having survived a potential coup against him in late 2016, Edvan tightened up control of the NIO. With a population of over 80 million, of which 99% are Muslim, Islam is the country's official religion, although the country is not strictly religious. It has become a popular tourist hotspot with western holidaymakers. However, Edvan seems to have double standards and supports some western views as well as the Muslim Brotherhood, Hamas, Turkistan Islamic Party, Turkistan Islamic Movement, Al Nusra, and various Al Qaeda affiliates.

Much to Patrick's delight, Deacon did pick up on the nuances he was hearing.

'Well, pal, it would be good to get together. I quite fancy a few days in the bazaars and fleshpots of the gateway to the Middle East. Where do you want to meet?'

'How about I call you in a day or two and let you know where I am?' Hythe replied before disconnecting the call.

With the niggling concern now clear from his mind, he ordered a bourbon from room service and sat in his room, waiting for the receiver to buzz.

<><><>

Nizip 1 Refugee Camp, Turkey

Weeks before, Adnan had walked away from the sergeant's tent, barely concealing a smile. The first part had gone as promised.

After a few more hours of waiting, he was transported in a small convoy of buses to Nizip 1, one of a number of refugee camps close to the banks of the Euphrates River. Nizip 1 is a tent camp housing almost 11,000 inhabitants, of which 5,000 are classified as children.

Within a five-mile radius are three more tent camps and one container camp housing a total of 30,000 people.

Crammed in, as everybody is, these camps are more like shanty towns or ghettos.

The queue of people waiting meant the check-in process almost took two hours. A guard demanded his yellow paper and then checked it on a computer screen. Receiving a positive match, he then half-guided, half-shoved Adnan against a wall that once may have been white, told him to face front and hold his paper up in front of him. Three photos were taken, one facing front, one of a left profile, and one of a right. He then had a self-adhesive plastic bracelet secured around his left wrist, similar to those worn by patients in a hospital. It contained his name Mohammed Yusef, a tent number (35G), and the details previously on the yellow paper. Once secured, it could only be removed with scissors. He was then finished, and a different guard pointed in the direction he had to go.

Unlike some refugee camps in Turkey, the Nizip sites are neatly laid out with pebbled or stone paths and tents in numbered rows. Finding tent 35 in row G took just minutes. This was one of the larger, single-sex tents housing twenty bunk beds, each with a small locker. Walking in from the bright sunlight reflecting off the dusty white ground and tents, it took a few seconds for Adnan's eyes to adjust to the gloom. The air outside had been cold, as is the norm in February, but inside, the tent was warm and stuffy, smelling of a mixture of food, strong tobacco smoke, and acrid body odor.

Finding an empty bed posed a problem. There was little spare room to move about, and the majority of the beds already had men lying on them. Trying not to cause conflict, he stopped by each empty one and asked whoever was closest if the bunk was taken. Three times he was told to fuck off, so he moved on. In the corner was one with a filthy stained mattress, no blankets or pillow, and the locker had the door hanging just from one hinge, but at least he now had a bed.

Settling down and sleeping in his clothes with his jacket rolled to make a pillow, he found it hard not to shed a tear or two. It began to dawn on him that if the second part of the plan didn't work, he could be stuck in this camp for years.

Adnan quickly found the camp had strict rules, and anyone breaking them would be punished. This could range from a verbal warning to permanent expulsion from the camp with subsequent deportation back to Syria.

As a refugee, basic food would be supplied by the camp. However, many of his fellow colleagues tried to find employment in the nearby town three miles away to provide some income. Salary for refugees was very low as the jobs were menial, but this allowed the purchase of extra food and essentials from the few camp shops or local traders. However, the vast majority of people merely stayed in the camp each day. The Red Crescent provided medical support for illness.

Although the site was officially run by the Turkish Government, within the camp it was under the authority of ISIS. Anyone breaking their rules was liable for beatings or even death. A dozen or so monitors were located around the vast site running adverts showing how those with money can get to Europe. TikTok adverts displayed images of the UK and highlighted the ease of crossing the English Channel. It also listed the benefits given freely to those that made the trip.

Adnan waited a few days to settle in before meeting the advert owner.

<><><>

'My name is Mohammed Yusef. I come from the Az-Zahabijja district of Aleppo. My family there are all dead, murdered by the American Satan followers. I want to go to England. I have a cousin there,' he said.

After a brief wait, two bearded individuals he believed to be ISIS motioned for him to follow. They headed to a quiet tent guarded by two more. Inside was a table with three chairs, two on one side, one on the other. He was roughly pushed toward the single chair and ordered to sit.

The two took their seats opposite and began their interrogation, reasonably politely at first but becoming more forceful and angrier as the questioning continued. Repeatedly asking about his view on Western culture; Is he a strict Muslim? How will he adapt to western culture? Does he pray each day faithfully? Would he fight to avenge Islam? Would he kill Americans or British soldiers? Would he kill non-Muslim civilians?

Having been fully briefed in Jordan, he was careful to give the correct answer and not to elaborate. He also highlighted that although he didn't have money on him, he showed them a letter from his UK cousin stating he would pay to have Adnan brought to London.

'Cost is ten thousand Euros,' the one on the left said.

'What? That's too much. My cousin will pay six thousand,' Adnan replied, by now feeling a little shaken.

The two men nodded at each other, and Adnan relaxed, assuming he had a deal. Then, before he could blink, the man on the right leaned forward and grabbed Adnan's right wrist with his left hand, slamming it down on a desk as he pulled a large bladed knife out from under his clothes with his right. He pressed the razor-sharp blade against the knuckle joint of Adnan's pinkie finger just hard enough to break the skin.

Adnan yelped in pain and surprise as the one on the left said again, 'Cost is ten thousand Euros,' as the blade was pushed a little harder and blood began to spurt.

'OK, OK!' he quickly answered as tears filled his eyes.

The knife was left pressing against his skin for a few more seconds before suddenly being removed. As Adnan clutched his bleeding finger and tried to stem the blood flow, the two men smiled, showing their yellowy teeth, and one said, 'Good, we understand each other.'

Standing and taking the letter, they said they would contact the cousin, and if the story matched, they'd be in touch.

On the evening of the ninth day he had been at the camp, two different men approached him and told him to be ready at 06:00 the following morning. They also confirmed that they would slowly and painfully kill both of them if he or his cousin failed to pay when he got to England.

14

AT 05:45 the next day, Adnan joined a group of approximately 80 people, mostly men, but 12 kids aged between five and fourteen and traveling without parents were included. All were crowded around various vehicles. Divided into two groups, they were then crammed into two large trucks.

As the truck accelerated away, Adnan slipped his right hand under his shirt as if holding his stomach and gently pressed the belt tang one-handed while trying to keep his balance.

The two trucks headed to Gaziantep before turning toward an industrial area and pulling into a disused warehouse about an hour later. As it approached, the roller doors opened automatically, closing again immediately after both trucks were inside. As they stopped, engines were switched off, and each vehicle's rear doors were slammed open. Male Turkish voices shouted at everyone to get out. Confused and a little scared, everyone climbed down and huddled in a large group.

One of the Turkish men started talking, 'You will be split up into smaller groups. There will be no talking onboard. There will be water and food in each van. We will stop again in four hours. Any questions? No? Good! Load up and keep quiet.'

At that stage, several men moved amongst the group pulling and pushing people into smaller groups of approximately a dozen. All the children were collected together and moved to one side, being looked after by three women. The remaining fifty, including Adnan, became four groups, two of twelve and two of thirteen people. Glancing around quickly, Adnan could see his group of twelve included two women - one looked to be in her mid-twenties and was very pretty, and the other was older in her forties. Those same four groups were then ushered toward the rear of the warehouse, where four dirty white Mercedes windowless panel vans were waiting.

Climbing aboard the second van, he could see two padded wooden benches bolted to the metal floor, one on each side, filling up the cargo area. A metal bulkhead was the van's width between that area and the driver's compartment, with a small sliding mesh-covered hatch. Half-meter-long ropes were attached to the benches to be used as rudimentary seat belts. There were also two blankets for each person as the weather was getting colder.

Adnan moved forward onto the front of the left wooden bench and sat leaning against the side of the van after kicking piles of rubbish aside. As others also took their seats, he pressed the belt tang again, under cover of making himself comfortable. The inside of the vehicle was dark, with the rear doors closed and locked. There were no windows in the rear, and only a minimal amount of daylight and fresh air managed to find its way through the small front opening. Each vehicle had a crew of three. Two were drivers, while the third was an armed guard in case of trouble.

<><><>

Hythe awoke having had a relaxed and peaceful night's sleep for a change. The top floor suite was decorated in the typical Byzantine style and had two king-size beds and a large window exiting onto a balcony. He stretched, called room service for breakfast, and was in the shower when the waiter rang the doorbell with the food cart.

The waiter quickly laid a place on the balcony table, poured a cup of coffee, and waited to serve Hythe but was dismissed with a healthy tip. Normally happy to be waited on, Hythe wanted peace and solitude this time.

Having checked that the belt receiver was working, he used the remote control to switch on the large, wall-mounted flatscreen television. He could even rotate the mount remotely so he could watch TV from the balcony. As the clock showed 06:30, he started watching CNN news and tucked into a fresh roll.

He had just taken the first bite when the belt receiver received an alert, having a soft two-tone beep similar to receiving an email or SMS. Swiping the screen and entering his pin on the device that looked the same as a smartphone, he got his first confirmation that Adnan was on the move. Cursing, he realized he'd missed some alerts, possibly not being detected due to the distance involved. Similar to Google Maps, the screen showed a map of about a ten miles radius with a flashing blue circle in the middle showing Adnan's last position. However, the system wasn't real-time. Unlike a GPS system, the map position pointer didn't automatically update until Adnan pressed the belt tang each time.

Nine minutes later, Patrick Hythe had packed, grabbed pieces of the breakfast to go, checked out of the hotel, and climbed into his car. Thankful he'd paid the parking attendant upfront and given him extra to keep the car close, he slammed the gearstick into *drive* and gunned the engine. The tires squealed on the asphalt loudly as the wheels lost their grip, spinning momentarily before road friction overcame, and the BMW accelerated rapidly toward Incili Pinar road.

Within a few minutes, he was on the D400 heading toward the main motorway to begin the long journey toward Istanbul via Adana and Ankara. Just as he started to eat another roll, another soft two-tone beep came through, updating Adnan's position.

15

BOREDOM, stale air, and poor lighting inside the van did little to encourage everyone to stay alert. After checking his watch, Adnan would press the belt tang to update his position whenever he was awake and found roughly an hour had passed.

Traveling all day, they managed over 1,000km, stopping three times in quiet areas to empty their bladders. Allowed a fifteen-minute break within thirty feet of the vehicle, they could stretch their legs and have some water or a simple snack before being herded back on board when the travel continued. Each time, the spare driver and guard armed with handguns would exit the vehicle and check the site thoroughly before allowing the passengers to disembark. Twice, Adnan tried to start a brief conversation but was aggressively silenced by the wave of a gun the second time.

After the first stop, the young, pretty woman chose to sit next to Adnan when they re-boarded. Smiling, she whispered her name and murmured that he looked kind, putting her hand close to his.

Surprised at her approach, he let his fingers brush hers briefly. Aisha, he thought; she said her name was Aisha, and I looked kind. He felt embarrassed and knew he was blushing, thankful the gloom of the van would hide his skin coloring red. His skin felt it was tingling - every bump in the road made her leg brush his. He'd never felt excited like this before. It was as though his skin was electric.

As the journey continued and some passengers began to doze, he was so excited he could hardly breathe. He could see enough in the darkness as her head began to loll forward, and as she put her head on his shoulder, he couldn't help himself. He gasped at her touch.

<><><>

As the hours driving dragged on, each position update confirmed to Hythe that the target was still somewhere ahead of him within a few miles, but he had no way of knowing which vehicle Adnan was in because the position update wasn't in real-time.

Come twilight and about 30km before reaching the suburbs of Istanbul, Patrick received three updates on the receiver within as many minutes. Patrick pulled over onto the road shoulder and waited as the receiver map updated itself. He guessed and hoped he was correct that they were heading somewhere to stop overnight while he examined his paper roadmap. The van had pulled off the main O7 highway and joined a smaller road leading north. His map showed the road reducing and narrowing from a single thick black line to a thin double line, passing through a couple of smaller and smaller villages, and reducing even further into a single thin line before ending as a dirt track heading to a remote farm.

Knowing any vehicle following those roads would stand out like bumps on a log, especially as they would need headlights due to the fading daylight, Hythe chose not to follow as detection was too likely.

His map indicated a small town approximately ten kilometers from Istanbul. Hoping to find somewhere to stay, he continued and was rewarded when a small family-run hotel sign appeared. Booking a room and meal, he settled down for the evening, ready to continue early the following morning.

<><><>

In the meantime, the van headed away from the main highway down narrower roads until the road finally became just a dirt track. With the driver refusing to reduce speed, everyone gripped the bench seats to stop falling on the floor in the rear. Finally, an isolated farm and outbuildings came into view. Surrounded by a sturdy eight-foot-high wire fence and patrolled by guards with dogs, other vans and trucks could be seen already parked there.

The van stopped with a final jolt, and the engine was switched off. In the moment's silence that followed, the only sounds were the creaks and groans of the engine cooling. Then the shouts of the guards filled the air as they opened the doors and began beating the van's sides with sticks, ushering the passengers into a large barn.

Adnan could see the barn's interior had been split into multiple areas, each separated by heavy cloth curtains. He and his fellow passengers were roughly pushed toward one particular location, ordered to stay within its confines, and instructed under no circumstances were they to attempt to communicate with anyone in another curtained area. They were also instructed to keep quiet and wait for food.

Aisha remained next to him, and together they waited. When it finally arrived, the food consisted of soup with a little meat and chunks of dark bread. There were no chairs, so they sat on old, threadbare filthy mattresses on the concrete floor and ate. Hungry from the day's travel, they wolfed it down before sitting together. Sometime later, Adnan eventually drifted off to sleep with one arm around her and holding Aisha's hand.

16

ISTANBUL lies on an isthmus of land separating Europe and Asia. The Black Sea is to the north; to the south is the Sea of Marmara. The Bosporus Straits is a waterway connecting these two seas. It is 30km long and only 700 meters wide at its widest point. It is also quite shallow in parts, and its fast flow is north to south. It runs directly through the city of Istanbul, making it a divided city located on two continents. There is only one tunnel and three bridges joining the two continents together.

Based on the van's travel the day before, Patrick guessed they would take the most northerly possibility, the *Yavuz Sultan Selim Bridge*, sometimes known as the *Third Bosphorus Bridge*. However, he wasn't willing to guarantee it, so he was up, showered, and dressed just after 06:00 and on the road ten minutes later.

The sun was shining, and with the sky a bright blue, the views of the Bosporus as he drove across the long central span were breathtaking. He carried on as far as Isiklar before exiting the main road and waiting.

The first position update was at 07:15, showing they are keeping clear of the city and remaining on the O7 heading for the northern bridge. Ninety minutes later, an update placed them just four kilometers east of Isiklar, heading toward Bulgaria. Congratulating himself on his correct guess and realizing he was only a couple of kilometers ahead of Adnan, he rejoined the highway. He followed closely behind each vehicle likely to be transporting immigrants for a few minutes each.

Making a mental note of each vehicle, he had narrowed it down to a full-size DAF truck or a white Mercedes panel van within the hour. Keeping just a few hundred meters behind the truck, he watched as it indicated and slowed at a rest area just as another position update came in, showing the vehicle still moving on the main highway. Accelerating again, Hythe closed the distance until he could easily read the vehicle's German license plate. He would contact Maj.Gen Ronaldson as soon as possible with the make, model, and license number for it to be tracked via each country's traffic camera network. Increasing speed, he slowly overtook the van before sliding into the same lane in front. He could see the driver and his two colleagues in the front by adjusting his mirrors. He left the highway at the next exit, rejoining it immediately, but now several hundred meters behind the van, and continued the drive keeping the target under observation but out of sight by them.

By late morning, just outside Edirne and a few kilometers from the Turkish - Bulgarian border, the van turned off the main road toward Sofia. Now heading on the quieter D535, the Customs Border Post appeared just forty kilometers later. Hythe's vehicle and the others waiting to cross were stopped and searched, with all paperwork being thoroughly inspected. However, it soon became evident that arrangements had obviously been made as the suspect van took only minutes to be waved through and pass both border checks when it finally reached the crossing point.

The van had almost a sixty-minute head-start when Hythe was eventually cleared. Driving as fast as the rural backroads would allow, Patrick was still at least thirty kilometers behind when the target van rejoined the autoroute toward Sofia.

Eventually, also able to increase speed, Patrick gradually closed the distance, relying on each position update as to the van's current position. The next border between Bulgaria and Serbia slowed both down. Again, arrangements seemed to allow the van to pass through virtually unhindered. At the same time, Patrick's Turkish rental BMW raised questions concerning insurance within Serbia and delayed him again.

Finally, as the sky darkened in the early evening, the van carried out a similar maneuver as the previous evening, close to a small Serbian town called Paracin. Patrick was still several kilometers behind when it turned off the main highway onto a minor side road before joining a dirt track out beyond the trees. He stopped and waited for the position updates to map precisely where they halted.

<><><>

Adnan had been getting increasingly concerned inside the van as the day progressed. Unsure if his belt was even working and whether he was successfully being tracked, he tried to discover as much about their route.

With no windows to indicate where they were, he religiously keyed his belt every hour or so, careful not to draw attention to himself. However, his questioning rapidly became a concern to his fellow passengers. He asked about their current position or direction a dozen times, and he was quickly shouted down each time to keep quiet. Even Aisha urged him to stop questioning.

After another long day just sitting there, the van finally turned off the main highway. Trying to alert his follower to the change in direction, he pressed his belt twice.

Aisha saw him and asked, 'Mohammed, what are you doing? Are you in pain? You keep rubbing your stomach.'

'No, no. It's just a bit of cramp from sitting here all day,' he murmured, realizing he'd almost been found out and would need to be more careful.

Everyone on board was feeling restless. The seats in the van were padded but became uncomfortable after a couple of hours just sitting on them. With nowhere to stand or stretch, everyone just wanted to get off and flex aching muscles.

It took another fifteen minutes of driving along bumpy dirt tracks before that day's journey was over. The headlights suddenly reflected off a pair of metal gates and eight-foot-high chainlink fencing as a remote farmhouse and buildings loomed out of the darkness. Braking and turning sharply in through the gates, the driver continued to the rear of the main building and stopped close to a large barn.

As the rear doors were unlocked and a male voice ordered everybody out, Adnan pressed his belt tang for the last time that evening. Intent on climbing out, he didn't notice Aisha had stared at him briefly just as he sent the signal.

The arrangements were similar to the previous evenings - the barn had been converted into an eating and sleeping area. One other van was already there and within an hour, four more arrived. The evening's meal consisted of a thin soup full of vegetables, small meat pieces, and two large chunks of bread. Better than the previous night's offering, there was also fruit available. Adnan grabbed a couple of apples for himself and Aisha, then spent a few moments looking around. He wanted to memorize as much as he could about the place and his fellow travelers. The sleeping arrangements were the same as before; each person was allocated a roll-out mattress for comfort, two grey woolen blankets for extra warmth, and a pillow. None of it looked particularly clean, with the pillow covered in stains from greasy hair, running eyes, and nasal secretions. Against the far wall were four portable toilet cubicles alongside two sinks. People were already lining up to use the meager facilities, unsuitable for sharing between sixty-plus individuals.

Looking around again, Adnan could only see a handful of women and none with young children or children alone.

'Aisha, do you notice? Where are other women? What about all those children that were traveling with us? Where are they now, and who's looking after them?'

Slipping her hand into his and cuddling closer, Aisha said, 'Hush, my love. You ask too many questions.'

<><><>

Following the GPS map, Hythe continued along the dirt track with all lights out. It was slow progress. Hiding the car behind nearby trees to provide at least a little cover, he proceeded on foot. He'd stopped about a kilometer from what looked to be a large farm building. As he neared the building he could see it was surrounded by a tall wire chainlink fence. Two armed guards were patrolling inside the fence, unaware Patrick had already detected them.

Their low voices faded as they moved further from view, but their body odor remained. Patrick waited another full minute until that had dispersed, then moved closer to the wire. He could see four other vehicles parked near the building, but with the darkness of night now complete and without night-vision-goggles, there wasn't enough light spilling to make out the vehicles' models and license plates.

Waiting behind a bush, he timed the guards. Their complete circuit of the fence took them six minutes. Watching them pass him twice more, he then delayed another minute before quickly climbing over the wire. He'd seen the guards brush against it, so he knew it wasn't electrified or alarmed. It took him less than fifteen seconds to scale it, swing over, and drop down the other side. He was hidden deep within dark shadows five seconds later, invisible to everybody.

There wasn't a moon, and the few farmhouse lights were all at the front, so he had to get close enough to each vehicle to make out their license plates. Climbing up onto the top of one van, he managed to reach the lip of a low roof. Swinging onto it, he crawled toward a dimly illuminated small ceiling window and carefully looked in. He could see approximately sixty people in various groups sitting, eating, or sleeping on the floor. He couldn't recognize Adnan in the gloom, but anyway, there wasn't any way to reach him. As he shifted his weight to leave, his foot dislodged a pebble or something that rattled down the sloping roof. Suddenly there was a shout followed by two others. Staying firmly in the shadows, Hythe rapidly ran the length of the building ridge before the guards appeared, lowering himself down and dropping the last few feet as they came into view. He remained firmly in the shadows and watched more guards arrive and shine torches onto the roof. He couldn't understand what language they were shouting in but knew he'd be detected if he remained where he was.

17

CRAWLING under one of the parked vans was difficult as its ground clearance was low, and his jacket snagged twice. The first time he quickly freed it, but the second time it caught solid. With his legs still outside the van's cover, he knew anyone looking would easily see him or trip over him. After what seemed an age, he finally managed to free himself and slid his feet under the side of the van just as heavy footsteps signaled someone's approach. The guards continued searching but, finding nothing untoward, soon lost interest and assumed it was a bird or a rat. Hythe waited another full hour before he ventured out. Gently sliding out from under the far side of the van, he stayed behind cover as he watched. Some guards had gone back inside, while the ones on fence duty returned to their earlier routine. He spent another thirty minutes checking before making his exit. Thirty minutes later, he was back in his car and heading toward Paracin.

The man hiding within the shadow of the trees where the dirt track met the main highway saw him as he passed. The man stubbed out his cigarette while raising his binoculars to his eyes and then dialed a preset number from a memory location on his cell phone. He passed on Patrick's vehicle license plate number, make, model, and color as soon as his call was answered

<><><>

Exhausted after two long days of driving almost 2,000 km, he checked into a '*Best Western*' type motel in Paracin. He paid for his room in cash and had to provide his Terry Johnson passport for examination and identification. Satisfied, the clerk photocopied and returned it, having issued him the key for a single room on the first floor at the rear. The room was typical of a million others. Bland wallpaper, fawn curtains, two single beds, a wall-mounted TV, and an ensuite bathroom. However, it appeared clean and looked reasonably comfortable.

He was famished, having eaten only snacks while driving, so he headed to the Paracin Best Grill & Bar, a restaurant he'd passed about a mile before. Having been cooped up in his car all day, apart from his brief evening adventure, he welcomed the fresh air and exercise, so he walked back along the main road even though it was drizzling.

He could see the place was only about a third full as he ordered a beer at the bar. Grabbing a menu, he seated himself at an empty table in the corner with his back to the wall. He ordered a steak, baked potato, and salad from the waitress. He texted Ronaldson a brief update and the other vehicles' details and license numbers.

An hour later, with the meal consumed and an empty second beer bottle on the table, he paid cash for dinner and left a good tip for the waitress. He jammed his hands in his pockets, pulled his jacket collar up against the heavier rain now falling, and headed toward the hotel. Heading back out, he realized that he'd walked in a big curve by following the road, and the quickest and shortest way back to the hotel was across an old disused parking lot.

He'd gone almost four hundred meters in darkness when his finely-tuned senses alerted him, and he became aware of their presence before he could see them. Three men appeared out of the night and blocked his path.

Paracin is only a small town. The leader of the three men had received a call. Find this stranger. Hurt him. Break a few bones. Stop him following us. It hadn't taken many phone calls to find which of the two hotels a stranger driving a Turkish-registered BMW X5 was staying in. Reception had called his room and confirmed the Englishman Hythe, or Terrence Johnson as reception knew him, was out. With the photocopy of his passport in their pocket, the three men had quickly split up and visited four local bars and two restaurants to find him. After quickly spotting him, it hadn't taken much guesswork that he would cross the parking lot. They waited for their chance.

'You no belong here,' was shouted at him.

Ignoring them, Patrick stopped ten feet short of them, fingers clasping some coins in his pocket as he considered his options.

'You hear? You no belong here,' the same person said again.

'How very perceptive of you,' Patrick answered.

'Ugh?... You no welcome here. You foreigner, go home. You follow my friends.'

'Have I?'

'He don't like it.'

'No, it's not *he don't like it,* it's *he doesn't like it.*'

'Uh? Shut up, you fuck.'

'Just trying to help, chummy. Just trying to help,' Patrick said, smiling.

Muttering something to his two colleagues in a local dialect, the three of them moved apart and began to approach.

Hythe tried to step past them, but they moved in front again. The one on the left was about the same size as him and pulled out a large hunting knife. The guy in the middle doing the talking didn't seem to be armed, but the one on the right carried a heavy meter-long chain and was a good four inches taller than Hythe, plus heavily built. Hythe thought he recognized him as the guard in the passenger seat from the van he had seen earlier.

Shrugging but with no option other than to fight, Hythe tackled the knife-wielding one first as the most dangerous. He lunged toward the knife holder while pulling some coins out of his pocket. Throwing them hard into his assailant's face, who instinctively turned his head away, Hythe sidestepped the hasty thrust of the knife and moved in close. Using his left hand, he blocked and pushed the blade arm further away as he jammed the heel of his right hand straight up into the guy's chin as hard as he could.

The guy's head snapped back with a loud crack before Hythe grabbed his shoulder and turned the two of them almost ninety degrees clockwise, putting his assailant's back toward the other two. With the middle guy still between the chain guy and Hythe blocking any move, Hythe had time to ram his knee hard up into his opponent's groin.

He then gripped the wrist holding the knife and slammed the arm down onto his raised knee, elbow first. His opponent's elbow snapped backward, and the guy screamed both from the pain in his arm and groin and doubled up forward. Hythe grabbed the hunting knife handle and slammed the bulbous end of the hilt hard into the back of his attacker's head.

One down, two to go.

Startled at the sudden turn of events, the middle attacker didn't react quickly enough. Hythe grabbed his jacket front with his free hand and yanked him forward. Hythe smashed his own forehead forward hard into the guy's nose as his head came within range. The force even made Hythe's head spin. The cartilage in the guy's nose splintered and shattered his cheekbones. The strength of the impact knocked him out for hours and would ensure severe headaches for weeks to come.

Two down, one to go.

'Just you and me, pal,' Hythe said, shaking his head slightly to clear it.

A chain can be deadly, Hythe knew, but a bit like wielding a sword, you have to telegraph your move first and be far enough away from your target. As his attacker swept his right arm back, with the chain extending out behind him, ready for the killing blow forward, Hythe darted in close and slashed with the knife at the arm holding the chain while kicking hard with his right leg into the guy's groin. With his arm now useless and blood spurting, the chain lost its forward momentum and rattled to the ground as the guy doubled up forward, gasping for air.

Hythe brought his knee up hard into the bowed head and slammed the knife's hilt hard into the side of the neck just below the ear as the guy's head came back up. The knee and knife hilt mixture took the big guy down in one.

'Hmmm, twelve seconds. I must be losing my edge, or maybe I'm just getting old,' Patrick murmured after checking that all three were unconscious, but their breathing was fine. Wiping the knife clean of his prints in the guy's shirt, he tossed it into a dumpster at the edge of the parking lot.

18

HEADING back to his hotel, Hythe locked the door, jammed the chair against it, and fell asleep. Waking early, he showered and was back on the road by 06:00, wanting to get a head start. Flicking the radio on as he pulled out of the hotel parking, he found a station in English playing local news. The second report on Serbia News was of three men murdered in Paracin last evening. All were stabbed with a large knife before having their throats cut. Police were looking for a foreigner from Turkey believed to be in the region.

He had planned to stop further along the road and wait for Adnan to pass him, but now he knew his only option was to get away from this area and dispose of his car as quickly as possible. The X5 was not a popular model here due to its cost, and one with a Turkish license plate would be easy for the police to spot. Being locked up by local police when accused of murdering people from the same locality would not be conducive to his health. Authorities in this part of the world had a reputation for severe beatings first, then questioning later. Allegedly, many Serbian politicians and police were corrupt paid members of human trafficking rings or criminal gangs. Serbia isn't part of the EU, and although political relationships between Britain and Serbia were reasonable, he could expect a lengthy jail sentence if he survived long enough.

The capital city of Belgrade was only forty kilometers away along a fast four-lane road. There he could melt into the crowds. He accelerated up to just under the legal speed limit and prayed the police would be slow off the mark.

<><><>

He saw police vehicles twice on the other carriageway across the median heading the other way, so he decided he'd pushed his luck enough. He exited the highway and continued on quieter backstreets, but it was a gamble. He would stand out more in that car on less busy roads, but there was less chance the police would be monitoring them.

As he neared the outskirts of Belgrade, he diverted again and kept to the suburbs. Standard evasion techniques include mixing with others and keeping as low-key as possible. Breathing a sigh of relief he'd made it that far, he drove into the underground parking area of Galerija Belgrade Shopping Center twenty minutes later, one of Belgrade's most extensive shopping areas. Parking in a dimly lit section, he wiped down all the areas of the vehicle he'd touched before heading up to the main concourse and toward the food court. All the shops were opening, but it was still too early for the main shopping crowd to have arrived. Ordering a black coffee and a chicken sandwich, he sat while keeping an eye on the toilet area while he ate.

Finally, a male of similar build, height, and age went in alone. Without rushing or making a scene, Hythe headed in. There was just the stranger in there who was just zipping up his clothes. Hoping no one else would venture in, Hythe swiftly grabbed him in a chokehold from the rear while dragging him into a cubicle and closing the door. The stranger struggled for almost fifteen seconds before the hold took effect, and he slipped unconscious. Placing him on the seat, he checked his pockets for a wallet and car keys. Grabbing both, he smiled as he took the one thing he needed before placing the wallet back in the stranger's pocket and quietly leaving, and closing the cubicle door.

Back down to the parking lot, it took him almost five minutes to walk up and down the rows of parked cars pressing the key fob until a car beeped and its lights flashed. Climbing in the VW Jetta, he drove around to his BMW, retrieved his bag, and gave the rear door a final wipe down. Two minutes later, he drove out of the parking lot and swung back up onto the E-70 for the seventy km drive to the Croatian border.

He had not wanted to hurt the stranger, and he knew the man would awaken after a short while, shaken and confused. Staff at the shopping center would assume he was ill and had collapsed or was drunk. They would likely call an ambulance to take him to the hospital. By the time anyone discovered his car had been stolen, Hythe would be across the border and in the EU country of Croatia.

He also hoped the two €500 banknotes he'd slipped into the stranger's wallet would help lessen the blow.

He slowed as he came to the border crossing just fifty minutes later. The news reports now confirmed the police were looking for a European male driving a BMW with a Turkish license plate in connection with the three brutal murders in Paracin the previous evening. Police were warning the public not to approach as it was believed the offender was armed and extremely dangerous.

Having deliberately chosen a busy traffic lane, Patrick passed over the driver's ID card and smiled at the guard. As with most ID and passport photos, the resemblance between the picture and the actual person can be pretty considerable. He was driving a Serbian-registered car and was approximately the same build and age as the person in the photo. The guard, who was overworked and was busy with a long line of traffic waiting with impatient drivers, swiped the card on his keyboard, didn't speak and hardly glanced at Hythe before granting entry, forgetting about him seconds later.

In Croatia, Hythe relaxed slightly as border checks are non-existent between Schengen countries, although Croatia has yet to sign up for that scheme. However, access from Croatia to either Hungary or Slovenia, both being fellow EU states, would be far more straightforward than the other borders he'd crossed recently.

Had his mission to follow Adnan been discovered, he wondered. Wanted by the Serbian Police, he needed to uncover who had set him up and for what reason. Someone had gone to a lot of trouble to murder the thugs who had attacked him and frame him for it. A beating to warn someone to keep away was one thing, but murdering someone raised the stakes.

By the time Hythe arrived in Zagreb in the country's north, Adnan's position updates also showed him inside Croatia, having just cleared the Serbian - Croatian border. Although Hythe was safe here, he wasn't sure how he'd been discovered; he didn't want to use his credit cards as their electronic footprint is too easy to track. He needed to change cars again, ideally something non-descript and with local or German registration, so he decided to steal one.

Zagreb is a popular weekend getaway location for German party-goers and is known for its fun nightlife. It only took him an hour to find an older model vehicle that didn't have the latest alarm anti-theft device fitted but was displaying German license plates. A broken side window, a large flat-headed screwdriver borrowed from the trunk, and removing the steering lock took moments only. Seconds later, the engine of the Passat caught on its first attempt, and with the big two-liter engine gently purring, Hythe continued on his journey toward Austria.

19

ADNAN had had a sleepless night in the barn near Paracin. Worried that he might now be on his own, he'd lain awake trying to devise a plan. He had escaped Syria along with his parents, his father managing to get them to Amman, Jordan. They had gone to the British Embassy at Abdoun to claim asylum. It had been granted to his parents, but he couldn't get asylum on his parents' application because he was nineteen. The British had refused him, finally only agreeing if he carried out an undercover operation for them first. So here he now was – a nineteen-year-old pretending to be a youth of fifteen. The British had drilled into him the need to play everything cool. Don't cause trouble, don't ask questions, and don't get caught using the belt. Just become Mohammed Yusef. In return, when you get back to the UK, your application will be fast-tracked, you will receive British citizenship, and you will be reunited with your parents

But Aisha was causing him concern. He'd never met anyone like her before. She was a few years older than him, and he was smitten. He became aroused every time she touched him. When she put her head on his shoulder in the van and slept, he thought he'd pass out from excitement. She had kissed him, just once on his cheek. He immediately became aroused and erect, quickly covering his groin with his hands to hide his embarrassment. As the days continued, she now always sat with him. Last evening, in the van's darkness, and before they arrived here, she'd gently pulled his hand in under her clothes until it was resting near her stomach on bare skin. He'd been too nervous and excited to move, his erection straining in his lap, but he was sure she could feel him trembling.

Then she moved slightly and gently pulled his arm up until her naked breast was cupped in his left hand, her skin velvety soft with her hard, pert nipple pressed into his palm. He'd fantasized about a moment such as this. He'd often masturbated, having found a discarded Playboy magazine near where he lived. He'd looked at the naked pictures of American women, all with shapely bodies, some with huge, enhanced breasts, but this was the first time he had touched a real woman, which was so much better than photographs. He couldn't help it. He didn't mean to, but with a soft groan, he orgasmed.

Hugely embarrassed, he tried to hide the dark stain spreading through his light-brown-colored slacks. But Aisha knew! She leaned in closer, kissed his cheek again, and murmured, 'It's OK. I'm glad you like me.'

Hardly drawing breath, he murmured back, 'I love you, Aisha,' as his hand gently caressed her breast.

Now, a couple of hours later, and laying on the mattress amongst the other fellow male travelers, he was torn. He wanted to spend every waking moment holding her. He wanted to kiss her and tell her he loved her. He wanted to spend the rest of his life with her. But most of all, he yearned to caress her naked breast again. He decided he'd tell her everything. He was going to spend the rest of his life with her, so he didn't want them to have secrets from each other. He'd find the right time tomorrow, and he'd tell her.

They would sit together, he with his arm around her and maybe, if he was lucky, a hand inside her clothes. They would talk and make plans. He would take her to

England to meet his parents, who'd love her as much as he did and plan to get married. Nothing too big or fancy, but in the Syrian tradition. Then he would get a high-paying job in London and buy her a big house. But first, he would tell her all about himself. She'd be so excited.

He finally fell asleep with a smile on his face.

<><><>

He awoke early the following day, still smiling. After a meager breakfast of stale bread and warm coffee, they were loaded back in the vans.

The opportunity came nearer lunchtime, having crossed into Croatia. They had already been traveling for almost two hours and had passed Belgrade, but Adnan hadn't found the right time to tell her. She was sitting next to him in the rear of the van, but others were sitting too close by, and he wanted privacy. As before, they were forcibly told by the guard to keep quiet as the van stopped at the Customs desk. The driver spoke a few words and then was allowed to pass through. They stopped on a quiet lane soon after to stretch their legs and eat. The meal on offer was the same as usual - a large bag of various pre-made sandwiches along with bottles of water, but he finally found them almost alone as the others were crowding around the food.

'Aisha, I love you and want to marry you.'

'Hush Mohammed, I love you too, but you'll have to wait until you're old enough. You are only fifteen,' she said.

'No, my name's not Mohammed, it's Adnan, and I'm nineteen. It's all a lie.'

'Wha... what? Why would you lie, Mohammed?'

'Honest! It's true. It's all made up. My name isn't Mohammed Yusef; it's Adnan Hussam. I'm not fifteen;

I'm nineteen and from Homs in Syria, not Aleppo. My parents aren't dead. They are alive in London.'

Shocked, Aisha said, 'You're serious?'

'It's true. There was a Mohammed Yusef, whose father was a doctor at Aleppo University Hospital. The mother was a secretary for a firm of architects. He had a sister of seventeen, Yasmin, and a brother of six, Karim. All of them are dead. Mohammed's brother and sister were killed when tanks belonging to the Syrian government forces blasted their building, wrecking it completely. ISIS shot the mother for daring to answer back. The father died when a Russian bomber aircraft attacking rebel forces misjudged it and hit the hospital. And Mohammed was killed when a suicide bomber detonated himself.'

'But why would you pretend to be someone who's already dead? 'she said.

And over the next twenty minutes, he explained how he was a spy working for the British to get his British citizenship. He said how the British had made him memorize everything about Mohammed Yusef and pretend to be him. He also told her about the special belt he was wearing and how he had to activate it at least once an hour and whenever anything different happened so that the people following him knew where he was.

'Adnan, that's fantastic,' she said after a few minutes of thought. 'That means we can be together and get married. I will get the guards to call ---'

'No, you mustn't. Anyway, who will they call?'

'The man in charge. The leader. He will be so happy we are to be married. He will arrange a private car for us instead of having to stay in this van, I think,' she said as she leaned closer and kissed him, this time on the lips.

He'd never been so happy.

Aisha smiled at Adnan as she went and spoke with the driver. He pulled out his cell and passed it to her. Smiling and waving at Adnan, she spoke for almost five minutes before handing back the phone and returning to him, still smiling.

'Adnan, it's as I thought. He is very happy for us and said he will pick us up later in his private car so we can travel together.'

They stopped less than an hour later for fuel. The driver motioned Aisha to come to him and spoke to her for a few minutes.

Returning to Adnan, she said, 'Moha—sorry, Adnan, it is still a surprise. It's as I thought. He is on his way, and we just need to wait here until he arrives,' she said, holding his hand, as the van left and continued its journey without them.

Two hours later, a long-wheelbase silver-grey Mercedes SUV with darkened windows pulled onto the forecourt. A male passenger alighted, aged in his late fifties, along with two well-built bodyguards.

20

'SO you want to marry Aisha?' the passenger said, extending a handshake. 'That's excellent news. Let me be the first to congratulate you both.'

Beaming with pride, Adnan shook his hand.

'Come, both of you, get in my car and travel in comfort. Luckily, I was only in Zagreb,' he said, arm extended and beckoning them.

As they moved to the Mercedes, Adnan was a little surprised to see he was being directed toward the rear to sit between the two bodyguards while Aisha slid into the front between the driver and the older guy. As they pulled away, the leader turned in his seat and said in a pleasant tone, 'So tell me what you told Aisha earlier, Adnan. This is very exciting. Please leave nothing out.'

So for the next fifteen minutes, Adnan told his story again, not watching what route they were taking, answering questions as they arose, and even slipping his belt off to show how it worked. No, he didn't know who was following him. He'd never met them. But he knew they were trying to track the immigrants' route. He had to play along and use the false name and details if asked. When he eventually arrived in Britain, someone would meet him, and he'd be reunited with his parents and be given his full citizenship.

'Splendid, splendid. Is there anything more to tell?' the leader asked.

'No, sir, nothing. I just want to be with Aisha. We want to be together.'

'Hmmm, unfortunately, that isn't going to happen,' he said. 'You see, Aisha doesn't love you. Never has, in fact. Aisha isn't even her name. It's Svetlana. A little bird told me there would be a spy amongst all the passengers this time, and we know someone has been tracking us. But I didn't know who the bad apple was. However, we suspected it might be you because something about you just didn't seem to fit right.'

'But you love me, Aisha. You told me so. You even let me touch you,' he said, tears welling up in his eyes.

Turning round in her seat, she looked at him with contempt in her eyes. 'You stupid little fuck. You're just a boy pretending to be a man. Touch my tit once, and you couldn't stop yourself messing your pants. You make me sick,' she said, finishing by spitting in his face.

He realized they were in the middle of nowhere, looking out the window. Just open fields and forests. The driver turned off the track they were on and headed in through the trees. Stopping, the leader told the bodyguards to get him out. As they dragged him out of the vehicle, terrified now by what he'd done and what was about to happen, his bladder relaxed, and the warm smell of urine arose around him as he wet himself.

'Little fucker's pissing himself,' Sveta laughed as she pulled out a pistol and kicked him hard in the rear of his legs. As his knees buckled and he collapsed to the dirt, she took aim and shot him three times in the back of his head, laughing hysterically like a child as his head exploded from the impact of the third round.

Leaving the body in a ditch, they climbed back into their car just as it began to snow lightly. As the vehicle turned and headed back along the track, the leader made a phone call before telling the driver to get back on the main road and catch up with the others but keep a distance of ten kilometers behind them.

<><><>

Hythe was concerned. He was now in a Ljubljana cafe waiting for an update. The easiest and most direct route between Turkey and the Channel Ports of Calais or Boulogne would be Turkey, Bulgaria, Serbia, Croatia, Slovenia, Austria, Germany, and France, or Belgium first, then France. Basically, along the route he was already taking, hence him already crossing into Slovenia.

But the van's position now appeared to be stopped halfway between the Serbian-Croatian border and Zagreb and had not been updated for almost four hours. Had his contact been detected? Had the radio belt malfunctioned? If there were no more location updates, perhaps the best thing to do was try and remain in front of them and intercept them nearer the Channel.

With that in mind, he continued his drive toward Salzburg and Munich, stopping that evening at a small hotel just inside Austria and close to the German border as snow began to fall more heavily.

21

AS the traffickers headed toward the main road, the leader had initially considered using one of his men to fool whoever was following and tracking Adnan off on a wild goose chase. However, after careful consideration, he had decided it would be more beneficial to capture this person and interrogate them. Accelerating past his people smuggling vehicles, they would head directly to his base in Austria and lay a trap.

Early the following morning, everything was ready. With guards deployed outside the forest, he fitted the belt around his waist and pressed and held the tang before repeating it every hour.

It worked. One of the lookouts was messaged by early afternoon. A car with a single occupant was heading up the private track in the distance.

<><><>

Hythe had woken up the following morning at 06:15, showered, dressed, and headed downstairs for breakfast. The hotel was small and privately owned, with just six ensuite rooms to rent. It was built in a traditional Austrian ski lodge style with a steep, sloping roof, heavy wooden beams, and timbers. It was also well insulated, extremely comfortable, and had beautiful distant views of the Alps as the snow had stopped and the sky was sunlit and blue.

As he tucked into a hot breakfast followed by fresh fruit and bread, all washed down with strong black coffee, he thought it would be easy to forget the mission he was on. Instead, he started thinking about how much his close friend and possible love interest, Gina Panaterri, would enjoy a holiday here.

Having still not received any position update, he decided he would finish breakfast and then continue the direct route toward Calais via Munich, hoping their paths would cross again soon.

Fifty minutes later, driving along the A8 he was suddenly pulled back to reality when the receiver in his pocket pinged with a new position update. With his mind now back in the present, he pulled the device from his jacket and pressed the *display* button.

Pulling off the A8 at the next junction, he checked the indicated position on the receiver against the map application he had on his phone. Quietly cursing, he realized they must have overtaken him as he slept. The flashing blue cursor indicated a position in the lower hills of the Austrian Alps. This was located several hours' drive further on from where he thought they were, and according to his map, now it appeared they were almost twenty miles south of his current position and in the middle of a forest. He wondered if it was from a random signal and decided to wait for another update.

Stopped with the engine off, the inside of the car grew cold. Changing the view on his map application, he could see the region's elevation from where the signal originated. It was at around 1300 meters above sea level. His current position was almost 600 meters. There were no higher hills or obstructions between where he was currently stopped and the signal source.

An hour later, the receiver pinged again, but its location hadn't changed. Although the line of sight put the device beyond its expected range of fifteen miles, Hythe knew from experience how atmospherics could affect radio signals. The temporary break in the snowfall and the clear blue sky might have made a difference. Changing direction, he headed toward where the signal was originating.

Nearing the region, he stopped and looked around. The entire area was hilly, mountainous, and had a thick growth of coniferous trees and shrubs. At this altitude, the air temperature was far colder, with trees already bending under the weight of the snow. It was also very sparsely populated. Drilling into the aerial map within his cell phone, he could see what looked like a set of buildings inside a walled perimeter, surrounded by dense woodland. The next closest structures appeared to be at least 10km away. Cautiously, he continued along the single thin access road as it weaved through the forest. When his GPS showed him still over a kilometer from the compound, he stopped the car in a small clearing completely hidden from the track.

Slipping a coat on to combat the heavily falling snow and the chill air, he removed his wallet, cellphone, and passport but kept his stolen Serbian ID card. He placed them in a bag before hiding them by burying them in the snow at the base of a tree located to his right. He tied a piece of cloth to the trunk of an adjacent sapling. He moved in the general direction for the first half kilometer but stayed hidden within the trees. Then he exited onto the track, carefully listening for any noise present in the silent world caused by snowfall. Already his footsteps were being covered and disappearing. The weather also masked the camouflaged infra-red beam he broke as he continued along the track. He had walked about a half kilometer when two men stepped out from behind trees. They were both armed with Heckler and Koch MP5 submachine pistols pointing at him.

With no chance to outrun their firepower and nowhere to hide, he stopped, raised his hands, and said in the best British accent he could, 'I say, chaps. I appear to be lost. You couldn't point me in the direction of Munich, could you?'

One guard covered him with his machine pistol without saying a word, while the other briefly frisked him for weapons before frog-marching him along the track to the gate. Even with his many years of SAS training, there was no way he could tackle either of them without the very real risk of being shot by the other. As they approached the high outer wall, a heavy wooden gate swung open, and a three-story gothic-style manor house came into view. Chiseled into the stonework above the doorway were the words *The Fortress*.

One of the guards moved in front of him and beckoned him to lower his raised hands. He saw the guard give an almost imperceptible nod to his colleagues as he did so. He heard the slight rush of air and managed to brace himself briefly before the reversed gun butt struck him forcibly on the rear of his head. His knees buckled, and the last thing he saw was the ground rushing toward him turn to blackness.

22

SLOWLY, as the darkness faded, the pain returned. He was sitting on a solidly built chair with his hands zip-tied in front of him. He was bound to the chair with rope or cord around his chest and ankles. His head throbbed from the beating. The slightest movements sent bright flashes of light to his eyes and severe pulses of painful agony through his skull. Very slowly, to minimize the pain, he looked up. Something felt tight on his skin around the rear of his head. He guessed it was dried blood from the wound where he'd been struck.

He was in what looked like the dining room of an old chateau or country house, with thick exposed stone walls, ceiling beams, and heavily built furniture. Looking around, he could see he was seated at one end of a long polished table. His place setting in front of him was empty. His outer coat had been removed and was lying on the floor.

The two who'd apprehended him were standing slightly behind him, one to each side. Two other people were at the far end of the table, over fifteen feet away, almost in silhouette from the glow emanating from the heavy logs burning in a large stone fireplace and from the light entering a full-length window made up of many smaller panes. It looked like lunch was in the process of being served.

'Who are you? What is your name, and why were you carrying a Serbian identification card? It's not even you in the picture?' a male voice said at the other end of the dining table.

'Me?' Hythe said. 'I was just trying to find Munich. I stopped to ask some locals, and someone hit me on the hea—'

'ENOUGH!' the voice shouted. 'Fuck me about, and I will make this slow and painful. I will ask you once more. What is your name? Who are you, and why were you following our vehicles? Why are you carrying a Serbian identification card of someone looking vaguely similar to you?'

Glancing around before answering, he finally said, 'My name is Terry Johnson.'

Slamming his fist down on the table, he shouted, 'We know you were following our vehicles. I want to know who gave those orders. You only have the time it takes us to eat our lunch to live, so make it easy on yourself. Last time. Who are you, and why were you following our vehicles?'

'Me?' Hythe said. 'I told you. I was just passing and trying to find Munich.'

'OK, you want to be a tough guy!' the voice said. 'So your name is Terry Johnson. The person you were tracking. What was his name? Mohammed Yusef or Adnan something. No matter either way. He's dead. We know all about you following him and this belt,' he said, holding it aloft. 'Your people sold you out. We'd received information from London that a spy was in one of the groups, and someone had been sent to track him. We didn't know who the spy was, but Sveta found him, didn't you, my lovely Svetlana? And, of course, he's dead, but now we have you, and you are next.'

Hythe could make out his hosts at the other end of the table now his eyes had adjusted to the gloom.

He tried to keep his expression impassive as the surprise of discovering the mission was already blown hit home. But along with the shock, something else was registering. Looking at the man from over a dozen feet away triggered something in Hythe's distant memory. There was something vaguely familiar about him, but the memory was too vague, too faint. It was like trying to grasp fog. There was something there, but he didn't know what.

Turning to the slim mousey-haired woman, who was already speaking, saying '… the English expression is.'

'What? Sorry, I wasn't listening. What were you saying?'

'I was saying,' she said in a raised voice, '*something about him stood out a mile,* the English expression is, although I prefer the American version of *Like tits on a bull,*' Svetlana answered. 'He just didn't seem right, so I spent some time with him. It was easy. Poor little boy fell in love with me. Then, with a bang, he was gone. Well, three bangs, actually,' she said, giggling.

'Not as good as Adam Paisley, though,' she continued. 'Put me off eating pork for a week,' she giggled louder.

'Who was Adam Paisley?' Hythe asked, already knowing the answer and vying for time.

Almost coyly, she answered, 'He was your predecessor. We met in a bar in Munich. Only once. He was quite cut-up about it,' she said, giggling even louder.

The man, who looked to be around sixty and still in good shape, pushed his chair back, stood, and strode toward him. Slightly taller than Hythe with salt and pepper hair, a greying goatee, and dark brown eyes, as he got nearer, he said, 'How long were you following us?'

'Let's be civil about this. I've told you my name, Terry Johnson. What's yours?' Patrick said, smiling.

A closed fist slammed into Patrick's cheek before he could even brace himself against the impact. Glancing at the outstretched arm thrust close to his face, he saw the shadowy shape of an old tattoo on the inner wrist of a curled and spitting python.

'Feodor Govorov. Major Feodor Govorov,' he said, rubbing his knuckles, although Patrick hardly heard it. The old tattoo had been like a flashbulb going off in his head. Random thoughts were being triggered.

Finally, Hythe said, 'I'm guessing of the Russian Armed Forces? And the skirt?'

'The FSB, now retired,' Govorov said, 'And the *skirt*, as you call her, is my partner, Svetlana Petrovich. Who do you work for?'

'You're a bit old for her, aren't you, or is she just a gold digger?'

Slamming his hand down on the table, Govorov half-shouted, 'Business partner... and executioner. Now answer my question. Who do you work for and how long have you been following us?'

Looking at Govorov's face didn't reveal anything apart from a look of anger in his eyes. Then Hythe noticed Goverov's right earlobe, distorted and scarred from previous fire damage.

Hythe answered, briefly confirming he'd been following them since Gaziantep.

Walking back toward Svetlana, Govorov tossed the belt and ID into the fire, where they began to smoke and ignite within a few seconds. He said, 'Well, you won't have any more use for these, but tell me, how did you overpower the three men I sent to attack you in Paracin?'

Not wanting to give anything away about his background, Patrick said, 'There was a group of four men walking by when your goons attacked me. They thought I was being mugged and helped. I just ran away.'

Not sure if Hythe was telling the truth, Govorov returned to his chair and sat down before saying, 'You seem a lucky man, Johnson, if that is your name. Unfortunately, your luck is about to run out.'

Over the next fifteen minutes, Hythe sat silently, thinking about Govorov and the FSB as Govorov finished his lunch of stew before ending with cheese and biscuits, all washed down with multiple glasses of red wine.

The FSB is the Russian Federal Security Service, or to give its full name, the Federal'naya Sluzhba Bezopasnosti. It is the principal security agency of Russia and the successor agency to the Soviet Union's feared KGB, itself a direct successor of preceding agencies such as the NKVD and, before that, the Cheka. Its headquarters are in Lubyanka Square, Moscow, the main building of the former KGB, and the director of the FSB is directly answerable to the president of Russia. Its primary responsibilities include counter-intelligence, internal and border security, counter-terrorism, and surveillance within Russia. It is also involved in countless covert operations against the West at the behest of the Russian leader, including assassinations of defectors and the president's political opponents.

Eventually, after placing his empty wine glass on the table, Govorov smiled and said to Hythe, 'OK, my lunch is finished. Time to die,' before turning to Svetlana and saying, 'Over to you, Sveta, my dear.'

Pouting, Svetlana looked up from eating and said, 'No, Feodor, I've not finished eating yet, and I still want coffee. It's cold and snowing outside. Have the guards hold him until I'm ready.'

'Not going to do what your lover tells you?' Patrick said.

'Lover? No. I think I'm a little too old for him now,' Svetlana said. Turning to the guards, she said, 'Take him outside and hold him.'

Govorov considered this before nodding toward the two men standing behind Hythe.

The guard standing on Hythe's right slipped open a razor-sharp flick knife. Hythe tensed, but there was nothing he could do.

23

LEANING forward, the guard used the flick knife to cut through the ropes around Hythe's chest and ankles before closing the blade and dropping it into his coat pocket. Hythe was violently yanked up from the chair, hands still zip-tied together before being half-dragged away by a guard on each arm as Govorov called out, 'Goodbye, Mister Johnson. We won't be meeting again.'

Under his breath, Hythe murmured, 'Don't count on it, pal.'

He was forcibly marched through the doorway, passing a room with its door ajar before being led down corridors toward the rear exit facing the woods and forest. Stepping through the outer rear entrance, they were on the top level of a row of seven snow-covered granite steps with a thick stone balustrade leading out into the grounds.

As they cleared the top step, the wind gusted and kicked up snow that had already fallen. Hythe's left arm guard relaxed his grip slightly as he put his free hand inside his jacket to pull out a suppressed pistol. This was just the moment Hythe had been waiting and praying for.

Suddenly slumping down caught both guards by surprise as all of Hythe's weight fell onto their hands holding him. At the same time, Hythe heaved to the left, unbalancing the guard who, already slipping in the snow, fell against the balustrade and who, in turn, loosened his one-handed grip on Hythe's arm even more. In an instant, Hythe yanked his left arm free and turned toward the other guard on his right, grabbing the front of his jacket and pulling him toward him. Jerking his head backward first, he lunged forward using all his strength. He smashed his forehead as hard as he could into his opponent's nose while firmly driving his knee into the guard's groin. The average human head weighs approximately 5kg. The thrusting motion would have multiplied the impact force to around 12kg, the same weight as a typical bowling ball. Hearing the crunch of broken bones and seeing the blood and snot running down his face Hythe knew the guard's nose was broken.

He also knew he had less than half a second before the first guard's pistol cleared his jacket. Turning and trying not to slip in the snow, Hythe grabbed the gun hand as it appeared, pushing the guard backward partly over the stone balustrade to keep him unbalanced. Bending the guard's hand and fingers back until he heard the snap of at least one finger, he closed his own fingers over those already on the trigger.

The suppressed explosion as the weapon discharged near his head was loud enough to momentarily deafen Hythe as the soft-nosed round exited the barrel. The bullet traveled up through his opponent's chin before continuing up into the brain, finally exiting through the top of the skull, spraying blood, brains, and gore into the air.

Snatching the gun from lifeless fingers, Hythe turned it toward the second guard, still heavily dazed from the impact to his face. Pulling the trigger for the second and third time, he murmured, 'Don't fuck with the SAS, pal.'

He ran down the steps ducking as a series of bullets peppered the stone balustrade, spraying sharp pieces of granite at him. Glancing right, he saw another sentry had ventured around the corner, saw him attack the guards, and had opened fire with an assault rifle.

With both his hands still zip-tied, Hythe turned, aimed, and fired four times on the run. His third shot caught the would-be shooter high in the shoulder as Hythe cleared the thirty or so feet of snow-covered flat lawn and disappeared amongst the bushes.

He could hear the shouts of other guards as he ran headlong toward the thickening trees. The covering of branches had limited the amount of snow landing on the ground, but it would still be relatively easy for anyone to follow the tracks his feet were making.

Slowing just long enough to relax and then flexing his arm muscles rapidly to snap the zip-ties, he ducked and dodged around the trees as his pursuers began chasing him into the wood, firing blindly. Although running in a straight line gives you maximum distance, it is the easiest to follow. Keeping changing direction ninety degrees or so forces those chasing to split up, making capture less likely.

After almost 300 meters, he came to the eight-foot-high walls he'd seen earlier, signifying the property's edge. The snow along its top was level suggesting it didn't have any glass or sharp inserts embedded in it.

Jamming the pistol in the rear of his waistband, he took a running leap at the wall, even though it was taller than he was. Scrabbling his hands through the snow and trying to get a grip with his feet, he felt exposed, just waiting for a bullet in the back. Then his foot wedged against something sticking out a little, and with a thrust from his legs, he swung his body up and over as five rounds thudded into where he'd been climbing moments before, spraying stone chippings violently around.

He twisted and jumped down to the ground in one smooth movement landing heavily just a few seconds later amongst bushes next to the same track he'd been on earlier. Gasping for breath and cursing a twisted ankle, he knew he had to get further away. The guards might not follow him over the wall directly, but it wouldn't take them long to find a way through.

As he half ran, half hobbled along the snow-covered track toward where he'd left his vehicle, he heard the roar of a powerful car engine accelerating somewhere behind him. He reached for the pistol in the small of his back, ready to take a stand, but it was gone. It had fallen as he'd cleared the wall or dropped when he'd landed awkwardly.

Running as fast as his ankle would allow, the engine's roar got louder as it accelerated toward him.

With no option to fight, Hythe half ran across the track, jumped the small embankment and ditch before dashing headfirst behind the thick foliage and tree trunks. His ankle was sore, but he knew he had to put enough distance between himself and his pursuers.

That's when the car began to lose traction and slip and slide in the snow. The driver panicked and over-corrected with the steering, then made matters far worse by jamming his foot on the brakes.

The front nearside wheel touched the embankment, plowing through the fallen snow until it found hard earth and jammed solid. The kinetic energy of the vehicle was to continue in a straight direction. These two opposite forces were to spin the car a complete 180 degrees until both the front and rear offside wheels rode up over the embankment and slipped down into the ditch resulting in the car ending up laying at a crazy fifty-degree angle.

The front passenger was trying to hold his door open one-handed and climb out, but the vehicle's angle, combined with the weight of the Mercedes door, kept causing it to slam back shut each time. The driver and rear passenger were trapped temporarily as their doors were now against the bottom of the ditch.

Hythe didn't hang about. He heard the sound of automatic gunfire as the car's occupants shot the windshield out before climbing out, but he was three hundred meters away by now. Trying not to laugh at the comedy show occurring in the crashed car, he hurried through the thickening forest, changing directions a few more times to throw any pursuers off his track. After almost a half-kilometer, he slowed and moved in the approximate direction he hoped he had left his car earlier.

It took him over thirty minutes to approach it silently, pausing every few minutes to make sure he didn't stumble into one of the guards searching for him. It had also occurred to him that although he'd hidden the car thoroughly from view from the track, they might have already found it.

The final two hundred meters took the longest. It was still snowing heavily, and Hythe was soaked and frozen, creeping through the forest and wearing ordinary clothes. He was sure his chattering teeth would give away his position. Then he smelled it. The faint but pungent, acrid smell of cigarette smoke was hanging in the air. Then he heard a soft cough, followed by two soft thumps as if someone was stamping their feet in the snow to keep the circulation moving. Carefully rounding the next tree, the rear of his Passat came into view just as he heard another cough. The source of the noise was behind the wide trunk of a large tree to the right of his car. It took him another twenty minutes to silently backtrack and move around to approach the noise source from a different direction.

His car had been discovered, but only one person was guarding it; the others were still trying to track him or were back at the Fortress. It was one guard with a hunting rifle slung over his shoulder and a 9mm automatic in his gloved hands. Hythe moved silently toward the tree, slightly behind the trunk, placing himself just out of direct sight. It was a straightforward decision, kill or be killed.

With his right hand clenched with his fingers folded under, his second row of knuckles formed a jagged edge of hard bones; he moved slightly forward and said, 'Psst!'

As the guard jumped and looked around, surprised at the sound so close to him, Hythe struck once hard and fast. He rammed his arm forward, the rigid knuckles of his right hand slamming into the guard's soft thyroid cartilage and larynx. The guard initially began raising his weapon, then realizing he couldn't breathe, he dropped his automatic and started clawing at his throat. There was nothing anyone could do. Even if a team of paramedics had been there, they couldn't have saved him. With his throat completely crushed, the seconds ticked away as he collapsed through lack of oxygen, his brain ceasing to function a minute later.

Hythe pocketed the fallen Glock automatic and the rifle. He had no compunction over what he'd done. It had been him or me, Hythe rationalized as he removed the thick overcoat and gloves from the body, grateful at last to have some warmth. He was even more surprised when he found a suppressor to fit the rifle in the jacket pocket.

He looked around to find the sapling with the cloth still attached. As expected, the snow around its base had been disturbed as the guard had searched the location. However, foraging near the tree's roots adjacent to it, Hythe quickly recovered his wallet, passport, and cell phone bag. He started the car again using the screwdriver jammed in the key lock, the engine noise dampened by the falling snow and tried to drive forward, but the front wheels failed to grip and merely spun in the snow. Checking the trunk, he found an old blanket. With it wedged under the front wheels, he slowly used the gears to gently rock the car forward and back under its own power. Finally, he'd set up enough momentum to keep going, and the front wheels found traction.

24

BACK on Route 8, Hythe continued on his journey to Calais. That evening he got as far as Saarbrücken on the border of Germany and France before stopping overnight at a Gasthof. His mind was still racing, and he couldn't relax, so he spent an hour typing a detailed email update of everything that had happened that day before sending it off to Ronaldson. After finally managing to fall asleep, he awoke an hour later, breathing hard and dripping in sweat.

The nightmare had returned in its most extreme form since childhood.

Intense noise … people screaming … extreme cold … water … not being able to breathe … locked doors … faceless man in black … fires … smell of burning flesh … bodies on the ground …

He lay there trembling and sweating for what seemed like hours. Gradually the nightmare passed, and he half-dozed for the remainder of the night, his mind still playing tricks on him. It was with some relief when the bedside clock finally showed 06:30.

Shaved, showered, and dressed, he was one of the first to be served breakfast, with only his red-rimmed eyes displaying his internal tiredness through lack of sleep.

With the sky finally clear of snow but with the daytime temperature only just above freezing, Patrick turned the heater on full and continued driving toward Calais that morning.

Arriving mid-afternoon, he noticed that it seemed to be a free-for-all. As he watched, vans, trucks, and even two old buses arrived and disgorged more people. The crowd consisted primarily of males, most seemingly aged between sixteen and forty, all willing to make the dangerous crossing to the UK, even in the cold snow of winter. Within thirty minutes of arriving, he'd located three campsites for the migrants on the outskirts of Calais, itself only a small town. Each site housed around a hundred and fifty to two hundred people waiting to cross the Channel. A larger encampment near the old disused site at Sangatte held several hundred more. Also arriving were various small trucks delivering dinghies and outboards.

Looking around, Patrick could see various small groups of French Police. Some were National Gendarmerie, and others were Municipal Police. However, they appeared to be merely keeping order.

After leaving the town, Patrick drove west along the coastline for thirty minutes or so toward Boulogne in one direction before retracing his steps and venturing east toward the town of Gravelines. He then walked along the beaches for a few hours, keeping a discrete distance, just observing. A small fleet of trucks had stopped in fields close to the beaches, with men unloading large, flexible bags with uninflated rubber boats. Teams of men were inflating the boats before attaching outboard engines. Each completed craft was camouflaged under netting before the men and trucks departed. As the daylight faded and the shadows lengthened, he managed to creep closer and photograph some of their license plates.

Leaving the area, he parked up and dialed his London HQ number.

When Ronaldson answered, Patrick quickly gave him a brief overview of events of what had happened so far before explaining in more detail where he was, what had happened to Adnan, and his capture and escape

'I'm on the outskirts of Calais and getting nowhere. It's a smugglers' paradise here, even in winter. The cliffs along this entire section of coastline rise in places to almost one hundred meters and the sand dunes are covered in grasses offering perfect cover. Then there are flat sandy beaches stretching from Le Touquet to Ostend in Belgium, making it perfect to launch dinghies from,' he said.

He continued, 'It's so easy for them to cross. The closest point between Britain and France is only twenty-one miles. An inflatable with a medium-sized outboard can manage that in just a couple of hours. I've already seen a steady stream of people arriving, some by bus, some just walking, and many being dropped off from overcrowded cars, vans, and trucks. They're all heading toward the camps or directly toward the quiet beaches or rough grasslands growing near them. Other crews are providing inflatables ready-to-go, including outboards. It takes just minutes to carry these boats the last few meters over the dunes to the water. There are some French police around, but they seem to be keeping clear of where the problems are. This isn't some half-arsed group of people trying their luck. This is being worked on an industrial scale and appears to be well organized. As migrants are being bussed in, boats are being delivered and made ready to take them the same evening. This is a fully organized exodus,' Patrick said.

Pausing for a moment, he continued, 'These bastards don't hesitate to kill. They tried with me and failed, but Adnan was just a kid, poor bugger. In the wrong place at the wrong time. The HMRC guy that was killed, Paisley, I think was his name. Have you managed to get a copy of his report yet?'

Ronaldson confirmed he'd finally managed to get a copy of Paisley's paperwork and gave a brief overview, but it was of little benefit. The report had been redacted but confirmed that Paisley had informed London he'd discovered a contact, a driver, who wanted to leave the smuggling ring but needed money. There wasn't any record of who this driver was, no name or anything to identify him by. Paisley had agreed on a sum of money with him and was ready to meet, but Paisley was killed before this happened.'

'Was his hotel room searched?'

'What?'

'Was his hotel room searched? Did anyone from HMRC go and search his room in Munich to see if he'd left anything of importance?'

Flipping through the brief report again, Ronaldson said, 'No. No, it doesn't appear they did. It seems they relied on the Munich Police who conducted the investigation.'

'I'll head there now. We might strike lucky,' Hythe said, noting the hotel name and address. 'It was weeks ago he died, but most hotels store anything left by a visitor for three months before its disposal. Although being a murder investigation, I expect the police took everything. Do you have the name of the lead detective in charge of the case?'

Hythe could hear the rustling of paper before Ronaldson answered, 'Yeah, it is Senior Detective Heinrich Baum based at police headquarters in Munich. I'll get Wainwright to arrange for you to have access and text you the address. What time will you be there?'

'I'll drive to Luxembourg tonight and get to Munich by lunchtime tomorrow. I'll try the hotel first. Make the appointment with Baum for mid-afternoon.'

25

AFTER abandoning the trusty Passat and picking up an Audi SUV rental in Calais, he arrived in Munich late the following morning. It then took all of Patrick's charm and persuasion. Gunther Schmidt, the hotel manager, had refused to assist at first. The furor by the local press and media after the body had been found had caused a massive decline in business for his establishment. The news had even spread internationally as various visitors from overseas also made cancellations. However, the incident was several weeks ago, and the last thing he needed now was for it all to be raked over again, so finally, he relented.

'Yes,' he answered when Patrick questioned him. *'The police had thoroughly searched the room, but little of value had been found. There was a power lead, but no laptop or cellphone was found. Yes, a female cleaner found the body two days later after complaints of a smell from other guests. The police had been called immediately. The room has been completely redecorated with a new carpet and bed. We had to; there was blood everywhere. And then the police left everything covered in black fingerprint powder. Yes, everything remaining was taken by the police.'*

Hythe spent a few minutes examining the room, but it was as Schmidt said. Everything was new, and there were no clues. Thanking him, Hythe left and headed to the Central Police Department.

Hythe was kept waiting almost an hour before Senior Detectective Baum arrived. 'I'm sorry to have kept you waiting. My superintendent received a call from London yesterday and has agreed I give you access to the case. What can you tell me?' Baum said, barely disguising the contempt in his voice.

'Nothing, I'm afraid. I've just been asked to examine anything Mr. Paisley left behind.'

'Are you suggesting we didn't examine everything properly and you can do a better job than us?' he said argumentatively.

'No, no, not at all,' Hythe said quickly, trying to pacify Baum. 'It's just for the paperwork. It's so we can tick a box in case next of kin, if there is anyone, ask any awkward questions. I guess you also have stupid amounts of paperwork to complete as we do?'

Slightly calmer, Baum spent ten minutes explaining the case was still open, and they had no leads. He then took Hythe to an inspection room before asking him to wait. He reappeared a few minutes later with a large cardboard box. Inside were the contents from Paisley's hotel room, with items protected in evidence bags. Hythe didn't request to open any sealed bags containing sheets and bedding because of the risk of contaminating forensics evidence. The other bags contained two pairs of trousers, three shirts, some underwear, an electric shaver, the missing laptop's charger, a can of deodorant, and a paperback book. After receiving permission to open these, he began examining each item in detail. He flicked through every page of the paperback, looking for anything underlined, circled, or highlighted, but was disappointed. Searching the clothes produced the same result.

Nothing.

Baum's phone rang, so he excused himself and left the room momentarily to take the call as Hythe started putting everything back in the box. As he reached for the can of deodorant, it rolled off the table onto the floor.

Leaning down and picking it up, he flicked the plastic cap off. It was the only thing he hadn't checked. Tucked firmly up inside the plastic molding was a small piece of paper. Pulling it out and unfolding it made him smile. It had a name and an address written in ink on it.

Petr Doležal.

Quickly slipping the paper into his pocket, he replaced the deodorant in the box as Baum returned.

Thanking him for his assistance, Hythe wished Baum good luck with the investigation and left.

<><><>

Patrick called Ronaldson, giving him the name and address details from the note. Ronaldson, in turn, contacted a colleague in the Intelligence Corps, who quickly responded. They confirmed Petr was a popular Czech first name for males, and Doležal was a familiar family name within the Czech Republic. Hundreds of people with the same two names were registered in various towns and cities throughout Europe, although most were located in the Czech Republic. As to the address, it was of an industrial area in Croatia close to the Serbian border. Beyond that, London didn't uncover anything of value. He would have to find a way to narrow it down more. Calling Ronaldson again, Patrick requested a list of items to be shipped overnight by special diplomatic courier to the British Consulate General's local offices at Möhlstraße 5, Munich.

The following morning, having picked up his delivery, Patrick headed back toward Croatia and Serbia. The falling snow reduced visibility, but the main roads had been cleared and gritted, so he made good progress.

The address Hythe had discovered turned out to be a particular warehouse in a complex of abandoned buildings in the small town of Lipovac, close to the Serbian border. London had already investigated its ownership and found the small industrial area had been empty and unused since the last tenants had moved out over six years before. A European shell corporation with registered offices in the Cayman Islands currently owned all the buildings and land surrounding it.

The long journey meant Patrick arrived late in the evening. He stopped over a kilometer from his target, changed into a newly acquired white camouflage winter battledress to lessen his chance of being detected, and began exploring the area. Within an hour, he'd found a perfect laying-up position half a kilometer from the warehouse. This gave him a slightly elevated view of the locality with clear visibility through night-vision goggles – also part of the delivery he'd picked up that morning.

The secret to any successful stakeout is patience and planning. Take time to check the immediate area for guards or patrols. Ensure you know how long a guard's circuit may take. Look for hidden alarms or tripwires and cameras. Patrick gave it a complete hour at his first observation position. Seeing no alarms and no signs of external movement, he moved closer. Six large waste wheely bins grouped a mere hundred meters from the warehouse provided perfect close cover. A couple of vehicles were parked, but both had thick undisturbed snow covering them and hadn't been moved for hours or possibly days.

Thirty minutes later, satisfied there was no one around and there were no signs of life, he headed over toward a corner of the building and scaled a drainpipe onto a low-level slanting roof. On his knees to stop himself from sliding back down, he climbed further to one of four tilt roof windows, brushed a small corner clear of snow, and carefully peered in.

The place appeared empty apart from a couple of small piles of rubbish on the concrete floor. The interior wooden window frame had two thin wires protruding - a clear indicator of a live intrusion alarm. Climbing back down, he approached the main doors. Access was through a large metal up-and-over roller door or a standard steel doorway to its left.

To anybody watching, they would have seen him slide his hands apart along the top, sides, and bottom of the heavily constructed doorframe. Enclosed within his palm was a pocket-sized ultrasonic imager. A small screen indicated two magnetic contacts set within the doorframe. Depending on how they were wired, the contacts would open or close as soon as the door was opened, triggering an immediate alarm or commencing a countdown sequence.

Using a lock pick gun to lift the tumblers, he pushed the door open and waited. The alarm system began to bleep its countdown.

26

THE alarm control box was key-operated and of the older square metal box type. Newer, more sophisticated versions rely on keypads that take longer to override. Using the same lock pick gun, he inserted the prongs in the key slot and pulled the trigger. The mechanism did its job lifting and jiggling the tumblers, but these were stiffer than those in the door lock. It took three sequences until all the tumblers were loose enough to align, but the pick gun finally turned, and the countdown stopped.

He stood in the doorway, looking around. He checked there was still no movement from outside before he closed the entry door. He entered the main warehouse area with his torch masked to produce only a thin beam of light. The narrow beam from his torch illuminated discarded sleeping bags, aluminum foil thermal blankets, woolen blankets, and thin mattresses stacked in the corner. Two large space blower heaters were positioned against the opposite wall, alongside a couple of stackable tables. There were four toilet cubicles along the left side of the warehouse and a small kitchen area with a sink, a benchtop, and a large electric-operated urn for hot water. There was also the smell of food well past its best-before date.

A sudden noise made him freeze. Then it happened again. Scratching and paper rustling. Torch in one hand and Glock in the other he slowly approached the noise source. Six large black plastic rubbish sacks were stacked in the corner. As he swung the light beam along their length, four small red spots of light shone back at him before quickly disappearing.

Two pairs of rat eyes.

Shuffling his shoes on the concrete was enough noise to make the rodents leave, taking another two of their colleagues from inside the sacks with them. Inspecting the bags, he found plastic and cardboard containers containing food remnants, empty drinks cans, and water bottles.

Exploring the rest of the warehouse uncovered two vans parked near the roller doors of the type he'd been following parked near the roller doors, and at the far end of the large building was a standard forty-foot road container. Next to it was a heavy-duty forklift truck and what looked to be two brand new forty-foot chilled refrigerated containers. The discarded rubbish, the container, and the forklift had no discerning information on them, but the refrigerated containers carried identification plates, including model and serial numbers. Patrick photographed the plates and sent them to Ronaldson at SAS HQ to see if they gave any information about the identities of those using the warehouse.

Trying the rear doors of the vans, he was surprised to find both vehicles unlocked with the keys in them. Apart from some rubbish and road maps, the first one was empty, but the second contained a large cardboard box in the rear. Inside were a dozen hanging sacks and sleeping bags. Inside a smaller box were dozens of silver mylar thermal blankets.

This was obviously another stopover location used by the traffickers

Satisfied he'd discovered as much as he could here, he reset the alarm and locked the door before heading to his car. He drove to the next small town, Podgradi, dozed in the car and waited until daylight. He checked into a local hotel. He kept a low profile during daylight, mostly sleeping, with a *Do Not Disturb* sign on the door. He planned to return to his lookout position each night to watch the warehouse hoping for the next traffickers to arrive.

On the third evening, his patience was rewarded.

Wrapped in heavy windproof winter gear to combat the cold and lying in the snow, he could easily see several panel vans and a container truck arrive. The roller doors were opened, with the vehicles driven inside, before the doors were again lowered, ensuring total privacy before their passengers were allowed to disembark.

Guards had been set but didn't patrol out as far as where Hythe was hiding. Some of the crew or drivers came out to smoke. Hythe didn't know or care whether that was a courtesy to their 'guests' inside or they merely wanted some time away and privacy; he needed to talk to one of them in private. It was over two hours later when the opportunity occurred. The voices in the background had stopped, and those seeking a new life in the UK had settled down for the night. The number of smokers had reduced as well. Avoiding the guards who were now half asleep in their duties, Hythe crept closer to the building. There were no outside lights, so dark shadows fought the whiteness of the snow.

He waited, utterly invisible to the naked eye in his snow-colored camouflage until a lone smoker appeared. Smiling to himself, he made quiet, mewing noises to attract the guy who crept forward, fingers clicking and extended in greeting. Instead of a furry nose nudging his fingers, the smoker received a sudden spoken 'meow' in his ear, followed by a swift karate chop to his neck.

<><><>

Waking ten minutes later, when somebody rubbed snow in his face, all the smoker could see was a narrow beam from a powerful torch shining in his face and feel the point of a knife to his throat. A computerized voice in German said, 'Wake up. Where is Petr Doležal?'

'Uhh, what?'

The light momentarily moved away from his face, but just as the smoker blinked, he was slapped hard across the face before the light returned.

'I said where is Petr Doležal?' Hythe said.

'Gone. He's gone.'

'Gone? What do you mean, gone? What was his job? Where's he gone?'

'He was a driver, like me. He disappeared about five weeks ago. Here one day, gone the next.'

'Is he dead?'

'I don't know. Miss Svetlana has been asking about him, but I don't know.'

'Let's keep this simple, pal. Where does he live?'

Maybe feeling a little braver or just being inquisitive, the smoker didn't answer at first, then said, 'Who are you? Why do you want to know?'

The knife's point moved slightly, drawing a small drop of blood, and produced a gasp from the smoker.

'I'm the guy who decides if you live or die in the next ten seconds. I'll ask once more. Last chance. Where does he live?'

'Prague. Zlicin in west Prague,' the terrified smoker blurted, 'That's all I know. Zlicin district in west Prague.'

Hythe thought for a few seconds before saying, 'Turn over.'

Terrified he was about to be killed, he reluctantly obeyed while beginning to murmur a prayer. Hythe slipped his forearm around the smoker's neck, ready to put him in a sleeper hold. As he began to apply pressure, he said quietly into his ear, 'You're not going to die. You'll wake up in about twenty seconds, but you'll be groggy for a while. I suggest you go and have a cigarette and tell anyone who asks you that you fell asleep. I will track you down and kill you if you say anything about me. Do you understand?'

Feeling his arm compress slightly as the terrified guy tried to nod, Hythe exerted more pressure, and the guy slipped unconscious within seconds.

<><><>

Leaving the smoker lying in the snow, Hythe removed the throat microphone plugged into his phone and stopped the voice masking app. Fluent in German from being stationed there when he was younger, he found many European people could speak English or German in addition to their native language. The masking app changed his voice's tone and timbre, making recognition almost impossible. He moved back to his lookout position to settle down and wait and watch, smiling as he saw the smoker stagger back to the warehouse and light another cigarette. When a colleague asked him something, his reply prompted a playful punch to the shoulder and a head rub.

Back at his hotel Hythe typed up a quick email to London before heading to bed for a few hours sleep. With the city and district within the Czech Republic identified, London should be able to narrow down the list of suspects.

<><><>

He felt he'd only just closed his eyes when the constant ringing of his cellphone forced him awake from his slumber. He checked the time and saw he'd only been asleep for less than two hours.

'Patrick, I have good news and bad news. Which do you want first?' Ronaldson said as Patrick tried to force himself awake.

'Good. Make it good news first.'

'We've identified eleven addresses that meet the search criteria for a Petr Doležal. Two can be rejected immediately. One due to his age being in his early eighties and the other being a wheelchair user six years ago after a serious road accident. That leaves just nine possibilities to try.'

'And the bad news?'

'You need to head to Prague.'

27

WIDE awake with renewed enthusiasm, Hythe showered, ate a quick breakfast, and was on his way within forty minutes. The 900 kilometers drive took him through Hungary and western Slovakia, passing Budapest, Bratislava, and Brno before finally arriving in Prague over eight hours later. Although the journey had been long, the road was a 4-lane smooth and fast highway gritted and salted, and it had only snowed intermittently.

Zlicin was a normal working and residential area of Prague. Not poor, but not particularly affluent either. Houses ranged from small two-bedroom types to larger three- or four-bedrooms. Cars on driveways and in the street were middle-range models. Mercedes and BMWs were two to three years old; the most popular models were Volkswagons and Skodas. Within two hours of arriving, Hythe had cleared two of the suspects. One wore a business suit when he arrived home, and the second spoke English and worked as a hotel chef. Neither fitted the mold of a truck driver.

Patrick decided to try one more that evening, leaving six to follow up the next day. Picking one of the seven addresses at random, he found it to be just a few blocks away. Parking a hundred meters from the house, he sat and watched. With the ignition off, the car started to feel cold. It wasn't currently snowing, but the ground was already thickly covered, and the air temperature was hovering below zero. However, sitting in a German-registered vehicle in a residential area in the dark with the engine running was liable to raise suspicion from anyone passing.

He was cold, tired from little sleep the previous night, and hungry. He decided to limit the time watching to thirty minutes. As the hands on the clock clicked round, he was just about to press the engine start button when a heavily built man wearing a thick overcoat left the house he was watching and walked to a local bar. Hythe followed five minutes later. Pushing the door open, he walked into a thick fug of stale cigarette smoke that stung his eyes and assailed his nostrils. It wasn't even decent tobacco, more like smoldering goat or camel shit, he thought as he moved toward the bar.

As his eyes cleared, he could see the man he was tailing sitting at a small table with a beer in his hand, talking to a couple of friends. Briefly looking more closely, this seemed the type of man he was after - older guy, work boots, old jeans, faded shirt, unkempt hair, and facial stubble. Turning to the barman, Hythe ordered four more beers, picked them up, and carried them by their necks.

Putting three down on their table, he said in English, 'If you are the Petr Doležal who knew Adam Paisley, we need to talk. Perhaps your colleagues would offer us some privacy?' All three of them looked Hythe up and down. Finally, Petr muttered something under his breath. The other two slowly stood and moved to a nearby table while eyeing Hythe suspiciously.

'OK, English man. What you want?' he replied, not fully conversant in English but understanding enough.

'Same deal as you had with Adam.'

'Paisley dead. Price doubled.'

'How do you know he is dead?'

'Man found dead with cock in mouth. Big news. Listen to German news DW and BBC. Price doubled.'

Not knowing what deal Petr and Paisley had agreed on, Hythe said, 'I'll give you €5,000, and that's it. Take it or leave it, but that's for full disclosure.'

'€5,000? Leave now, Englishman. You insult. Deal was €10,000. Now €20,000.'

'€10,000.'

'Twenty.'

Hythe waited a few seconds, finished his beer, and stood up. 'Fifteen or I leave, and you get nothing,' he said and walked toward the door.

As his fingers wrapped around the door handle, Petr said, 'Tomorrow night. Small bar, Lucaž, in street at back. By Husova and Skorepka in Old Town. Eleven hours. Come on own. Bring money.'

28

PATRICK spent the morning typing up a detailed account of everything that had happened so far and this evening's planned meeting. Being his first time in Prague, he spent the rest of the day exploring the city as a tourist and checking out the location to meet Petr. He had no reason to believe he was being followed but used the old trick of doubling back momentarily to double-check. Satisfied he was alone, he found a quiet restaurant to enjoy a peaceful meal before heading to the meeting place.

It had continued snowing on and off all day, leaving the streets and ancient cobbles covered in deep snow. Soft and pure white in parts untouched but grey and compressed where footsteps had trod. The breeze was bitterly cold, keeping tourists and locals indoors as he made his way along the empty backstreets. Patrick had walked past the bar twice earlier, checking entry and exit points. For all he knew, this meeting tonight could be a trap. Petr would expect him to be there carrying cash. Lots of it. Three or four of them against just him might seem good odds to them, so he'd brought his sidearm.

He arrived at ten, ready for the meeting at eleven, but remained outside. Three doors along and on the opposite side of the narrow road were two large metal waste bins. Standing in the deep shadow behind, he had a complete view of the entrance to the bar, watching who entered and left.

At ten-fifty, he saw Petr Doležal arrive. Alone. Waiting another twenty minutes to check on any other attendees, he crossed the road and walked in just as Doležal was about to leave.

'I think you not come, Englishman?'

'Sprichst du Deutsch?'

'Of course. Doesn't everyone?' Petr replied in perfect German.

Replying in the same language, Hythe said, 'I thought you might. Just checking. Let's continue in German. Now sit down. Over there,' pointing to a table in the corner, well away from the two other drinkers present at that time, two old men easily into their seventies.

Ordering a couple of beers, Patrick turned to Petr, 'I have a lot of questions. I also have your money. Here's half,' he said, passing over an envelope containing a wad of Euros while showing Petr the remaining. 'You answer all my questions; you get this other half as well. Verstehst du?'

Seeing the eager nod from Petr, Patrick placed his cell phone on the table between them, started the *'Record'* function, and began.

'How long have you been working for these people?'

'Ten years, give or take.'

'Doing what?'

'I am just a driver. I drive the vans or trucks to Calais or Zeebrugge, sometimes to Antwerp.'

'And the van's contents?'

'People wanting to get to the UK. Mostly men, but some women and some children.'

'What is the name of the top person running this?'

'Major Feodor Govorov and his lady colleague, Svetlana Petrovich.'

Hythe paused for a moment, not wanting to give away his knowledge about these two. He'd often found that sometimes playing dumb elicited more information freely given. 'How does Govorov get so many past UK Customs and Border Force?' he continued.

'Quite simple, my friend. We flood the market. For every four dinghies crossing, at least three make it. The French, your Border Force, and the RNLI are all so obliging. Always there to help. The few that get turned back simply try another time. For those, Major Govorov even gives them a credit toward their next attempt. And the French even help close inshore by escorting the dinghies out into the Channel far enough for your Border Force or RNLI to take over.'

'But, what about those that pay a premium to get across? I can't imagine them being happy to be stopped and detained before having to try again?'

'They sometimes put people on special faster boats when they have paid a lot more. Boats that don't show up so well on radar. I know one of the boat drivers, and we often chat. He said the boats get sent out slowly, letting them merge amongst all the other traffic in the Channel. It's really busy sometimes. There are ferries, cargo ships, tankers, fishing boats, and lots of charter and pleasure craft in the summer. Then if need be, he or a colleague will report a fake incident on one of the many fishing charter boats, perhaps a radio call claiming someone's fallen overboard or something. It ties up all the emergency services from both sides looking.'

'So the boat drivers don't just drop these people off on the nearest beach?'

'No, of course not. If someone's paid a premium price, they expect a premium service. Our fast boat drivers make a quick trip over to a quiet port in the UK, and it's arranged to have someone waiting to pick them up to travel to London or wherever they want to go. I think Major Govorov arranges all that. Nothing to do with me; I just drive the vans.'

'Okay, just a few more, Petr. What about those that don't want to chance it going by little boat? What about those going by land?'

'Even easier. Just hide them well enough so they aren't found. We put them in standard containers containing other goods; the UK only checks one in ten due to the amount being shipped. Another good one is in the hollowed-out floor area in a coach. Can easily get four or even six people in there. Your customs people never seem to examine coaches very much. They pay some English customs people to look the other way. They check the passengers, match passports and tickets, and often remove baggage for x-ray but never seem to think about x-raying the coach itself. I watch BBC. Your prime minister has been saying he wants to stop the crossings for many years, but it has been good for British companies, has it not? German news DW say cheap labor to do all the jobs you British don't want to do. It was tough getting people across the Channel back then, but then you all voted for Brexit, and it got easier. DW say part of the Brexit deal was reducing immigrants arriving, but it made it easier. BBC say all imported food and fresh products arriving in the UK from the EU are meant to be checked. The EU has been doing this from the UK since day one of Brexit. But the UK has been very good in helping us by not implementing this. They've even announced they won't be doing this until at least 2025. We have even put people in a chilled meat container. We gave them blankets to keep warm, wrapped them in sleeping bags, and maybe gave them a little ketamine to help them sleep and keep quiet if it was a long journey.'

'So how do the paid customs people know which trucks to ignore?'

'That's simple. Most truck drivers have charms or objects showing through the windscreen. The customs people know what to look for. Those vehicles don't get examined.'

'Petr, how come you know so much about this?'

'I've been driving trucks for years all across Europe and to the UK. Biggest problem is always paperwork, so it pays to know all the rules of what is needed for each country outside the EU. Lots of questions asked in Europe about why Britain wanted to leave EU. Nobody here cares, but I listen to BBC and DW, so I hear things.'

They stopped to replenish empty beer glasses twice and once to use the toilet. By 2:00 am, Patrick decided he had everything Petr could tell him and called it a night. The owner barman had started making snorting noises hinting he wanted to close for the night as Hythe and Doležal were the last two customers in the bar.

Patrick asked one last question before passing the second envelope over. Then, when rising to leave, 'Petr, why did you agree to speak about all this with Adam Paisley? Why did you choose to leave Govorov's team?'

'I am sixty-two. Two months ago, I was diagnosed with lung cancer. It's terminal. They always tell you longer, but I have maybe six months. I want to spend them with my wife and leave her enough money to live after I'm gone.'

Opening the door, they see that the snowfall has increased in the three hours they've been together. Petr turned to Hythe and asked, 'Where are you staying, Patrick?'

Coughing as the cold air hit his throat, Patrick answered, 'I'm at the King's Garden.'

'That's a taxi ride away, but you won't get one here this time of night. You need to cross the river. C'mon, I'll walk you to the Charles Bridge. There should be some on the other side.'

'And you, Petr? How will you get home?'

'I can get a metro train from near there back to my car.'

They started to walk back down the deserted streets toward the bridge, their footsteps soundless in the snow. Patrick thought to himself how every street was a perfect Christmas card vista. The buildings were old in this part of the city and extremely picturesque. With snow settled on their roofs and ledges and lying thickly on the roads and paths, it looked like a typical depiction of a Charles Dickens Christmas scene.

Earlier in the day, Patrick had read one of the many tour guide books available.

It read, *Prague is the capital city of the Czech Republic. Located in the heart of Central Europe, this historic city was built on the banks of the Vltava River. In the 14th century, it became the cultural and religious center of the entire region, also known as the Kingdom of Bohemia. Known as the "city of hundred spires" for its many gold-tipped towers and medieval church spires that puncture the skyline and are untouched by the devastating wars of the 20th century, Prague is one of Europe's best-preserved old cities.*

One of its most famous and popular tourist attractions is the 600-year-old bridge spanning the river.

The Charles Bridge is a medieval stone arch bridge that crosses the Vltava. Building commenced in 1357 and was dedicated to King Charles IV. It was completed in the early 15th century. As the only means of crossing the river Vltava until 1841, the Charles Bridge was the most important connection between Prague Castle and the city's Old Town and adjacent areas. This land connection made Prague important as a trade route between Eastern and Western Europe.

At 516 meters long and nearly 10 meters wide, it was built with 16 arches and three bridge towers. The bridge is decorated by a continuous alley of 30 statues and statuaries, most of them baroque-style, originally erected around 1700.

As they neared the bridge, a few more nighthawks could be seen. Romantic couples, arm in arm, silently strolling across the UNESCO World Heritage site enjoying its ambiance lit only by the glow from its thirty or so gas lamps, one of the very few cities worldwide still lit by gas.

Even Patrick was impressed. He had seen it in the daylight earlier, but at night it looked stunning. Covered in a thick layer of fresh snow, few footprints in the cobbles showed through as more flakes gently settled.

As they approached the middle, with the far side still not visible through the snow, Petr said, 'I'll leave you here. The taxi rank will be on the right after the tower. Order in English because your German accent is terrible,' he said smiling.

Shaking hands and thanking him for the information, Patrick wished him well and walked on as Petr turned and walked back the way they had come.

Out of the gloom, a slim, attractive woman with blonde hair and a scarf covering her mouth and nose against the cold air walked toward and past him. She glanced briefly at him and smiled just as a party of four, two men with two women, walking in the same direction as he was caught up and overtook him. As the woman carried on by him, Patrick was deep in thought, thinking about everything he had learned that evening. He was also trying to remember something he'd heard a few days before about refrigerated containers.

A sudden thought interrupted him as his brain clicked into place. He spun around and started running back the way he'd come, slipping the Glock out of his waistband.

'Shit, shit, shit,' he murmured as he heard two soft *kerchings* and a splash a few seconds later. Keeping running, he skidded to a stop near one of the arches. The darkened spray of crimson red was in fierce contrast to the pure white snow blown against the bridge parapet support. Straining to see the water of the Vltava River through the falling flakes, he could just make out Petr's body slowly floating away amongst small ice floes, blood still swilling from two bullet holes in the back of his head.

Hearing the gentle thud of footsteps running away, he started to give chase, swerving around a young couple arm in arm. As he neared the end of the bridge, he saw a swirl of blonde hair.

'Svetlana!' he hissed as he saw her stop, turn, and raise her right hand and point toward him before three bright flashes from her pistol lit up the area.

Diving sideways toward the cover of a parapet, he felt the pull of his coat as one round passed through it, missing his body. The other two shots missed him entirely, but he heard a thud of a body landing, followed moments later by a woman's shrill scream.

Glancing up, he saw Svetlana climbing into a waiting dark Mercedes, slamming the door behind her as the driver gunned the engine. With snow spraying everywhere, the car sped away.

Regaining his feet, he ran toward the still-screaming woman, holstering his weapon as he ran.

Her boyfriend or husband lay face down in the snow, two bullet holes in his back, blood pooling around him. A quick check for a pulse confirmed there was nothing Patrick could do, and with other people now attracted by the woman's screams, he reasoned he needed to leave before the police arrived. Being caught with a dead body on the bridge, a second dead body floating downstream, and possessing a handgun, even one not fired, would take a lot of explaining.

29

LEAVING the hotel early the following morning, after another restless night visited by his recurring nightmare, he headed back toward the Austrian Alps via Munich. He knew he needed more proof with his witness dead and only the recordings as evidence. The only place to obtain that was back at the Fortress.

Early afternoon found him waiting in the International Arrivals section of Munich's Franz-Josef-Strauß Airport for the passengers from Washington D.C. to walk out. As a crowd of twenty or more people walked out all at once, ex-US Navy SEAL John Deacon spotted Patrick waiting before Patrick saw him. With a big grin on his face, Deacon bounded over.

'Hiya pal. Howya doing?'

'Hey, good to see you. How was the flight?'

Deacon had several pre-arranged meetings in Dubai to drum up business for Phylax, his executive and VIP close personal protection business. He'd planned to fly later that week but had brought forward his flight and diverted through Munich after speaking with Patrick in Gaziantep. After handshakes, back slappings, and general greetings camaraderie, they headed outside to the parking garage and Hythe's Audi.

'So I got your WhatsApp call and understood the basic gist, but tell me more,' Deacon said as they raced down Autobahn 92 and headed in the direction of central Munich. 'Before I left, I convinced Melissa to give me a couple of goodies that might come in handy,' he continued.

'As the saying goes, there's something rotten in the state of Denmark,' Patrick began. 'This mission I've been given stinks. The UK public is pissed off at the number of illegal migrants entering the UK across the Channel, mainly by boat from France. The Prime Minister and the Home Secretary are being made to look like fools by the media and the opposition party in government and want something done to stop them.'

'Where are all these people coming from?

'Mostly the Middle East, Syria, Iraq, Iran, Yemen, Sudan, North Africa, Afghanistan...'

'Well, in the US, we have many illegals trying to cross from Mexico, but that's because we are the safest country. But yours are coming in through Europe, which is safe. Why don't they stop there? Why do they want to get to the UK?'

'A number of reasons, John,' Patrick said. 'Some have relatives already in the UK and want to join them. For others, it may be they speak English as it's a more popular language than, say, German, Italian, or French. However, the main reason is other European countries greatly limit benefits given to illegals. These countries have made it hard for illegal migrants to find work, obtain medical cover, and find accommodation unless they apply for refugee status or asylum. Britain, by comparison, is a real soft touch. They get put up in hotels, paid weekly cash, and get free medical cover even if they have major health problems. Their applications take months or even years to process. Even if rejected, many have gotten into relationships with other UK citizens, giving them a right to stay. On top of that, Legal Aid is a free legal service paid for by UK taxpayers that helps these illegals stay in the UK and fight any deportation orders.'

'So why doesn't the government put a stop to this?' Deacon asked.

'They say they are trying to, but many businesses want immigrants or low-paid foreigners for cheap labor. Also, they've found that illegals who have been given everything, including the right to stay, will vote for that party at election time. So the public is finding the government is heavy on words and slogans, but light or non-existent on any action.'

'And your current mission?'

'Last year, almost 30,000 migrants crossed the English Channel from France to the UK in small inflatable boats. In the summer months, it was in excess of 1,000 per day. Some are individuals who may be escaping poverty or persecution. They have made their own way across Europe to the Calais region, but it is believed the majority are being assisted by gangs of people smugglers for large sums of money.

'My job was to work with a Syrian youth that wanted to get to the UK. His family had escaped Syria and been granted UK residency, but he was an adult at nineteen and couldn't get in under their 'family' scheme. So the UK government held him to ransom by offering him a visa if he successfully carried out a mission for them. They placed him inside one of these gangs to monitor the routes and resources they were using. I followed my source from the Turkish border with Syria to here en route to Calais, but his signal is now dead, and so is he. A while back, a colleague from another branch of the government running a similar operation managed to find a driver who wanted to leave the traffickers and was keen to sell his story for money. Unfortunately, the colleague was discovered and murdered a couple of weeks back. I tracked down the driver and interviewed him in Prague last night. On his way home from our meeting, he was murdered.'

'So what is this rat you are smelling?' Deacon asked.

'I'm not sure. The guy leading this is ex-FSB Major Feodor Govorov. He hinted that they have an insider in London tipping them off. Three days ago I used London to try and find this driver. Then two days ago, I informed London I'd tracked him down and confirmed I was meeting him that evening. The same evening he was killed by an assassin named Svetlana Petrovic. Possible coincidence, as she was searching for him, but I don't think so.'

After pausing, Patrick continued, 'Everything about this mission smells. Somewhere there is a leak. Orders from Whitehall were for only me to cover a 4,000km route. No backup, no support. If our mole was discovered, there were no extraction arrangements for my young ransom guy, no involvement with Interpol or individual countries' police forces. Then there's a concerted effort to stop me by setting me up for the murder of three people. Finally, the murder of my latest source last evening – the assassin knew my whereabouts and route.

30

AFTER a shower and a late lunch, the two were sitting in the empty bar area of their Munich hotel, nursing a cold one. 'OK, pal, what's next?'

'I need to find a way to verify some of this information Petr gave me about Govorov. I need to get inside his office and look around. Our IT department has said they can't easily gain access to his computers – it seems his firewall is military-grade.'

'Well, lookie here,' he said while rummaging through his bag, 'the good 'ol US of A comes to the rescue,' as he dropped what looked to be an ordinary USB thumb drive into his hand. 'This, according to Melissa, my man, is just what we need.'

'A memory stick? What's special about it?'

'No, it's more than that. It allows her to hack into his computers! Mel gave it to me in case we needed it. I don't know the technical stuff of how it does it, but all we need to do is plug it into a USB port on one of their computers, call her, and it will give her access to their data.'

'Looks like we're working tonight and won't be getting much sleep,' Patrick sighed. 'Let's rest a few hours later and leave at 22:00.'

The remaining time was spent analyzing images of the location in and around The Fortress.

<><><>

At 02:00, Deacon leaned against the wall, knee-deep in snow, with his hands clasped together, supporting Patrick's left boot. With a quiet exhalation of breath, Deacon hoisted Patrick up high enough to climb over the eight-foot-high wall. Sitting astride it, Patrick turned, leaned down, clasped Deacon's outstretched hands, and pulled. After a lunge and a little scrabbling, both ended up sitting on the wall.

'You fat fuck,' Patrick whispered, smiling to Deacon, the taller and heavier of the pair.

'Just 'cus you've got a bony ass, you undernourished Brit,' came the quiet reply.

Climbing down, they headed along the inside of the wall. Coming to the end of a straight section Patrick removed his rucksack, and from it, he withdrew a small reel of detonation cord along with a miniature radio detonator. Cutting a twenty-foot length of the cord, the two of them placed it against the wall in an eight-foot-high, two-foot-wide rectangle shape, having brushed the snow briefly from that area of the wall with their hands.

Everything was ready with the cord pushed into place and the radio detonator connected but hidden in the snow.

Det cord, or detonating cord, to give it its full name, is a flexible hollow cord (usually plastic) filled with highly explosive pentaerythritol tetranitrate (PETN) explosives. Originally designed to be used as a fuse/primer to detonate explosive charges, it was found to burn at a speed of about four miles per second, so fast it appears to explode instantaneously. Used against a door or wall, the forces when it explodes will match the shape it is positioned in when triggered.

Having sorted out a potential escape route and both armed with suppressed Glock handguns and Deacon with a rifle, the two of them moved cautiously through the trees until they reached the rear corner of the garages.

They'd arrived undetected and parked a kilometer away over three hours previously, having researched the location. Initially, they used a US classified system similar to Google Earth but with far higher resolution and detail. Then, using one-day-old satellite images from a CIA black website that Deacon had illegal access to via Melissa Rogers, they could see an up-to-date, clear, detailed image of the house and land surrounding it. The entire area was very hilly and made up of dense forest. The five acres of land surrounding the house were enclosed by an eight-foot-high stone wall with an entranceway on both the north and south walls. Both entrances were fitted with closed solid wooden gates with a guard positioned at each.

The house itself was toward the southern end of the land with a seventy-five-meter clearance around it consisting of lawn. Beyond that, mature pine trees covered the remaining area up to the exterior wall. The land dropped away slightly at the rear of the property, and there was a ten-step balustrade leading from an exit door to ground level. The front of the property opened up to a parking area with a water fountain located in the middle. The day-old CIA images showed the entire area covered in deep snow with the fountain frozen and enclosed in ice.

The house was Elizabethan Gothic in style and consisted of three floors. There were three outbuildings, thought to be a garage for vehicles, a storage barn, and a dry wood store for the open fires. An infra-red image taken by the CIA showed heat concentrations in three areas; the kitchen, the large meeting/dining room, and a smaller room off the main corridor. This was assumed to be where the computers were located.

The roof of the garage was determined to be the best overall viewing position. Although covered in snow, low-hanging tree branches protected its roof, meaning anyone hiding on the garage roof would be almost impossible to detect from within the house or gardens. However, the roof's position also meant it had unfettered views of the ground floor, the first floor, and across the garden.

Using night-vision goggles from Patrick's delivery, they observed the guards' routine around the building. Only two patrols were covering each leg of the exterior of the wall at fifteen-minute intervals, so it had been simple to time their incursion.

Hythe had boosted Deacon onto the garage roof and left while he was getting into position. Unobserved in the shadow of the doorway at the top of the steps, he waited.

'I'm in position and got your six,' Deacon stated over the miniature transceivers.

It then took Hythe just seconds to open the heavy oak door using the lock pick gun. He brushed compacted snow from his coat and boots and crept upstairs to avoid leaving a trail. Twice the hushed voices of other guards on duty could be heard, but luck was with him, and he wasn't detected. One advantage of guards being on duty meant it was less likely any alarms would be set. Arriving at the door that had been ajar on Patrick's previous visit, it was now closed. Gently trying the handle, he found it was locked. Relieved that it was unlikely anyone would be working inside a locked room at that time in the morning, he set the trusty lock pick gun in motion again. Three seconds later, with a faint, barely audible click, the lock disengaged, and the door opened.

Two powerful computers, various routers and devices, and a mass of colored cabling greeted him, all being cooled by an industrial-sized air-conditioning unit. This was the main computer room. Connecting his cell phone by cable to one of the unused sockets on a router, Hythe selected a particular app and then made a call. Pressing the screen display on his phone, the app activated, and the computer's IP address was sent by secure encryption direct to Melissa. The direct line on her desk at the FBI headquarters in Quantico rang once before she answered. A close friend of Deacon's, she was always willing to help.

'Hold on,' she said, her fingers flying over her keyboard. 'It's good. It's very good. The firewall is excellent… this is going to be a toughy. Every time I try, their system will send an alert saying they are trying to be hacked. It'll take a while, but I'm not sure I can before being detected. Hold on … '

Five minutes later, which felt to Hythe hiding inside and Deacon observing from the garage roof as nearer five hours, Melissa said, 'No, it's better not to do this. There's too much risk it will trigger an alert. Use the device instead as we discussed.'

Taking a tiny device about the size of a regular USB stick out of his pocket, Hythe plugged it into an empty port at the rear of the computer. The fifty seconds of waiting as it scanned the airwaves for a suitable 5g mobile network seemed far longer. Finally, it was a welcome relief when Melissa said, 'Got it. Make sure it can't be seen easily and get the hell out of there.'

Confirming he'd call her again as soon as they got back to their hotel, he exited the room, locked it, and moved toward the external oak door he'd entered. Seconds before he reached it, Deacon's voice came over the radio. 'Two targets approaching. Twenty meters.'

With no other option, Patrick backtracked to the computer room, hastily trying to unlock the door again before he was spotted.

'Ten seconds,' Deacon announced. 'Five.'

Just as the outer oak door opened and an icy blast rolled in, Patrick's lock pick gun finally clicked, and the handle turned. He lunged into the room before gently closing the door and wedging it shut with his foot. He leaned his weight against it but kept the handle still turned, so the latch bolt remained silent and didn't click as it re-engaged.

The voices grew louder as they approached, although their owners were only murmuring at such a late hour.

Then the voices stopped moving.

It was obvious to him that the noise source was just the other side of the computer room door.

31

LATER, back in their hotel on the outskirts of Munich, Deacon and Hythe called the same US number. It was 05:00 in Munich and still late evening in Washington, but Melissa was still at her desk, waiting. Rechecking her computer, she confirmed there was a lot of data. The 5g connection had failed and resorted to 4g. The problem was this connection was slow, so a full download would take five to six hours. She was about to leave and go home, leaving the data collection running overnight. She would be back at work at her desk at 07:00 the following day, lunchtime in Germany, so she suggested they call it a day. She would call them later that day as soon as she had anything to report. In the meantime, she had set up an auto-forward option that retransmitted every piece of data to their private accounts.

Hythe was still relieved the guards hadn't tried the computer room door. He had his silenced handgun ready and wouldn't have hesitated to put down the two men if necessary. Luckily, the targets had finished their conversation a few seconds before moving up the staircase. Waiting another half minute, and with Deacon confirming no one else was around outside, Hythe quietly exited the room, locking the door again before heading to the exit. Outside he headed to the rear of the garages.

As Deacon moved across the roof and quietly climbed down, Hythe whispered, 'You may be the better marksman, but next time I'll be the lookout and spend the evening laying down.'

The snow outside had been trampled on repeatedly, masking their footsteps and aiding their escape. With hands cupped, Deacon hoisted Hythe just enough to see over the wall. Thirty seconds after the guard walked by on his rounds, they gently let themselves down outside the wall before hurrying back to their vehicle.

<><><>

They spent the morning discussing Patrick's mission and how things were going at Phylax. Then Patrick moved on to Gina. Gina was Deacon's office secretary, organizer, assistant manager, left arm, and good friend. Ex-Secret Service, she held the Washington office together whenever Deacon was out or away on business. She was also a very close friend of Patrick's.

She had been close to a breakdown when her daughter died last year from a drug overdose. On Patrick's insistence, she had flown to the UK and spent time with him recovering. Patrick had hired a river cruise boat on the Norfolk Broads, a large area of peat bogs and old navigable waterways. With no phones or email distractions, she had slowly come to terms with what had happened, and they had grown closer. Much closer.

He had flown to Washington twice more since then to see her. Their relationship was as close as a 3,600-mile separation allowed, and he was keenly looking forward to their next time together. He was explaining to Deacon he would be flying over to spend a few days in Cancun with her soon when Deacon's phone rang. He immediately answered it on speaker mode.

Melissa said, 'I've received masses of data. There are details of journeys, dates, monies paid and by whom, and contract details of boats, dinghies, life jackets, and outboard suppliers. There are also names and payment details of employees in Europe and some in the UK. All the names, passport details, and monies paid to get them across the Channel and their travel method are stored in one database. There's a list of names and numbers of men, women, and children shipped and addresses for some residing in the UK. Unfortunately, there are references to a second computer not on the network that I cannot access.'

'But I thought you could find anything once you had access to their network?'

'Yes and no, John. Each computer device has an IP address - a unique number that identifies it. Depending on the device and if it is connected to a network, you may be able to access it remotely. Once you are connected to a network, you can move around within it and connect to other connected devices. The network will have firewalls and passwords, but these can all be overcome. The more sophisticated the network, the longer it takes for someone to break through the firewalls and passwords.'

'But if this other computer is in the same room as the others, why can't you connect to it?'

'It may be in the same room, but either it's standalone and not connected to anything, or it's behind an extremely sophisticated firewall, a top-of-the-range military standard version.'

'But the device we connected last evening. Didn't that give you access?'

'It did, hun. It did. Let me explain, 'cus I know you're a bit of a Luddite,' she laughed. 'I couldn't easily break through their firewalls without being detected, so you plugged in the WiFi Dongle—'

'The WHAT?' Deacon said. 'What the fuck is a dangle?'

'Dongle, hun. Dongle. It just means a device plugged into a computer port or connector. It's a computer buzzword. So this one connects to the computer, then looks around for a fast 5g cellular network signal, like the data signal on your cell phone, and connects to a network. The dongle has its own IP address, and I can connect to it through the relevant telephone companies' networks, and voila! I am connected to the computer and network it is plugged into. But it's a bit more sophisticated than that. Normally, when you plug anything such as a USB memory stick into a computer, the computer senses or detects it and loads any needed software.'

'Yeah, I know what you mean. A little display pops up on the screen.'

'Correct. But that would also set off alarms that something has been connected. The device you connected had been modified by me. As soon as you plugged it in and the computer detected it, the device ordered the computer to delete its record of it being connected. Therefore as long as no one physically sees it, it stays working. The only drawback is it's connected to Telekom Austria's network. Their 5g signal is very weak halfway up the Alps and inside a big stone building like the Fortress. So it reconnected to Telekom Austria's 4g network instead. But 4g is an older technology and slower, especially halfway up a mountain. That's why I have taken so long to get the data.

'But, what that means, and I'm sorry to say, boys, is that unless I can break through their firewall without being detected, the only way to gain access to this second computer would mean connecting the dongle directly to it,' Melissa said.

Turning to Deacon, Patrick said, 'I need the information on that other computer. If the only option is to swap this dangle or dongle thing, I think we have to go back and do it. Thoughts?'

Reluctantly, Deacon agreed they'd make another attempt that evening.

After completing his latest update report of everything Petr had disclosed and what had happened subsequently in Prague, Patrick emailed it to the office of Maj.Gen Ronaldson in London. Within the hour, he received an urgent email reply from Whitehall clearly stating his mission was canceled. Feodor Govorov was not to be injured or arrested. The email stated, "… clear and concise orders … the highest level … Whitehall instructs … mission canceled … ordered to return immediately … International incident … Govorov unharmed … Europol to arrest … report for duty immediately … . "

'What the fu…?' Deacon said. 'You're here completing a 2-3 man mission on your own, but having found the top guy, they decide the mission's canceled and you now gotta let him walk, and someone else arrests him and gets the glory.'

'Like I said, there's a leak somewhere. I'm just glad I omitted our incursion last evening from the report.'

<><><>

Careful not to be observed, Patrick drove the last kilometer with lights out, relying on his night-vision goggles and the overall brightness of the snow. Pulling in off the main track in the same place he'd stopped before, they spent ten minutes moving around, checking the Audi couldn't be detected from any direction.

Satisfied, they removed some gear from the car and fitted the radio transceivers in their ears. Quietly moving uphill toward the Fortress's outer walls, they stopped and watched the guard's routines. Nothing had changed, confirming their ingress into the Fortress the evening previously hadn't been detected. Timing, as before, was everything. While the patrolling guards were walking away from each other, Deacon approached the wall, bent down, clasped and joined hands together, and waited. Hythe put his left boot in Deacon's hands and was hoisted high enough to grab the snow-crusted top of the wall. Sliding a leg over, he reached down as Deacon handed him a holdall of equipment before dropping it over the wall. Leaning down again, he hoisted Deacon. Within seconds, both were safely on the ground, unseen, unheard, and inside the compound again.

They moved around the grounds keeping within the tree line until they were close to the explosive det cord they'd fitted the day before. Fresh snow had covered what footsteps they had made, and the installation was as they had left it. Satisfied it may need to become their escape route today, they split up with Patrick heading toward the same steps as previously. Checking everything was all clear, he moved silently up them until he was in shadow just as Deacon's voice came over the transceivers they were wearing.

'In position. Clear view. All quiet,' he whispered from the sloping roof of the wood store building where he'd headed and set up position.

Like the night before, the place was deathly quiet and seemed deserted. Patrick unlocked the outer door and ventured in. He quickly gained entry into the computer room again and found the device still in situ. He promptly removed it, plugged it into the other computer, and waited. A minute later, he received a text from Melissa confirming a WiFi connection had been made.

Relocking the computer room door, he moved back toward the entrance door when he was blinded by a flashlight shining in his eyes and the shout, in German, of *"Freeze! You as much as blink, you're dead."*

32

TEN seconds later, accompanied by the noise of running feet down the staircase, another one of Govorov's guards rounded the corner wide-eyed and pointed a submachine gun at him.

Raising his hands and keeping them raised, Patrick said, 'I want to speak with Govorov.'

With his weapon aimed directly at Patrick, the guard used his radio to speak to someone.

It took almost ten minutes before Feodor Govorov appeared along with a sleepy Svetlana. Although not necessarily together, both had been asleep as they were wearing dressing gowns over their nightclothes. Govorov was also carrying a Makarov 9mm pistol at his side. Now in the main dining room again, Govorov moved closer to Hythe, sitting in a chair at the end of the table. He aimed his gun directly at Hythe's face while inspecting the items found on him.

After a quick but thorough pat-down search, the guard had placed Hythe's cell phone, silenced pistol, and lock pick gun on the table, well out of his reach. Now with a guard standing six feet behind and to his side while aiming their machine guns directly at him, Hythe didn't need to be secured. Govorov's command to shoot him if he moved at all was clear.

Govorov moved away and took a seat next to Svetlana in front of the full-length multi-pane window, facing Hythe. 'So you have come back here to be killed?'

'No, not this time. Your bit of skirt got the wrong guy. He'd already told me everything he knew, and then she missed when she tried to shoot me. Should've gone to Specsavers, love,' Hythe said, directed toward Svetlana.

Fuming, she cursed, 'Well, I won't fucking well miss next time.'

Turning to Govorov, he continued, 'Don't you want to know why I'm back?' Seeing a vacant look on his face, Hythe continued, 'I intend to make a citizen's arrest of you both so that you can stand trial for your crimes.'

Svetlana laughed and said, 'The only thing arresting will be your heart when I pump a couple of rounds through it,' as she pulled a snub-nosed pistol from her nightclothes.

Addressing Govorov, he continued, 'Major, before you get your little dormouse to shoot me, why don't you answer a question for me. You know, condemned man, etc.'

Realizing the position Hythe was in, he nodded his agreement. He patted Svetlana on the arm to lower her pistol, 'OK, ask away.'

'How did your dormouse know where Doležal would be in Prague?'

'Mr. Johnson, some of your questions are so naïve. It was simple. You told us. It was in your report you sent to your Maj.Gen Ronaldson.'

'What? You're saying Ronaldson works for you. No fucking way!'

Exhaling loudly and slowly, Govorov continued, 'I didn't say HE worked for us. I said it was in the report you sent him.'

Hythe was quiet for a moment or two before he continued.

'Just one last question?'

Seeing a nod from Govorov, Hythe continued, 'OK. Children. You smuggle children in on their own. Why?'

Govorov paused and didn't reply for almost a minute. When he did, his tone had changed, becoming noticeably hostile. 'You ask a lot of questions, Johnson. What makes you think we smuggle in children on their own?'

'A little bird told me.'

'A bird?'

'Just a manner of speech. Your former colleague in Prague, Petr, told me. Before the bimbo killed him,' Patrick said, looking at Svetlana. 'He said you had promoted him to take kids as young as four. They went by container through Zeebrugge in Belgium. He had to dope them up with ketamine in their drinks to keep them asleep.'

With that, Govorov clicked his fingers and said, 'You're wrong. Enough. I'm bored, I'm tired, and I want to go back to bed. Sveta, I think you should kill him now and do it here.'

As she reached for her pistol again, Govorov suddenly placed his hand over hers, lowering her weapon again.

Standing, he walked toward the center of the table and picked up the lock pick gun. Turning, he said to the guard who'd initially stopped him, 'Wait. Where was he?'

'In the corridor, Major.'

'Where exactly, you idiot?'

'Outside the communications room, sir.'

'Search it. NOW! Get Hans out of bed. NOW, MOVE, DAMN YOU.'

Six minutes later, a bleary-eyed Hans, in charge of IT, entered carrying the wifi dongle. 'Major, this was plugged into the frame of system B,' he said, holding it aloft.

'And? Explain. What does it do? NOW!'

'It allows someone to bypass our firewalls and gain access to that system, sir.'

He raised his Makarov and shot Hans in the forehead, his face red with anger. Turning to Svetlana, he said, 'Kill Johnson.'

'Just before you raise your weapon, Sveta, you should know that the guards here will die when I snap my fingers. If you pull the trigger, you will also die. Then, you, Major, will also die to round off the evening,' Patrick said, smiling as he raised his right hand.

The guard looked a little startled, but Govorov merely laughed as Svetlana's fingers closed around the grip, and she began to aim it. The click of Hythe's fingers and the crash of one of the small window panes behind Govorov shattering seemed to occur together. The wet plop of the guard's head exploding as a high-velocity round from a hunting rifle penetrated his skull was a millisecond later. Before anyone could move or register what had happened, a second pane exploded, and the second guard's head also exploded.

'If you move a muscle, you're next,' Hythe said to Svetlana, frozen in mid-action. Bending to pick up the guard's fallen weapon, his own weapon, and cell phone, Hythe turned to Govorov and said, 'There is a laser spot on the side of your head. I'm leaving now. You will die if either of you moves or tries to stop me. I expect Europol will be paying you a visit soon.'

Exiting, Patrick ran down the stairs and out into the garden as he radioed Deacon. Although Deacon's rifle was fitted with a suppressor, the glass window exploding had alerted the guards, who were all rushing to the house. Those patrolling outside the walls ran to the single front large access door. Two bright floodlights were switched on, illuminating the outside of the house, the drive, and the gardens out as far as the trees. Hiding down by the balustrade steps, Patrick heard the dull retort of a third shot, followed ten seconds later by two more aimed at the lights. He was up and running again as the grounds were plunged back into darkness, reaching the wood store just as Deacon slid down off the low roof.

A quick glance at Patrick, a nod in return, and Deacon pressed the transmit button.

As the det cord exploded, the boom echoed around the walls and seemed to echo around the hills and mountains. A section of the wall almost twenty feet long had disappeared. The blast had blown the stones outwards, with many adjacent also being displaced. Two guards running past it were blown over and killed in the blast. Overall, it produced two effects. First, it disorientated and stunned anyone in the near vicinity into inaction. Secondly, as they recovered from the shock, they wrongly assumed Deacon and Hythe would be leaving that way, so they rushed to guard and defend.

In fact, both men had run through the trees retracing their steps back to their unguarded ingress point. In the darkness, they climbed over the same way they'd arrived, scrambled down, and raced to their car.

'You were lucky they didn't find your transceiver. I heard everything going on.'

'Yeah, it's right down inside my ear. But I'm surprised it took Govorov so long to realize I wasn't there to arrest him.'

'That, pal, is the beauty of waking people up in the middle of the night. Takes them a while to get it all together.'

'You fired a third shot?' Hythe asked as they drove away, 'Before the two that took out the lights.'

'Yeah, the woman, Svetlana, started to move. I shot another window pane out. Scared the shit out of her. She froze,' he laughed.

33

THEY arrived back in their Munich hotel just as Melissa called. She confirmed the link to the new computer had been working but was suddenly disconnected.

'Did you manage to get anything at all?' Hythe asked.

'Loads, hun. And very disturbing it is too. I was only connected for about fifteen minutes, but this computer had a lot less data than the other. I think I got about ninety-five percent before the connection dropped. It appears to be just a backup copy of Govorov's laptop. As before, I'm forwarding everything to your accounts again, but some of the content makes it challenging to read. I'm finding details of multiple pedophile rings in various European countries, including the biggest one in the UK. There's a password-protected database I've gained access to that lists the pedophiles themselves broken down by country and even region. Dark website details, screen names and titles, passwords, email addresses, credit card details, contact numbers, dates, and venues of meetings. There's even a list with details of the kids' ages, gender, and where and to whom they've been shipped. Everything,' she said, her voice beginning to crack. 'It's horrible, and it gets worse.'

Taking a moment to compose herself, she continued, 'I've seen some vile things in my life and some photos bad enough to make you want to puke, but these take the cake. I didn't even believe what I was seeing at first, but it's an auction house of kids. An auction house for sick motherfuckers to buy kids for sex. Each child, boy or girl, is listed along with a photo, either a head and shoulders or a top-half body shot. Their first name and age is listed along with a *"suggested"* starting bid price. Sick fucks can log in and raise the bid, and they can even select if they want private use or shared use,' she managed to say before her voice broke again.

Deacon had known Melissa for years and knew she was one tough cookie. If this was upsetting her, it must be really bad.

'If all that isn't enough, when you select *"shared use,"* you can see obscene pictures of that child performing some sort of sex act with an adult. I knew some of the child abuse sites were bad, but I never imagined anything like this,' she sobbed. 'I'll have to call you back,' she said as she disconnected the line.

It was almost thirty minutes before she called back. 'I'm sorry, guys, but I had to compose myself. It's late, but I'm still in my office in Quantico. If anyone had seen me bawling like a teenager, I'd have some explaining to do looking at this stuff. I'm OK now, but you've got to stop this guy. He is one sick individual. They all are, and I feel so bad for those poor kids.'

'So is Govorov just a supplier or is he a user as well?' Patrick asked.

'Both. The way this is structured, he seems to be running it. At the very minimum, he's supplying the kids for the UK. Looking at the data, when someone from the UK wins a bid, he arranges to ship the child over to them. All the kids are under twelve years old and are refugees and orphans. None are with any form of adult or older sibling. He is also a user of the kids - he's listed the ones he's personally used. God, he's sick... I've found out some other things as well. There's a copy of an email about four refrigerated truck trailers to be acquired. For acquired, read stolen. Details about their location, the security details of the manufacturing plant, the employees' working hours, and the times the night watchman makes his rounds. They're based in Wies--.'

'Wiesbaden, Germany,' Patrick interrupted. 'I remember hearing something on the news a few days ago about them being stolen.'

'I've also seen multiple references to a Belarus company located outside of Minsk. They were a government-owned pharmaceutical manufacturer taken to court by the European Medicines Agency, charged with manufacturing counterfeit drugs. The EU are the world's biggest trader in medicines and medicinal products, and the EMA are the pharmaceutical governing body for the EU. This court case resulted in this company, called Zhizn which means *"Life"*, being closed down. But in the same folder, I've uncovered lists of shipment dates, quantities, locations in third-world countries, and journey plans, all originating from this company, Zhizn. Bear in mind that Belarus is a puppet regime under direct rule from Moscow. Almost anything goes, and there's a distinct lack of law and order. A bit like the Wild West, I think,' she said.

Deep in thought and absentmindedly stroking his chin, Patrick said, 'Melissa, can you do something for me, please? Can you pick three or four of these third-world countries and check if their relevant health departments have placed high-value pharmaceutical orders from the major European manufacturers?'

Almost ninety minutes later, Melissa called back. 'I've tried four countries; Ghana, Chad, Niger, and the Republic of Congo. All their relevant public health departments have ordered vast quantities of Covid-19 vaccine, but the makers in Europe are all short of stock fulfilling existing orders,' she said.

After thinking for a moment or two, Patrick said, 'I think Govorov is planning to ship or is maybe already shipping counterfeit Covid vaccine medication. Bear in mind that he is Russian, ex-FSB. What if, with or without Moscow's support, he has managed to get this company Zhizn to manufacture counterfeit Covid-19 vaccine? I've been wondering why he needed four more refrigerated trailers. He'd need them for shipping the vaccines. Even fake ones need to be chilled; otherwise, the end customer authorities would suspect something was wrong immediately. He would only do it for money, but enormous profits will be made with the millions of vaccines needed. Just hard luck to all those who think they are vaccinated and then catch the disease and maybe die, but Govorov and Moscow wouldn't give a shit.'

'Is it possible Zhizn is making real vaccines but needs help distributing them?' Melissa suggested.

'No, I don't think so,' Patrick said. 'The major manufacturers wouldn't be working with a company already charged with counterfeiting their products, especially one based in Belarus. No, they're making fake shit and trying to pass it off as genuine.'

<><><>

The three of them spent the next few hours discovering as much as possible about the company Zhizn. Their headquarters had been near the center of Minsk, but this was just office space for the senior executives. There were two manufacturing plants, the largest being about 30km northeast of Minsk in the industrial town of Barysaw. This plant was shut down after the court case brought by the European Medicines Agency. Zhizn was found to be in breach of contract and law, and with pressure also applied by the EU, the outcome was its closure. The smaller manufacturing plant had been sold to a private firm registered in the Caymans. It was to be refitted to be a manufacturer of agricultural fertilizers. This plant was located in the small town of Bastuny.

Delving deeper, Melissa uncovered the owners of this company registered in the Caymans are no other than some of the Government ministers running the larger company previously.

'So let me get this straight. This company, Zhizn, is set up by the Belarusian government. It produces counterfeit drugs and gets taken to court by the European Medicines Agency. They win, and the company gets closed down, but some key members of their government transfer ownership of one of the manufacturing plants to a private company they own, allegedly to produce fertilizers. But with the set-up the same as before, they can just go on producing knock-off drugs?'

'Exactly, Patrick. What a farce!'

'How big is this site?'

'Can't be a hundred percent sure without the latest photos, but Google Earth shows it as a medium-sized single-story warehouse factory,' Melissa replied.

Turning to Deacon, Patrick said, 'I may have to leave Govorov alive, but I'm going to find out if what we suspect is true about the factory. If it is, I'm putting it out of action. Are you in?'

With a broad smile, Deacon said, 'Of course!'

34

'SHANE. Deacon. How are you doing, pal?'

'Good to hear from you, bud. How's Dubai?'

'Ahhh, haven't gotten there quite yet. Stopped off in Germany en route to give Patrick a hand. Got a question. I need to quietly get to Bastuny, a small town northwest of Minsk about sixty klicks from the Polish border.'

'No way, man. You been watching the news?'

'Not a lot this week. Been busy,' Deacon said.

'Russia is stirring up a shitstorm. Looks like they will invade Ukraine at any moment. Thousands are fleeing Kyiv, with most heading west to Poland. Belarus is aiding Russia in grouping Russian tanks along the Ukraine - Belarus border. If that wasn't enough, to further confuse the situation, Belarus has emptied one of its migrant camps and moved thousands close to their border with Poland to overwhelm the Polish border force and provoke a new refugee crisis in Europe. Both Polish and Belarus border guards are on full alert. There's no way for a quiet in and out,' Shane said. 'Hang on a minute, let me look,' before he put the receiver down, and Deacon could hear the clicks of a keyboard.

Shane Walker was an old friend of Deacon. He was also a long-time CIA operative. Currently, he is a Captain at the US Embassy in Baghdad in charge of intelligence gathering.

'John, you there? The easiest way to Bastuny is from Lithuania. Let me speak with a colleague in our Embassy in Vilnius. Is this official? Can I ask what it's about?'

'Shane, No, and it's safer if you don't know. There will be two of us going and returning a day or two later, along with some equipment.'

'Equipment? What sort?' Shane asked.

'Oh, you know. Just usual stuff Patrick and I carry in backpacks. Might need to pick some up locally.'

'OK, bud. For you, anything. As long as it doesn't come back to bite me on the ass. Send me a secure list of what you need and give me twelve hours,' he said before disconnecting the call.

<><><>

It was late that evening when Shane dialed Deacon's encrypted cell phone.

'All go, pal. Get close to our Embassy in Vilnius tomorrow by four pm and call the number I'm about to text you. Ask for Brad Thorndike. He's expecting your call and won't ask questions. He'll meet you fifteen minutes later on the corner of Gedinmino and Jaksto. He'll have the items you requested available. He'll also have the name and address of a local guy who will escort you where you wish to go. In English, the password is *"Do you have a cigarette? I've lost mine."* The correct response is *"I only have Marlboro Lights."* The cost to this local guy will be fifteen hundred American cash. OK?'

After making notes of the address, Deacon thanked him profusely. Shane was due home leave in Washington in a few weeks, so they agreed to meet and catch up then.

<><><>

The two-hour Lufthansa flight arrived fifteen minutes early due to a strong tailwind. Entrance through Customs was easy, and twenty minutes after landing, and with only carry-on, Deacon and Hythe shared a taxi into the city. There were plenty of cafes and restaurants close to the Old Town section, so they stopped and had a late lunch.

They made their way toward the chosen meeting place at three-thirty, stopping to make the call first. Sure enough, Brad Thorndike arrived on the corner of Gedinmino and Jaksto fifteen minutes later. Stopping briefly, he handed over a bulging holdall and an envelope before getting back in his vehicle and driving away.

Deacon flipped the cover open briefly. Satisfied, he ripped open the envelope and read the single page inside.

'Lukas and Filip Meizys will be our hosts. Let's go meet them,' he said before looking around and whistling for a taxicab.

It was only a thirty-kilometer journey, but the cab driver took almost an hour to find the old unlisted farmhouse in amongst the trees. After paying the driver, they waited until he'd driven away before walking toward the barn. A teenager stepped out of the shadows, holding a shotgun aimed at them.

Dropping the holdall, they both slowly raised their hands to chest height.

35

CAREFUL not to make any sudden moves, Deacon said in English, *'Do you have a cigarette? I've lost mine.'*

The shotgun barrel lowered as the boy smiled, turned his head, and shouted something in Lithuanian before replying in English, *"I only have Marlboro Lights."*

Maybe in his sixties, an older man came into view, also carrying a shotgun but aimed at the ground. Walking over, he extended a hand and said, 'Jūs esate amerikiečiai. Sveiki.'

Both showing a blank look extended their hands in return but said nothing. Patrick eventually tried, 'Sprichst du Deutsch?'

The boy laughed and said, 'I speak English. My name is Filip, and my grandfather's name is Lukas,' as they all shook hands. 'My grandfather speaks Lithuanian and Belarussian Russian. He said *You are Americans. Welcome.*'

Hythe didn't feel the need to correct him.

Moving into the barn, Filip pulled a bottle of Stakliškės, a traditional alcoholic drink made from fermented honey and water and similar to mead, from his rucksack on the floor, along with four glasses.

Pouring a good-sized measure into each, he said, 'It is a Lithuanian tradition to welcome guests. Drink!'

The amber-colored liquid slid gently down their throats, smoother than they expected as they toasted each other, Lithuania, and America. Then they got down to business.

After moving to another farmhouse, Lukas's wife, Rosa, fed them a tasty evening meal of Šaltibarščiai, a cold beetroot soup. This was followed by potato dumplings stuffed with spiced minced meat called Cepelinai, all washed down by a couple of large jugs of beer.

At 22:00, the four of them climbed into a VW Polo almost as old as them. Little of the original paintwork remained, and none of the door colors matched. The tires had seen far better days, and the wind blew in from various gaps as they drove. However, the engine started on the first turn and seemed to run OK.

Patrick kept an eye on their overall direction using a compass. Slightly perplexed, he said, 'Lukas, we appear to be heading southeast. Wouldn't it be better to be more southwest? The border is closer to Bastuny that way?'

Filip translated for his grandfather, who answered with a rapid, angry, and long speech as he jammed his foot on the brake, making the little car skid to a stop.

'My grandfather says, why do you Americans come here and tell us what to do? If you want, I will take you southwest. There you will be stopped at the border. If you do make it across, you will be shot leaving. I lived here many years, so do you want to live or die?' Filip said.

Realizing he might have made an error, Patrick apologized and indicated that Lukas should carry on the way he was going. With a large sigh and obviously cursing the stupid Americans (Filip was about to translate before suddenly stopping and blushing), Lukas put the Polo back in gear and continued on the journey.

Lukas, talking almost continually in Lithuanian, drove them down smaller and smaller roads until these ran out and changed to dirt tracks in one of the many forests surrounding the border area. Stopping again, Lukas switched off the car's headlights, reached into the glove box, and pulled out a set of Russian night-vision goggles weighing at least a kilo. Fitting these heavy and bulky metal glasses to his head, he plugged the cable into the lighter socket to power them. They gradually powered up with a loud hum, light spilling from around the perished leather eye shields. They were so heavy that Lukas groaned each time the car hit a pothole as his head and shoulders shuddered from their weight.

Trying not to laugh, Patrick murmured to Deacon, 'Fuck me, they must be 1900s vintage.'

Filip continued translating Lukas's ongoing rambling as best he could until Lukas suddenly slapped his hand down hard on the faded, split plastic dashboard.

'We are in Belarus now,' Filip said.

Ordering Lukas to stop the car, Patrick climbed out and looked around until he found a small rock. He moved to the car's rear, raised the stone, and smashed the rear lights. Raising a hand to stop Lukas from arguing as he climbed back into the car, Patrick said to Filip, 'The stoplights would glow every time your grandfather hit the brakes and give away our position. Tell him I'll pay him extra for repairs.'

As Filip translated, Lukas reluctantly nodded acceptance, put the Polo in gear, and pulled away. Keeping to quiet backroads and tracks, Lukas kept them clear of villages and the few main roads in the region. However, it still took another sixty minutes before they stopped in a heavily wooded area near the outskirts of Bastuny. Lukas explained, translated by Filip, that this entire area of Belarus up to the Lithuanian border was mainly local small farms and forestry.

'Grandfather says he has brought you to Bastuny as promised, and you are still alive. He says you follow the train track south for about twelve hundred meters. There are only two warehouse-type buildings in Bastuny, and the closest one repairs tractors and farm machines. He thinks the one you want is the furthest on the far outskirt of the village. It has secure fencing and sharp wire around it.'

Thanking them both and instructing them to wait in the same place until 04:00, Patrick handed over a quarter of the money. He said, 'You will get the rest when we get back to safety. OK?.' The old man merely nodded, having removed the heavy Russian goggles and was currently massaging his neck.

They moved away from the vehicle and quickly changed into black pullovers, balaclava masks, night-vision goggles, and miniature transceivers. They also wore black backpacks filled with C4 explosives and timers and carried AK-12 Russian-built assault rifles fitted with suppressors. Deacon had specifically requested Russian weapons to add confusion if they were left behind or captured.

Separated by fifty meters and with Patrick in the lead, they walked silently alongside the raised railway track, careful to keep low by the side of the embankment so as not to present a silhouette in the darkness.

Bastuny, more a village than a small town, was dark and sleeping. The snow on the ground reflected little natural light, but total cloud cover helped keep the entire area dark. As with many small villages in Europe, there were no streetlights.

Skirting around the outside of the village to reduce the chance of being seen, they approached their target. There was just one dim light glowing above the loading dock on the side of the warehouse building. As they approached, they could see through the wire link fence the front of a large DAF truck with a refrigerated container waiting at the loading dock. A second one was parked further away but still within the enclosed area. Both vehicles were covered in snow and had been there a while.

They moved around the perimeter fence until they found a section hidden from view inside the compound by two large waste bins. Keeping watch for patrolling guards, it took just minutes to cut the fencing away to allow access. Once through, they split up to arrive at the loading dock from different directions.

'Didn't see any sign of life. The entrance door is locked, but there are lights on inside,' Deacon murmured.

'Yeah, the loading bay is closed for the night. Hopefully, if anyone is inside, it's just a night watchman.'

Moving back toward the entrance door, Patrick crept forward and used his lock pick gun to align the tumblers. The lock disengaged with a gentle click, and he turned to Deacon and whispered, 'It's open. On the count of three, I'll go left; you go right.'

He gripped the door handle gently and turned it just enough to lift the inner catch. 'One, two, three—'

Patrick pulled the door open as Deacon brushed past him and was already in.

36

IT was dark inside, but there was a glow from lights escaping some inner rooms. There was also the sound of voices and soft music playing. Having split up, they each moved around the inside of the exterior walls of the building. Exploring right, Deacon approached a canteen area, two empty offices, and the toilets. He also passed a large printing and packaging machine. Heading left, Patrick walked by the loading dock and the goods inward and outward areas. The place was stacked with pallet loads of boxes. Using a small torch, he examined the stamped and sealed cardboard boxes labeled with all the correct logos and information identifying them as legitimate Covid-19 vaccines.

All carried the European Medicines Agency (EMA) stamp of approval as well as the individual manufacturer's name, logos, and details: Pfizer-BioNTech, Janssen, Novavax, Moderna, and Oxford-AstraZeneca.

'John, it's as we thought. They're making counterfeits but packaging them as legit from the main five manufacturers,' Patrick radioed.

'Yeah, I've got printed boxes by the hundreds over here. All neatly stacked but empty, just waiting,' Deacon replied.

Moving toward the center of the warehouse, they came to the central group of self-contained rooms, all with lights on. The voices and music were louder here, able to be heard over the dull hum of working machinery. As they approached, a set of frosted glass double doors suddenly opened with a loud hiss of escaping air. Two men wearing traditional cleanroom clothing stepped out directly in front of them. They saw Deacon dressed all in black, wearing a balaclava, night vision goggles, carrying an assault rifle, and froze. One just stood there, but the other was quicker off the mark. Turning, he ran back through the closing doors, shouting as he pressed an emergency button.

Overhead, arc lights came on, temporarily blinding Hythe and Deacon as an alarm began to wail.

'Fuck,' Deacon said as the doors slammed shut.

Motioning the one worker to move to the left by the flick of his rifle's barrel, Deacon reversed his weapon and slammed the butt against the glass.

Nothing happened.

Patrick looked around for the source of the alarm. Seeing a tannoy near the roof, he carefully aimed and fired a three-round burst. In the sudden quiet that followed, they could hear people shouting. Bending low so the upward trajectory would miss anyone on the other side of the doors, they aimed at the center of the frosted glass panel of the left door. After thirty or so rounds of three-round bursts concentrated all in one place, the glass finally gave way. It shattered, allowing the remaining shards to be kicked clear.

Grabbing the worker and pushing him through the doorway to stop him from running away, they leaped in, weapons ready. The unexpected burst of withering machine-gun fire caught all three of them by surprise, especially the worker hit by a dozen rounds to the chest. Diving for cover, Hythe and Deacon immediately returned fire, hitting at least one whose initial scream changed to a faint gurgle as he died seconds later.

A few seconds later, screams of *"Мы сдаемся, Мы сдаемся"* were shouted.

Patrick turned to Deacon and said, 'I don't speak much Russian, but I think that means *"We surrender"*.'

Covering each other, they moved in. Two more people wearing cleanroom clothing, including the first man who'd run back in and triggered the alarm, were cowering behind a filing cabinet. A quick scout around confirmed there had only been three workers in cleanroom clothing supported by one armed guard.

Deacon ushered the two survivors outside to the spare refrigerated container parked against the fence. Pulling a couple of pairs of cable ties from his pocket, he secured them to each other and the trailer legs. He also covered their mouths with rags he'd found on the floor in the warehouse to keep them quiet. The rags weren't particularly clean, but he reasoned they'd be happy to be alive and not worry over swallowing a bit of dirt. They'd be cold sitting in the snow, but he reckoned assistance was already on its way.

Patrick checked the two bodies. The worker had died instantly, having been shot by the building guard, who was then hit by Hythe's and Deacon's rounds. After examining the laboratory, Patrick was reassured he'd made the correct choice. Hundreds of small glass vials were being moved around a production mechanism that filled each one to the brim with a clear fluid. They then progressed along a conveyor belt where a metal, plastic, and rubber top cap was firmly attached to the vial. The next stage resulted in the attachment of a label bearing the name of one of the major manufacturers. Finally, each vial was loaded into a waiting cardboard box after insertion between two protective foam pieces.

These larger boxes, holding 144 vial units each, were waiting to be loaded onto a wooden pallet and then into a waiting refrigerated container for shipment worldwide.

While Deacon was busy securing the prisoners, Patrick started laying C4 charges before grabbing paperwork and a few of the filled vials.

The alarm wailing and the sound of gunfire had alerted the locals, who, in turn, had called the police located in Voranava. Sirens could be heard in the distance approaching. The rhythmic flash of blue lights began reflecting off the walls as Hythe and Deacon rapidly retreated through the open section of the chainlink fence.

Ten seconds later, the sky lit up as an enormous explosion blew off part of the warehouse roof. Keeping low, they both ran along the side of the railway to where they hoped Lukas and Filip were waiting as flames licked up toward the sky.

They ran the twelve-hundred meters back to the car in record time, gasping and breathing heavily when they arrived, thankful Lukas and Filip were still waiting. Pulling off their balaclavas, Deacon climbed in the rear seat from the right, but Hythe stopped.

Turning to Filip, he said, 'Tell your grandfather to keep the lights off, even here amongst the trees. Here, tell him to wear these. They're far more powerful than those old Russian ones,' as he pulled off his night-vision goggles and handed them over.

Slipping the new goggles on, Lukas pressed the power switch and gasped. After speaking rapidly for a few moments, Filip managed to translate, 'Grandfather said they are fantastic. It's as good as daylight. And so lightweight.'

Climbing in, Patrick tapped Lukas on the shoulder and said, 'C'mon, let's go.' Nodding with much less effort now, Lukas pulled away before the loom of any approaching police vehicle's headlights could reach them. With a massive grin on his face as the black landscape showed bright green through the goggles, he drove down dirt tracks in total darkness at speed.

Three times they had to divert, having detected Belarusian security forces, either police or military. The first two times, they saw the loom of headlights from a distance, and it was easy to turn and head away to avoid being seen. The third time was harder.

Lukas suddenly slowed and stopped while driving through the forest near the border along a track hardly wide enough for a horse and cart, let alone a car. Somewhere up ahead, he'd seen the flare of a match. Hythe and Deacon rolled out through the rear doors before the vehicle had even stopped, exiting the car and readying their weapons. Lukas carefully selected reverse and gently let the clutch engage while keeping the engine revs at tick over. He steered the vehicle slowly in reverse at a walking pace, knowing any increase in engine revs would be heard. At the same time, his two passengers walked slowly in reverse, ready to open fire if challenged. They would never have made it without the goggles, but the slow and steady approach eventually paid off. A small clearing came into view almost a kilometer back. Turning the car around, Deacon and Hythe piled back in as Lukas headed the vehicle further into Belarus before turning along an even smaller dirt track.

This track wasn't being guarded, and Lukas proudly removed his goggles and reused his headlights as he announced they were back in Lithuania. Forty minutes later, he drove his battered VW and three weary passengers into his farmyard just as the sky was beginning to lighten.

There was fresh coffee brewing on the stove, and Rosa had made sandwiches.

Later, after a shower and a three-hour sleep, Patrick happily handed over the remainder of the money and their weapons. Deacon's NVGs went to Filip, and after heartfelt thanks and handshakes, they headed by taxi to Vilnius Airport.

Waiting in the lounge for their flight, Patrick said, 'It was a gamble, but we were right. Whatever's in those vials is the same in all of them. It might be just saline or even water, but it sure ain't a vaccine. All to be shipped to poor countries paying through the nose for a genuine product. How many poor bastards will die?'

37

THE flight back to Munich was uneventful. Deacon planned to catch an onward flight to Dubai two hours later, so they stopped in one of the airport sports bar restaurants for a quick meal. Every TV channel had the latest news running. Russia had started attacking Ukraine. They had crossed the border, and it was open warfare, although Russia was choosing to call it a *special military operation.*

'Sorry I can't stay longer, but I've got meetings planned for tomorrow morning in Dubai. What are you going to do now?'

'I don't know what the fuck's going on. Been ordered back to London, so I need to finish my report and submit it before I head back to the UK tonight. That factory's out of action, but I guess there'll be others. Need to find out what the bosses plan to do about Govorov. Then I have three weeks of leave to take, and I promised my godson, Peter, to look into an accident he was involved in. But it'll all depend on what's happening with this follow-up and with the Russia – Ukraine shindig. I also want to head over to Cancun to meet with Gina for a few days. Then it's off back to the Shiners in Tidworth, I expect,' Patrick said.

'The Shiners? What?'

'The nickname for the Royal Fusiliers. Where I came from before I joined the Regiment. Officers only get to do two tours of duty with the SAS, then it's back to their old regiment. And I'm well overdue. Don't know, though. I quite fancy something completely different ... Anyway, enough about me. What about you?'

'Business is booming. Might even need to expand. Ahh, they're boarding. Look, I'll give you a call when I'm back in the office.'

The two shook hands and embraced, with Deacon heading off to catch his flight while Patrick headed to the parking lot to retrieve his Audi.

<><><>

Having checked out of the hotel, Patrick returned to the British Consulate General Munich offices, where he deposited the remainder of the gear and weapons. He then drove to the airport and returned the hire car. He caught the next flight to Gatwick, picked up his X5, and headed to his apartment.

The following morning at 08:30, he entered meeting room 3G in Albany St Barracks, pulled up a chair, and said, 'Well, that was a total fucking waste of time. One trafficking group identified with links to a pedophile gang and information that at least three traffickers are working the route, with a war between two of them, a Serbian and an Albanian group, both vying to be top dog. And what happens? Mission canceled, and I get called home.'

'Were you able to identify either of those two groups?' Maj.Gen Ronaldson asked.

'No way! I'd need more resources than just me. I'd need at least one extra colleague, potentially two. I don't know who it is, or who they are, but I reckon there's a mole either in the Home Office or somewhere with access to my reports. Some bastard is setting us up to fail!'

Coughing to cover his embarrassment, Ronaldson handed Patrick a brown manilla folder. Inside was the original two-page report from Adam Paisley stapled together. Attached to it by a paperclip was a photocopy of the same report. Patrick glanced at it before looking back at Ronaldson and raising an eyebrow questioningly.

'The photocopy is the one I was sent from the Home Office after I requested it officially. It has various parts redacted, including the name Petr Doležal,' Ronaldson said. 'This one is the original that contains the name, along with some other useful information. This came from HMRC direct,' he continued.

'And you came across this ... how?'

'I, umm, I have a friend at the HMRC, and I called in a favor. It had seemed strange Paisley wouldn't provide the name of his contact to his bosses. I thought it was either deliberate because he didn't trust someone in HMRC, or somebody either in HMRC or the Home Office didn't want those details leaked. The fact it was in the full report, but redacted before handing it over ... Well, it answers that question. But as to who didn't want it known, I don't know.'

'So, how do we move forward with this?'

'We don't! The mission was to identify one of the trafficker groups which you've done. The Home Office has informed me they will liaise with Europol to arrest and charge them. As for you, you are about to go on three weeks' leave, starting in a couple of days, before you head off to Wiltshire. Like before, you need to go to Credenhill to sign large amounts of paperwork, complete your expenses for this last trip, and hand back any equipment. They shouldn't keep you more than a day or two. You know how sorry I am to see you go, and I have tried every which way to keep you here, but rules are rules. You have my heartfelt thanks for all you have done, and you have been a valued member of the regiment, but this mission is over. Now we leave it to Europol.'

With that, they shook hands and left. Hythe walked back to his car, Ronaldson to his office.

<><><>

Patrick was fuming. This same thing had happened a number of times in the past. Something was started and then stopped before completion. The last time it happened to him was last year in southwest Chad chasing Boko Haram. The UK government had sent the SAS in to support the Chad army in tracking down and eliminating Boko Haram. Twenty SAS were chasing over sixty BH, and the UK government pulled them out at the last minute. Rumors were the Chad government wanted to claim the glory. But it left a really sour taste in all their mouths, especially as after the SAS left, over eighty percent of the Boko Haram they were chasing had managed to escape again. One of his colleagues said it was like starting to paint a door or a wall and then leaving it half-done.

This latest mission was the same. Leave it to Europol to arrest them sometime in the future when it suits them. *No,* he thought, *this isn't over.*

He was glad he hadn't submitted a report on the counterfeit Covid vaccine and his and Deacon's attack on the manufacturing plant. Someone high up was controlling this, and he intended to find out who.

<><><>

Two hours later, he was approaching Queen Elizabeth Hospital Birmingham. After parking, he headed into the Royal Centre for Defence Medicine, a specialist division within the NHS providing medical support for military personnel.

Patrick was early for his lunch meeting with Captain Christopher Youngman, a long-time colleague, and friend. They had met after several of his men had been injured in training or in action many years before. After handshakes, back slaps, and twenty minutes of catch-up, Patrick discussed his reason for being there.

'Chris, I have a favor to ask. I came across these two vials recently, and I wonder if you could get the contents tested in one of your path labs to see what they contain?'

'Where did you get them?'

'I can't say yet, Chris. I don't believe they contain anything dangerous or poisonous. I think it may be just water or saline. Can you get them checked without this having to be official?'

After a moment or two of silence, Chris said, 'Patrick, this is pretty unusual. If this turns out to be something weird ... Look, I'll do it on one condition. It'll take me a couple of days to get results, but when I do, you must promise me you will tell me exactly where you got these from?'

'Deal, my friend. And I promise you will get the full story,' Patrick said, smiling.

THE MIDDLE EAST

38

THE United Arab Emirates, or UAE, is often considered a single entity but comprises a federation of seven hereditary tribal monarchy-styled political systems called Sheikhdoms or Emirates. Although a nation-state, all seven emirates in the UAE are ruled by different royal families, with the present rulers being direct descendants of the founding Sheikhs of the UAE. The emirates comprise Abu Dhabi, Dubai, Sharjah, Ras Al Khaimah, Ajman, Umm Al Quwain, and Fujairah, with Abu Dhabi being the capital and the richest, with Dubai a close second.

Deacon's first meeting with four of the third-level senior members of the Maktoum ruling family of Dubai went without a hitch. All four regularly traveled on business with their guards, who were armed with sidearms for use within any of the seven emirates.

However, when traveling outside the Middle East, their insistence on having their guards armed often fell on deaf ears, as many of the countries they visited insisted on foreign security staff being unarmed.

When visiting the USA, for example, the level of security offered depends on the aspect of their visit and their seniority. At their level within the diplomatic regime, if they are on official government business, they are classified as dignitaries, with their security provided by the Diplomatic Security Service, a division of the Department of State. If, however, their visit is not official and merely business-related or even vacation, they are classified simply as VIPs. In those instances, armed security is not supplied as standard. Instead, in-country licensed private security organizations are often contracted to offer these services.

With Deacon selling and promoting the virtues of Phylax and with armfuls of satisfied Middle Eastern customer references, he had signed up all four for their forthcoming trip to New York and Los Angeles within two hours.

Keeping the impetus going, he was recommended to arrange a meeting with third-level senior members of the Nahyan ruling family of Abu Dhabi, just a seventy-minute drive away. They also experience similar issues when traveling on non-government business. His host made one phone call, and the meeting was arranged for that afternoon. A quick taxicab ride, a brief presentation followed by a conference call with the four senior staff from that morning, resulted in a very successful outcome. Deacon signed another six senior clients.

Surprised and extremely pleased that his trip had been so productively completed on the first day, he decided to enjoy his remaining two days exploring the city and taking in several tourist activities before returning to Washington.

He spent the remainder of the day visiting Abu Dhabi's Sheikh Zayed Grand Mosque. It is one of the world's largest mosques and an architectural masterpiece that stunningly combines Islamic architecture and design. He'd visited it before but always in daylight, only seeing it floodlit from the Al Khaleej Al Arabi St to the airport. Here was a chance to spend time exploring its wonders as the fading amber sunlight bathed the white facade to create a beautiful orange glow until the sun finally dipped below the horizon. As the sky quickly darkened, as it does in those latitudes, the true majesty of the building showed through, tastefully illuminated by lights.

Although Deacon wasn't religious, he could still admire the skill, design, and love that went into buildings such as St Basil's Cathedral, the Duomo, and St Peter's Basilica. The Sheikh Zayed Grand Mosque is a modern building of equal wonder.

He spent two enjoyable hours slowly walking around before evening prayers were called. He sat quietly at the rear of the building during the call to prayer *Adhan,* followed minutes later by the *Iqamah* before the full sunset *Maghrib* was completed.

He casually looked around the prayer room, and his eyes swept briefly across many faces. Something triggered his brain to return to one particular face, but he didn't know why. As he swung his gaze back for a more detailed look, other worshippers moving into place blocked his view. The face he'd seen had disappeared, but two companions he had been standing next to were still there. He continued looking for a few moments but then, assuming he'd imagined the experience, didn't give it any more thought.

When the prayers had finished, he headed back to Dubai before taking an evening sightseeing cruise on a dhow in and around Dubai Creek. Sharing the small craft with a pair of middle-aged Australians and a group of Chinese tourists all enjoying vacations, everyone seemed to be impressed and often speechless at the views of the floodlit skyline, illuminated hotels, the Creek itself, and the Burj Khalifa tower. Deacon hit it off with the Australians, and together they spent the rest of the evening sharing a meal and a few too many beers. By evening's end, he even had to promise to look them up the next time he was in Sydney.

The following morning he hired a jet ski and spent two hours acting like a large kid. He reluctantly returned it with a smile as wide as a pizza dish, knowing he had business calls to make that afternoon.

Established as a small fishing village in the early eighteenth century, Dubai town remained primarily unchanged until after WW2. Once oil had been discovered, the town went through multiple renewals and rebuilds, culminating in the impressive ultra-modern city it has now become. However, unlike some of the other oil-growth cities of the Middle East, Dubai kept parts of its Old Town where ancient meets new.

At the northwestern end of Dubai Creek, close to its outlet into Port Rashid and the sea, lies the Deira region, and within that, Dubai Old Town - an area of approximately one square mile where time appears to have stood still. On the west bank, souks sell everyday items under shelters and lean-to's dating back a hundred or more years in narrow alleyways even older. Take away today's vehicles, and it's easy for the visitor to imagine Ahmad Ibn Majid, one of the most famous Arab navigators of all time, strolling the alleyways and passages without a care in the world.

Crossing the Creek in an Abra is an experience not to be missed. These open-air small water buses are cheap and plentiful, taking just minutes to cross the busy waterway or longer if further travel is required.

Once on the water, restore the engines in the dhows back to masts and sails, and suddenly you have traveled back in history a thousand years. Goods come in, are bartered for and sold, placed on dhows, and leave. It had been this way since before Christ was born.

<><><>

Deacon always enjoyed this region of Dubai and decided to spend his last evening here. Having just spent an enjoyable hour re-visiting the west bank, he stood at the water's edge watching the next Abra water bus arrive. For less than the equivalent of a dollar, he stood on the crowded deck as the small, heavily overcrowded vessel turned and plowed its way across the churning water. The 120-yard trip only takes a few minutes, but the warm evening air, even in February, the salty smell of the sea, and the distinct aroma of a thousand other smells and perfumes brought the wide-mouthed smile back to his face. *You can have all the latest hotels and apartments, but to me, this is Dubai,* he thought. He headed first to the Perfume Souk - rows of stalls and small shops selling every scent under the sun, from the latest western VIP 'must-haves' to local bouquets unchanged over generations. He picked a regional perfume he knew his on-off partner, Wendy Fitch, would like, along with four others for his mother, two sisters, and Melissa, his close friend in the FBI and one of the best ex-gray hat hackers around. Now running a division in the FBI tasked with investigating cybercrime, there wasn't anyone better at cracking firewalls and computer code. Paying in cash, he smiled to himself, knowing for once he had remembered to bring them presents from his travels.

After strolling through the Old Souk, selling everything from the latest Artificial Intelligence voice assistants to Bluetooth sunglasses to vacuum cleaners and fruit, he purchased a few hundred grams of dates before heading to the Spice Souk. Here, every conceivable spice and herb was on offer, presented in hand-woven baskets of many shapes and sizes.

Then came the Gold Souk. Security was obviously present but very low-key. Having been raised in America with its incumbent crime, he was always amazed at how many millions of dollars worth of gold was casually on show. *However,* he mused, *Arabic justice for theft is a pretty good deterrent.*

Heading back down to the quay, he stood looking at the large dhows. Originally they would all have been sail-powered, but now all relied on powerful diesel engines, although a few still had both. The traditional hull shape had not changed in centuries, still built of Indian Mahogany or Teak. In years gone by, and even up to the turn of the century, the wood would have been imported from India or Africa with local skilled craftsmen building the boats by hand, but those local skills had slowly been lost. Now, most new large dhows are made in the coastal ports of India, Pakistan, or Yemen. However, workers in sheltered creeks and bays of Ras Al-Khaimah still manage to produce one or two every few years. Although these workers have access to modern equipment, much of a dhow is still cut and shaped by eye and hand using the simplest of ancient practices and tools.

Large ocean-going dhows, typically between eighty and one hundred thirty feet, still play a significant role in the modern economy of the UAE. Loaded with merchandise ranging from foodstuffs to furniture, they regularly leave Dubai Creek en route to Iran. They are also still used for fishing and more and more for tourism, with some being turned into floating restaurants. Making deals, making money, and moving goods to other parts of the world is still a multibillion-dollar business at Dubai Creek.

Leaning against the wall idly eating his dates, Deacon watched a heavily loaded dhow making ready to sail. Two crew were at the bow and stern with the mooring lines ready as the captain started and revved the engine. A large puff of grey-white smoke emerged from the black funnel but quickly disappeared, leaving behind the steady rhythmic beat of a highly loved and well-maintained hidden iron beast.

A shiny black top-of-the-range Mercedes pulled up close to the gangplank, and three men climbed out. The first seemed to be the lead passenger, while the other two were his guards. From the cut of their suit jackets and the slight bulge under their arms, it was obvious to Deacon they were armed. They looked familiar. Then it clicked. It was the same three people Deacon had noticed praying in the Grand Mosque.

Because they appeared to be armed, he watched them out of professional curiosity. Whether the passenger felt Deacon's eyes on him or was glancing around out of habit, their eyes met.

It took two seconds.

Two and a half heartbeats.

The time it took for a bag of dates to fall to the ground.

Deacon saw recognition flare in his opponent's eyes just as he mouthed the word, 'Saif!' and his opponent said, 'You!'

39

THE spell broken, Saif ordered his guards after Deacon. One pulled out an automatic handgun while grabbing a suppressor from his jacket pocket and trying to fit it. The second guard pulled his jacket open, exposing and raising a short-barrel Heckler & Koch MP5 submachine gun on a shoulder strap.

Deacon didn't hang about. Unarmed, he didn't even have any dates left he could throw at them. He ran. He heard two *zings* as rounds from the handgun peppered the wall, and he dived into the first alleyway he reached. He could hear his pursuers' footsteps as they ran after him. Ducking and weaving to throw off their aim, he reached another alley and skidded around the corner into it as something buzzed close to his ear before *zinging* as it hit the wall next to his head.

'Fuck me,' he murmured, haring around the next corner as he felt his jacket twitch as it was hit.

Relieved a little as he ran back into the crowded Old Souk, he suddenly realized the fragrance of multiple perfumes was assailing his nostrils. Only small bottles; he'd stored his purchases in his jacket pocket. The silenced round had missed him but found another target. Cursing, he weaved and ducked through the crowds, having to push some people out of the way. Glancing back, he saw his pursuers hide their weapons. Dubai Police do not take kindly to people brandishing weapons, especially in an area of high tourism.

Moving as quickly as he could, he rushed to get through the passageways and out the far side of the souk into yet another alley. Turning left and accelerating, he glanced back to see he now had almost a two hundred meters lead on them. But then they split. One followed him while the other chose a different route. They were obviously hoping to out-maneuver him. Turning right, he was again at one of the Spice Souk entrances. As he ran into it, veering left and right down busy lanes of people, trying to lose his assailants, he was looking for some sort of weapon.

Anything.

One stall holder was holding a wooden pole, about three feet long, used to draw the sun cover over his stall. Deacon grabbed the stick out of the shocked stallholder's hands as he ran past. Ignoring the shouts and bluster, he sped on.

Making a sharp right, he accelerated down a long alleyway, shouting to get people to move aside and let him through. Those that didn't budge were pushed out of the way while he also tried to keep a lookout for his tail.

One stall, on the corner of a junction, was longer than many of the others. It had woven baskets and metal trays displaying their goods, ranging from herbs and nuts to dozens of powdered spices. As Deacon was running past, the other pursuer crossed in front of Deacon.

Glancing down, Deacon grabbed the first tray of spice he could reach without stopping. Scooping it up, he threw it directly into the face of this new assailant raising his MP5. The metal tray slammed into the gunman's head, making a dull *dong* sound, as the contents covered his entire face before Deacon side-swiped him with the wooden pole to the side and back of his head and kept running.

Glancing back, he was amazed to see the gunman collapse to the ground, hands gouging at his eyes, and he could hear him beginning to scream.

Already trying to stifle a laugh at the tray's noise as it bounced off the gunman's head, he realized that with all the dozens of spices available; Cinnamon, Bay Leaves, Thyme, Oregano, and more, he'd struck gold with Hot Chilli powder.

He couldn't help it; he laughed out loud.

<><><>

Thirty seconds later, Deacon rushed out of the Souk, turned sharp right, and found himself back on the busy quayside road just yards from an Abra pontoon. One half-empty water bus was just leaving. Jumping down from the stone dock and sprinting the last few feet of the small pontoon, Deacon held his breath and leaped. Both feet landed on the Abra, but with its rocking, he would have toppled off backward had hands not grabbed at him, pulling him inboard.

Offering a nod of thanks to his helpers, some of whom were looking at him strangely because of the odor coming from him, he quickly moved amongst them to hide from those after him. The craft was almost halfway across the Creek before both gunmen appeared on the quayside, one helping the other, who had a cloth wrapped around his head. They were looking around trying to spot Deacon, but the area was too busy.

As he exited the water bus back on the western bank, Deacon took shelter in the shadows and watched from a distance. The dhow with Saif onboard had left the dockside and was slowly turning across the busy waterway to head out to sea. Saif could be seen on deck angrily waving his arms and threatening the two guards, one who was leaning back, staring at the sky while the other poured bottles of water over his face.

Grabbing his cell phone, he dialed. 'Mitch, John. Sorry pal, but no time for niceties. Can you patch me through to the Admiral?'

Twenty seconds later, Admiral Douglas Carter picked up the extension and muttered in his gruff voice, 'Commander, speak.'

'Sir, I'm sorry to disturb you at lunch. Steve Caan, aka Saif Khan or Saif the Palestinian, is still number four on the FBI's ten most wanted list. I believe I've just seen him getting on a dhow in Dubai Creek. The dhow left a few minutes ago. I need it tracked ... Yessir, I'm a hundred percent confident it was him ... About sixty yards, sir ... He recognized me as well. Sent two of his goons after me.'

'Commander, head to the US Consulate General building. Keep this line free,' the Admiral said.

In fast-walk mode, Deacon reached the entrance eight minutes later. Although closed to visitors at that time of the evening, the armed US Marines at the entrance examined his passport. Not sure what to make of a disheveled man appearing at the guardhouse after the Consulate was closed and stinking of multiple perfumes, they picked up the phone to call their superiors at the Embassy in Abu Dhabi for instructions. Before their call was answered, Deacon's phone rang.

Answering it, Deacon said, 'I'm being held at the guardhouse. Yessir, I tried to explain.' After listening to a reply, he turned, handed his phone to the senior of the two guards, and said, 'For you,' before standing back and gently smiling.

The Marine Corporal took the phone, warily placed it against his ear, and said, 'And who the fuck are you, pal?'

Even replaying it in his mind afterward, Deacon was never sure whether the grin on the Corporal's face left before the color drained from it or it was the other way around. He also couldn't remember seeing anyone snap to attention quicker.

When Deacon told the story after, he said the Admiral's voice was so loud he could hear both sides of the conversation.

There were plenty of 'Yes Sir's, No Sir's, No Sir, I don't want to be assigned to Alaska' that Deacon had to turn his head away to hide his grin.

A very red-faced Corporal handed Deacon his cell phone back a minute later, saluted, and asked him to follow him into the offices.

As they stepped inside the mostly unlit building, an older man, greying at the temples and quite heavily built, approached, saying, 'I'm Larry Helm, acting Head of Station. I have an Admiral Carter holding on the phone for you,' as he passed an encrypted handset over.

'Commander, there are currently over ninety small craft within a ten-mile radius of Dubai harbor. Some are speedboats and power yachts, with at least thirty vessels in the eighty-to-one-twenty-foot range. Can you offer identification marks?' the Admiral said.

'Sir, it has a double-height, full-width wheelhouse roof that is a dark, faded red color. Hull was the same dark red with faded blue rubbing strake. The dhow was heavily loaded with tarps covering most of the cargo on the foredeck. Some large crates were secured on both quarters. Any good, sir?'

A few minutes later, the Admiral answered, 'I'm looking at twelve possibilities from an E-3 Sentry feed that seem to match your criteria. Head of Station Helm will take you to the comms room. I'll get CAOC to get you the live feed,' the Admiral said before hanging up.

Handing back the handset to Helm, they both walked toward the stairs. Helm said, 'I don't know who you are, and I guess I don't want to know, but you must be pretty high up the totem pole for the Chief of Naval Ops to call?'

Not bothering to answer, Deacon was relieved by how quickly the Admiral had reacted. The E-3 Sentry is an airborne warning and control system, or AWACS. Typically, it is a modified Boeing 707 with a massive rotating radar dome on top of the fuselage. Anything in the air, on land, or on the sea, moving faster than at walking speed could be detected, and high-resolution aerial views could be shown in real-time.

Multiple screens came to life in the communications room, streaming a live feed of different views and aspects of the Gulf from the Middle East Combined Air Operations Center in Qatar. Deacon could immediately see the twelve vessels the Admiral was referring to. Navy operators had already detected these as possibilities as they were circled in red. Deacon selected each highlighted object using the keyboard and mouse before zooming in for a closer look. In the dark, colors were not detectable, so he only had the shape of the craft and superstructure to try and determine which vessel was his. He ignored those staying within a mile or so of the shore or close to the entrance to the Creek, as these were most likely evening cruise or restaurant tourist boats. With the gain of the cameras turned up full, the shape of cargo on three dhows didn't look familiar, so he reclassified those as unlikely.

With seven vessels now accounted for, the remaining five became his focus. Vessels tagged as one to three were staying within a few miles close inshore as they headed along the coast toward the Strait of Hormuz. Two others, tagged four and five, were heading further northwest up the Gulf toward Qatar or possibly Kuwait.

All five were located within distance to have left Dubai within the previous forty minutes, so all he could do was wait and watch.

40

THE hours dragged on. The distance from Dubai to the northern part of Oman bordering the Strait of Hormuz is ninety-six nautical miles. The average speed of a fully laden cargo dhow is between ten and fourteen knots. Deacon knew it would take between five and six hours, assuming their rate didn't vary for the three inshore ones to enter the Straits. If dhows four and five were heading up the Gulf, the earliest one would reach Qatar at two hundred miles distance would be almost twelve hours, and Kuwait at over twenty-five hours.

The Strait of Hormuz is a narrow waterway that connects the Persian Gulf and the Gulf of Oman - the only passage from the oil-rich Gulf to the Indian Ocean for maritime traffic. Considered one of the busiest narrow channel shipping routes in the world, and at only 21 miles wide at its narrowest point, it is an obvious choke point.

With the Islamic Republic of Iran occupying the entire northern shore with its political views and instability, the whole area is often considered to be a powder keg just waiting to explode.

The Strait itself has shallow water areas and a sharp ninety-degree bend; therefore, tankers and commercial shipping constrained by their draught are confined to an internationally recognized Traffic Separation Scheme. This consists of two two-mile-wide shipping lanes: one for incoming traffic and one for outgoing. These two shipping lanes are separated by a two-mile buffer zone. Overall, the narrow confines of the scheme offer tankers and other large commercial or military ships very little room for maneuver.

However, local smaller craft keep clear and remain inshore whenever possible.

By 03:00, it was clear that two of the inshore dhows, tagged as four and five, had passed through the turn of the Strait and were now heading south toward the Gulf of Oman, having followed the coastline closely and kept to the inshore of Musandam Island.

However, the third dhow was approaching the narrowest part of the Strait, crossing the Traffic Separation Scheme at a right angle and heading north to Iran.

The minutes ticked by as Deacon watched the slow northerly movement of the dhow. Soon after it passed to the left of Larak Island, a fast patrol boat out of Bandar Abbas approached the dhow. It went alongside before leaving it and heading inshore to the naval base a few minutes later. The resolution wasn't clear enough to see individual bodies, but Deacon assumed Saif and his colleagues had been removed and were heading ashore.

Iran has two independent naval forces: the Islamic Republic of Iran Navy (IRIN), predating Iran's 1979 Revolution, and the Islamic Revolutionary Guard Corps Navy (IRGCN), which was formed during the Iran-Iraq war in 1985. Both the IRIN and the IRGCN continue to operate as distinct services, with parallel chains of command; the IRIN is seen as Iran's blue water navy with submarines, larger longer-range surface vessels, and is primarily responsible for the Gulf of Oman, while the IRGCN is more ideally suited to be a coastal defense force within the Persian Gulf, consisting of small fast-attack craft armed with machine guns, rocket-propelled grenades, torpedoes, and missiles. Both naval forces share responsibility for the protection of the Strait of Hormuz.

After the dhow's passengers had departed, the captain continued his route toward the coast to the small busy commercial fishing harbor of Haqani Port. Eager dock hands helped the crew unload his goods, both legal and illegally smuggled.

<><><>

It was 04:30 in Dubai, 20:30 the previous evening in Washington, when Deacon made the call.

'Admiral, this is our chance to finally capture Caan, aka Saif. We know he's in Bandar Abbas. Authorize an incursion team, and we can go in and get the bastard.'

'Commander, I'm sorry, but no can do. The President would not sign off on aggressive action against Iran at present. Washington is currently in delicate negotiation with Tehran, and he doesn't want anything to upset the talks.'

'But Caan is number four on the FBI's most wanted?'

'I know, Commander, but my hands are tied. Now that President Wexford has recovered and is back in the White House, he has been keen to get Iran back to the negotiating table. The nuclear talks stalled when the President collapsed, and VP Derwent took over, but now he's back; it's full steam ahead. Even if that wasn't the case, making an incursion into Iran based on possible recognition from a two-second glance at sixty yards of someone we don't have current photographs of and that you haven't seen for over three years ... Need I say more, Commander?'

Realizing it was an argument he couldn't win, Deacon thought for a moment before answering, 'Obviously, you're correct, sir. I apologize,' while brainstorming ideas of how he could get to Haqani Port without being arrested or shot.

41

DEACON awoke later the same day, having gotten to bed by 6 am. The Emirates Airline direct flight to Washington left each day at 11:40. It was too late to get to the terminal in time for today's fifteen-hour flight, so he called and changed his booking until the following morning. Instead, he would enjoy one last lazy day before returning to work. He had allowed three days for meetings in and around Dubai when booking flights and intended to use all of them thoroughly.

Pulling up his customer list, he phoned a couple of very satisfied clients who'd been using Phylax for over a year and offered to take them to lunch as a courtesy. He also wanted to replace the broken perfume presents he'd bought yesterday, so he planned to return to the Perfume Souk later that evening.

The lunch at the Pink Orchid restaurant overlooking the beach was a great success. The service was perfect, and the food was excellent. His guests, three local government members involved in banking, were regular visitors to New York. Deacon had first met them almost eighteen months previously and convinced them to let him and Phylax look after all aspects of their security when visiting the USA. It had been the start of an excellent working partnership. They had passed Deacon's and Phylax's details on to various colleagues who were now also customers.

<><><>

As Deacon and his guests sat down together and decided on pre-dinner drinks, Salim al-Ghulam walked through the restaurant. Salim was in contact by cell phone and miniature earpiece with his twin brother, Faiz, sitting astride a powerful black motorcycle parked across the road. He casually eyed and compared Deacon's face against a US Department of Defense photograph taken of him in uniform a few years back. He murmured in Arabic, 'It's him, Inshallah,' before continuing and leaving the restaurant by the side door.

The phone call had come in earlier that morning to Salim. *Find and remove this person. He's American, his full name is John Patrick Deacon, and he's an ex-US Navy SEAL, so be wary. The caller didn't know which hotel Deacon was staying in, but being an American, try the American franchise ones first.* As he listened to the caller, a photo was sent to his phone.

It had only taken them twenty minutes to track down Deacon's hotel. Having discovered he was staying at the Four Seasons, Faiz had called and asked to speak with him to be told he was out at lunch. A simple question was whether they knew where because they needed to reach him urgently, and a helpful receptionist confirmed she had made lunch reservations at the Pink Orchid.

Thanking her, both of them headed to the restaurant, with Salim completing the positive identification while Faiz stayed with the transport.

<><><>

With excellent food, great service, and good company, the two-hour lunch passed all too quickly. When they had finished, the restaurant called an executive taxi cab for them. Deacon and his guests climbed in the rear, and

Deacon suggested they all head to a local hotel bar to enjoy another drink or two.

Sitting an hour later, enjoying an ice-cold Pepsi while talking, Deacon felt uneasy. Something was wrong. Without drawing attention to himself, he idly glanced around. A stranger in business clothes was sitting at the bar drinking a coffee and looking at him. He glanced away as soon as he saw Deacon had noticed him, but he was too slow by a fraction of a second. Instantly on alert, Deacon recognized him as the same person who had strolled by in the restaurant. To be looked at once was ok; twice if in the same location would be unusual but not necessarily alarming, but twice on the same day in entirely different locations made the hairs on his arm stand up. Always alert, he'd completed enough eyes-on walk-throughs to know he was a target.

Unarmed, he kept a close eye on the bar entrance while casually slipping a table knife up his sleeve. Finishing his drink, he made his excuses to leave but left his three guests with an open bar and instructions to enjoy themselves. He knew the bill wouldn't be excessive – his guests were Muslim and didn't drink alcohol.

Heading out, he waved down and jumped into a passing taxi, instructing the driver to take him to the Dubai Mall, located downtown next to the Burj Khalifa, the tallest building in the world. As the taxi drove along the busy roads, Deacon twisted around on the back seat until he could glance out of the rear window without looking too obvious. Sure enough, a black motorcycle was tailing the taxi with a rider and a passenger. The rider was dressed in black leather with a full-face helmet, while the passenger was also in a black leather jacket and helmet but wearing business clothes underneath.

<><><>

Cursing as Salim realized he'd been made, he had hurried outside the restaurant to Faiz and put on the leathers and helmet. Salim knew he shouldn't have completed a second ID check at the bar. He knew the more you place yourself near someone, the more chances they will recognize or remember you, but he did it anyway.

Parked two hundred yards from the doorway to the bar, they saw their target leave a few minutes later and immediately wave down a taxicab before leaping in. Dropping into position four vehicles behind Deacon's taxi, they followed him as he headed back downtown. Both armed with silenced handguns, they were just waiting for the chance to catch him alone and unaware.

Salim and Faiz al-Ghulam had grown up in a poor farming family in the backwaters of Iran. Seeing their parents work their fingers to the bone scraping a living from the soil hadn't inspired them to follow suit. Salim, three years older than Faiz, had attended the local school, albeit in one room with a male teacher trying to teach kids to read and write. He was conscripted to join the Iranian Army for two years when he turned eighteen. This was after the Shah had been deposed, and Iran was under the strict Islamic law based on Sharia rulings, with all its hatred against the West, particularly America. After finishing his conscription, Salim had a choice. Remain in the Army and commit to a long-term career in the military, or seek employment elsewhere. He left and joined one of the underground street gangs making money selling alcohol, protection, and illegal imports.

Within the first month, he made more money than in twelve months in the Army. Faiz, now approaching eighteen ignored his call-up papers and joined forces with Salim. Together they became enforcers running illegal protection rackets in Tehran. They were brutal and efficient. Many older generations still remembered the freedoms under the Shah's rule. They yearned for the luxuries of the past, including western cigarettes and alcohol, now banned under strict Islamic Law. Then, seeing a business opportunity in the rich states of the UAE, the brothers gathered their money, took their chances, and headed to Dubai.

Although Islamic countries, the UAE interprets the religious laws and rulings more leniently than some. Dubai, in particular, spent billions of dollars becoming the playground for the rich and famous, even lowering their standards to welcome the not-so-rich to capitalize in the tourist holiday market. One thing Dubai has large quantities of is alcohol for the non-Muslim western workers and tourists. It was relatively easy for the al-Ghulam brothers to tap into that market and ship regular amounts by dhow to Iran.

Then the Russian Mafia moved in. Known as Bratva, meaning Brotherhood, they also saw opportunities to supply what the rich and famous desired; alcohol, drugs, and women. Heavily into human and drug trafficking, extortion, smuggling, prostitution, and pornography, Dubai and Abu Dhabi provide a perfect market for most of these activities. As with many of the world's uber-rich, both residents and visitors want what they want, and money talks. Many of them also believe the laws of the land do not apply to them, only to those of lower social standing.

Alcohol is only sold to non-Muslim residents in the UAE on the production of a residency card showing their religion. However, it is also sold extensively in hotel bars and clubs. Many of these bars and clubs also contain dozens of stunning young Eastern Bloc women for hire by the hour or overnight. Discretion is paramount and enforced by men you wouldn't want to argue with.

It didn't take long before members of Bratva visited the brothers. Bratva announced that all alcohol shipped into Dubai would be through a company they owned. Prices would immediately rise by twenty percent, but as good business people, Bratva offered the brothers a choice. Carry on smuggling their drinks into Iran purchased through Bratva at increased cost or end up buried in the desert.

Their decision had been a simple one. The brothers quickly realized it was better to work for and with the Russians than against them. With a tidy income from their alcohol smuggling business, Salim and Faiz were happy doing what they enjoyed most - working as enforcers for the Russians with a regular overnight pretty young freebie thrown in as and when.

Senior members of MOIS, based in Tehran, were also interested in the al-Ghulam brothers. MOIS, the Iranian Ministry of Intelligence and Security, knew of the brothers' smuggling enterprise. Their task was to protect the Islamic Republic's interests at home and worldwide by infiltrating internal opposition groups, monitoring domestic threats and expatriate dissent, arresting alleged spies and dissidents, and exposing conspiracies deemed threatening. Therefore, the opportunity to expose the UAE's western corruption and lack of adherence to Muhammad's teachings was fuel to their fire.

The al-Ghulam brothers' ability to smuggle goods or people into and out of Iran undetected was of great interest to MOIS. A simple threat against the lives of Salim and Faiz's family and relatives still residing in Iran was enough to guarantee their support and compliance.

This morning's call from Bandar Abbas to eliminate an individual in Dubai wasn't unusual. Refusal or failure was not an option.

42

AS Deacon's taxi neared the Mall, the traffic was heavier, and the driver had to queue to reach the taxi rank. Keen to be out of a potential enclosed target zone, Deacon dropped a wad of cash, including a sizeable tip, on the front passenger seat, thanked the driver, opened the door, and was gone before the driver could object.

Disappearing quickly amongst the crowds' Deacon glanced back in time to see the passenger strip off his outer leather jacket and deposit it, along with his helmet, into the cycle's luggage bin before the rider rapidly pulled away. Turning, Deacon dashed up the escalator amongst the crowds.

<><><>

Salim tried to keep an eye on Deacon as he pushed toward the crowd gathered around the bottom of the escalator. A Mall guard had seen Deacon move quickly through the crowds and called after him to slow down. Salim knew if he did the same, the guard would likely raise the alarm, so he chased after him as rapidly as he could without drawing attention to himself.

The Dubai Mall is enormous, covering almost 80,000 m2 and 1,200 shops. As big as a village, it has concourses heading off in multiple directions from every entrance and multiple floors. Exiting at the top of the escalator, he looked around, but Deacon had gone. Cursing, he chose the concourse directly in front and started moving along it.

From behind a rack of shirts in a men's clothing shop, Deacon watched his pursuer rush by, eyes darting left and right, trying to spot him. He moved to the doorway, watching and waiting until Salim had gone over fifty meters before stepping out to follow. Salim was glancing around, but Deacon kept to the side of the walkway and moved into each shop entrance as he reached them. At the end of the first concourse leg, where it joined another three, Deacon moved into another shop and watched Salim from a distance.

Not sure what to do next, Salim called his brother on his phone while still looking around. He then waited almost ten minutes until a figure wearing motorcycle leathers approached. Faiz had removed his outer leather jacket and helmet but was still wearing his protective leggings and heavy boots. Deacon watched as they argued before splitting up, each taking a different concourse leg. Deacon knew both of them were trying to find him. Although he hadn't seen the face of the second pursuer close enough to identify him, Deacon decided anyone wearing black leather motorcycle leggings in the Mall would be easily recognizable from a distance, so he decided to follow Salim instead.

Deacon tailed him for another hour, watching him twice make a call before meeting with his motorcycle accomplice. After making sure they were both separated again and heading in opposite directions to each other, Deacon decided to up the game. He circled around in front of Salim and walked across his line of sight. As expected, Salim saw him immediately.

Deacon then headed to the restrooms and entered the men's block. He'd already checked and seen it had two entrances, one at either end. Inside, he found one other man drying his hands and just leaving. Standing just inside the door, ready to attack, Deacon waited. With the place empty, he wanted to speak with his tail and find out why they were following him.

<><><>

Salim had been getting angrier and angrier. He knew his masters in Iran would not be happy if his target escaped. He and his brother had never failed before, but so far, they were being outwitted by a damned American. Then he had the lucky break. The target appeared out of nowhere, heading to the john. Sending a quick text to Faiz, he followed Deacon. As he approached the outer door, he slipped his right hand in under his jacket and gripped his handgun. The suppresser attached to the barrel made the weapon slightly unwieldy and awkward to draw quickly, but he couldn't afford to walk in with it already exposed.

A stranger walked out as he pushed the outer door open, shaking additional moisture off his hands. Their eyes didn't meet, and he ignored him even though the stranger murmured something. Leaning forward, he pushed open the inner door and walked in.

<><><>

Deacon heard the outer door open and a word or two spoken. Then the inner door began to move. As he saw Salim's body appear, he also saw the handgrip of a weapon being pulled from his jacket. In an instant, everything had changed from being a simple interrogation to a fight for his life. Armed only with a blunt dessert knife, Deacon knew he had to react fast.

Leaping forward, he grasped Salim's jacket lapels and pushed hard while twisting the two of them away from the door. The pressure on Salim's chest stopped him from withdrawing his right hand, still gripping his handgun. Deacon's forehead smashed down on the bridge of his nose, making him dizzy at the same time as Deacon kneed him firmly in the groin. Deacon grabbed him by the back of his neck as he began to buckle and thrust his head down toward the porcelain washbasins.

He turned his head slightly at the last moment, making the edge of the washbasin strike the side of his head and chin instead of his face. That move momentarily saved his life, although the pain from his smashed jaw made him want to vomit. As they pushed against each other, both of them lost their footing on the polished floor. Salim collapsed, with Deacon still grasping his neck almost on his back. Trying to roll, Salim finally pulled his right hand out from under him, still grasping his handgun. Deacon grabbed the weapon and twisted it clear, breaking two of Salim's fingers as he wrenched it away.

Turning the weapon back on Salim, Deacon jammed the suppressor tip into Salim's right ear, yanked his head up by his hair, and growled, 'Who the fuck are you? Why are you following me?'

Before a semi-conscious Salim could answer, the far restroom door was kicked open, and his brother, Faiz, was standing there, weapon in hand.

<><><>

As Faiz saw what was happening, he shouted, raised his weapon, and fired. At first sight of Faiz, Deacon had already begun rolling off Salim's prone body while still holding his hair. The weight and length of the suppressor always made the weapon front heavy. In his panic and rush to shoot, Faiz didn't allow enough time for his weapon to be fully raised before he pulled the trigger. The sub-sonic round exited the tip of the suppressor at a little over 800 feet per second. In a fraction over four-tenths of a second, the soft-nosed round traveled the thirty-five-foot length of the restroom block and embedded itself in Salim's chest before smashing through ribs and ending up causing massive internal trauma resulting in virtually instant death.

In response, Deacon's right hand holding Salim's weapon was dead on target. Two quick pulls of the trigger slammed Faiz back against the restroom door while it was still dawning on him he had killed his brother.

Quickly checking in the mirror that he didn't have any noticeable amount of blood on him, Deacon needed to get away. Wiping his prints from the weapon he'd fired, he placed it back in Salim's hand. He was tempted to keep one of the handguns, but he quickly reckoned if he were stopped with an illegal suppressed weapon just used in a murder, it wouldn't be an easy situation to resolve. Trying to explain to Dubai police what had happened would not go well. Instead, he took their wallets and phones, leaving both bodies where they lay, and made a hasty exit.

Just outside the restroom door was a cleaning cart. Deacon wheeled it in front of the doorway and slipped the sign over the door handle stating *Cleaning in progress.*

Three minutes later, he was two floors down and lost amongst the crowds.

43

'MELISSA, I'm at the Consulate. I have two names, a Salim al-Ghulam and his brother, Faiz al-Ghulam. Both are Iranian citizens living in Dubai. I also have their UAE residency cards. I'll get Larry Helm to scan and send them over. Please find out everything you can about these two and get back to me asap,' Deacon asked, passing the cards to Helm.

Continuing, he said, 'Larry, I've also got two phones, both locked. Anyone here able to unlock them?'
Receiving a positive nod and a 'Sure, no problem,' Deacon then requested a listing of all names and numbers stored in both phones and a printout of all texts and any emails. Again, Larry Helm confirmed it would be with him within the hour before disappearing toward the comms room with the two phones.

Deacon had decided the safest place for him, at least for now, was the Consulate until he knew more about who was after him. Leaving the Mall had been easy. He was halfway down an exit escalator heading toward a taxi rank when the alarm went up. Suddenly guards were running around looking worried, and the sirens of approaching police cars could be heard. It would be impossible to lock the Mall's doors with everyone still inside, so he casually waited in line for a few moments until a taxi was available.

The police had already announced on the news two men were shot and murdered today in the Dubai Mall.

The police were claiming it was fighting between rival gangs of unlawful non-UAE workers.

Melissa called him back after forty minutes. After checking he was alone and able to talk, she explained basic details about the al-Ghulams. They'd been in Dubai for almost fifteen years. The Dubai Police had records on both of them as suspected accomplices of Bratva but little proven evidence.

As they finished speaking, Larry Helm reappeared with a couple of sheets of paper. The first list was phone numbers Salim had called or received calls or texts from. The second was the same but from Faiz's phone. The final sheets of paper were the transcribed text SMS messages or emails from both phones.

Examining them more closely, Deacon could see Salim had received a number of texts and calls today. At 08:15 this morning, his DoD photo in full Navy uniform was received by Salim, who forwarded it on to his brother a few minutes later.

It had come from a +989 dialing prefix.

Iran.

<><><>

The latest texts on both phones were from each other concerning Deacon's whereabouts. The last one sent by Salim to Faiz concerned seeing Deacon cross in front of him and heading to the restrooms. The other texts and emails on both phones were related to instructions from Bratva. Most names and numbers were for persons in the UAE, but half a dozen were for their parents and relatives in Iran.

There were a few Iranian numbers with names that might interest the CIA, Deacon thought, but nothing with the name Saif associated with it, much to his disappointment.

Calling Melissa again, he asked her if she could track the location of the phone that sent the photo of him from Iran.

It took her over an hour. She called him back and said, 'Being a mobile number, it wasn't area-specific or network-specific apart from being Iranian registered. I had to connect to their various networks to see which it was registered with and then check if it was still physically in Iran or roaming. Then I had to detect which cell towers it was connected to at that time in the morning.'

'Melissa, ... I don't need all the background info, just the answer. Have you found the location?'

'John, I was keeping the best to last. Yes, I have. It is currently located in Suza on the island of Qeshm just south of Bandar Abbas in southern Iran, and I can locate it within a half-mile radius.'

'That's fantastic!'

'That's not all, John. The area it's in is semi-rural and has a low population. There are only four villas close by. The phone is still active and in one of the villas!'

44

AT 06:01 the following morning, Shane Walker's cell phone rang in his apartment at the US Embassy in Baghdad. Walker left it to ring nine times, hoping the caller would give up, but when it became obvious they wouldn't, he answered it on the tenth ring.

'Shane, Deacon. Why so slow answering?' Deacon said before Shane could get a word in.

'It's 06:01, and I was asleep. Duh!'

'OK, well you're awake now. I need some help. I'm in Dubai and want to get to Qeshm Island by Bandar Abbas. Any ideas?'

'No "Good morning, my friend. How is sunny Baghdad? I hope you are well and enjoying life? Sorry to wake you this early, but ..." OK, I might have some ideas after I've had a coffee and fully woken up. Text me your number. I'll call you back in ten,' Shane said, laughing before hanging up. Yawning and stretching, he climbed out of bed and did what ninety percent of people worldwide do on awakening. He headed to the bathroom.

Feeling a little more comfortable, he moved to the kitchen, flicked the coffeemaker on, and poured himself a mug before booting up his laptop. After checking a couple of things, he picked up his cell phone and called Deacon back. 'Can I ask why the fuck you want to go to Qeshm Island?'

'Two evenings ago, I watched Steve Caan, aka Saif, get on a dhow in Dubai, and I tracked him on radar to

Bandar. I believe he's now on Qeshm. I wanna go and get the bastard.'

'Why didn't you get him that night, if I might ask?'

'Yeah, alright, wiseass. He sent his goons after me. By the time I evaded them, he was headed out. Then yesterday, he sent two more Iranians who also failed. So how can I get there?'

Thinking for a moment before answering, Shane Walker finally said, 'When I worked there in the Consulate, I was a handler to one of the dhow captains who sometimes worked for us. He is an Emirati and is pro-American, hence him supplying me with information. He regularly delivers small goods between UAE, India, Pakistan, and Iran. He lives with his wife and child in Dubai. He was always open to a little bribery, and he owes me big time. He passed on a lot of information and rumors about what was happening and when. He's never given me a bum steer yet. Occasionally he'd drop stuff off or pick it up for us. I'll try contacting him. How are you going to find Saif when you get there?'

'I have four potential villas to go kick the doors down. Two are on the coast, and the others are about a half-mile inland. The entire area looks to be fenced off, and there's only one road access to it. Satellite images show soldiers guarding it. No idea which villa Saif is in or if he's even still there. He might have left Qeshm and be in Bandar or even somewhere like Tehran, but that's where I'm going to try first.'

<><><>

At 6:00 pm sharp, just as daylight had faded, Captain Yusef's dhow, the al-Shalifi, dropped its mooring lines and gently motored away from the Dubai quayside before heading north toward Iran. Hidden down below, out of

sight of any prying eyes, was Deacon. After the call to Baghdad, Shane had managed to make contact with Captain Yusef. The captain wasn't planning on heading to Iran for a couple more days but agreed on Shane's insistence.

And a price.

For US$5,000 cash paid up front, he would cut in close to Suza on Qeshm Island for Deacon to swim ashore and, if Deacon was in the agreed spot on his return, would pick Deacon up on the way back later that same day.

The captain spent the remainder of the day loading refrigerators, air-conditioning units, washing machines, flat-screen televisions, and dozens of smaller items into the hold of the al-Shalifi to be sold in the markets of Bandar Abbas. Captain Yusef had previously supplied a list of all the items he could provide, along with their prices. The market stallholders had customers wanting these hard-to-obtain items, so they sent orders for them to the local senior Customs Official at Haqani Port and paid him. He, in turn, passed their combined orders on to Captain Yusef by text. On arrival at the port, Captain Yusef would be paid for all the items delivered minus a fee of ten percent of their value as an import tax to the same senior Customs Official. He also had to give the official a crate of the finest Scottish whiskey to sweeten the deal.

While Captain Yusef had been busy organizing the loading, Deacon had thoroughly examined satellite images of the area surrounding the villas. The depth of the sea along the entire shoreline was no more than five meters until out to approximately a mile offshore. In contrast, the shoreline itself was rocky with small sandy coves, perfect for an unobserved stealthy landing. Two of the villas were mere yards from the shore, although almost a mile apart. The other two were on elevated sections with excellent sea views but closer together. He had also raided the store room of the Consulate. He signed out a black wet suit, fins, mask, and a waterproof backpack into which he placed a SIG Sauer P226 handgun and suppressor, two spare ammunition clips, a miniature GPS receiver, a few small tools, a torch, and a set of night vision goggles.

Deacon moved up from below to the wheelhouse after they had cleared the entrance to Dubai Creek and turned north. He was amazed at the sturdiness of the dhow. Built by hand over ninety years ago, its condition was excellent. Although suffering exposure to the incessant Middle East sun, the captain and crew obviously maintained everything about it with love and care. The major frames were attached to the keel with large wooden dowels called trennels, and the hull planks were secured with copper nails. The mast and sails had been removed in the late 1900s, and a hefty 6-cylinder slow-revving Cummins diesel was fitted. Twenty-five years later, it still ran as sweetly as the day it was installed. The wooden decks were polished smooth, and he could walk barefoot without fear of injury.

One of the two crew members brought him a cup of hot, sweet tea - a traditional drink from the region - which he downed along with a couple of high-energy bars. After leaving instructions he was to be awakened if anything out of the ordinary happened; he settled down in the corner and promptly fell asleep.

By 22:00, the distant glow of lights on Qeshm Island could be seen. This, the largest island of Iran, is a popular holiday destination for Iranians. Qeshm Island is 80 miles long, with a population of approximately 130,000. The city of Qeshm, named after the island, is the largest habitation and is located at the eastern tip.

The direct route from Dubai to Bandar Abbas passes between Qeshm Island and Larak Island. Today, Captain Yusef kept closer to the Qeshm shore than usual, straying off the direct rhumb line route and closing to within two miles of the shoreline. Yusef normally would have slowed the al-Shalifi to allow Deacon to climb into the sea safely; however, with the entire area closely monitored by Iranian naval radar, he knew any slight deviation of course or speed would be investigated immediately by one of the numerous Iranian Navy fast patrol boats prowling around.

At 23:45, Deacon trailed an extended length of canvas over the stern, connected to the stern rail. Dressed in his wet suit and mask, holding his fins, and with the other items safely stored in his backpack, he sat on the stern rail, turned facing aft, and with a cheery wave and a '*See you soon,*' he was gone.

As he slid down the canvas, his rearward speed almost matched the al-Shalifi's forward speed, making a net effect of gently sliding into the wake of the dhow before he went under the water. As he resurfaced, the dhow was already ten meters away, with the distance increasing every second.

Checking his backpack was firmly attached, he slipped his fins on, sighted on a particular star, and set off swimming with long, slow strokes. Sixty minutes later, his feet touched the seabed. He was less than ten meters from the shoreline.

45

SWIMMING parallel to the beach, he passed an area of rocks before a thirty-foot-wide sandy inlet opened up in front of him. Climbing ashore, he quickly removed his fins and clipped them to his belt before using the night vision goggles. He scanned the coast in both directions after climbing to the top of the small rocky outcrop.

It was 01:00 and another six hours before the sun rose. The entire area was deserted. The two villas nearest the shoreline could be seen a few hundred meters away. The other two inland ones were too far away to see them clearly, but one of them had lights glowing. The only sound apart from the waves lapping the shore was a dog barking somewhere in the distance.

Removing his swim gear and leaving it hidden behind rocks, he quickly dressed in dark shorts and a T-shirt and slipped a pair of rubber-soled shoes on from his backpack before moving stealthily toward the first darkened villa. The ground was sandy dirt full of stones and small rocks. Armed with NVGs and his handgun, he approached and circled the property from two hundred meters before moving closer.

After careful examination, there was still no sign of life. The lean-to carport was empty of vehicles, and the access pathway to the front of the house was covered in weeds. Checking for any trip wire triggers or infra-red alarm triggers, Deacon slowly approached until he reached a window. The NVGs magnified the available light by a thousand-fold. Peering through the windows, he could see the furniture was covered with dust. Moving to the front door, Deacon pulled out his lock-breaking tools, and five minutes later, the door swung gently open, accompanied by the acrid aroma of something dead and the buzz of flies.

Although this could have been a trick to make the place seem deserted, the house was emitting the peculiar aroma of dust, decay, and decomposition. The stale air hit his nostrils, and he knew the house was empty. Doors and windows hadn't been opened for months, not since the end of last year's summer. This was just a holiday home closed up for winter. The smell of death came from two dead birds on the floor in a bedroom. A small opening high up in the laundry room wall was protected with wire mesh to allow airflow, but the mesh was broken. The birds had found a way in but couldn't escape. Flies and maggots covered the floor.

<><><>

The next villa was also dark at ground level, but the glow of internal lights showed upstairs. Deacon moved around the exterior completely, looking for any way in, but all options relied on breaking cover. Finally, he took the plunge and moved closer. Looking in through one of the windows, he could see the bottom of the staircase through an open door. The glow of the light was brighter nearer the top of the stairs. Tempted to break in and discover who was living there, he moved around to the rear first to a clear glass sliding door. Propped up inside against the far wall was a walking frame. Looking around more, he could see the furniture and furnishings were quite old and worn. They didn't seem to be the sort of things someone like Saif would own.

Deciding to move on to the third and fourth villas, he silently moved away, planning to return if the next two proved negative.

The next two villas, close together, were over half a mile further inland, built on a raised section of earth. Although further from the shore, their higher position gave a far wider view of the immediate area and sea. The one on the right was dark, but the other one was larger and floodlit.

As Deacon moved up over the barren, rocky scrub, he could see the entire area of all four villas, and their surrounding gardens and ground was about six hectares in total and was surrounded by a six-foot-high chain-link fence topped with razor wire. He'd seen the shadow of something from the satellite photos and assumed it was just a small fence to keep stray dogs out, but this was far stronger. Tracks from each of the villas merged into one access road, which then went through a manned barrier gatepost about 500 meters away in a slight depression.

A military jeep was parked to the side of the gatepost with a bright floodlight backlighting the building. A soldier could be seen standing near the hinge of the barrier. Deacon could just make out the shape of a rifle slung over his shoulder.

Whoever lived in the villas obviously enjoyed a high level of privacy and security.

Not wanting to disturb the guards who could likely call for reinforcements, Deacon headed to the darker of the two buildings. A quick scout around outside suggested this one was also empty. The outside trash bin was empty, the garden and path a little overgrown with weeds, and by laying on the ground and putting his eye as close to the small gap at the bottom of the garage door as possible, he could see the parking area was empty.

The time was 02:45, and he needed to move. He had thirty minutes before the al-Shalifi left Bandar Abbas, assuming the unloading had happened on time. Captain Yusef had stated he always did his deliveries to Bandar in the middle of the night because only the senior Custom Official would be on duty at that time and didn't want the public observing. The customs guy would have a couple of willing colleagues standing by to help with the unloading, and he'd have trucks waiting to take his purchases to a secure warehouse where he would sell them to the market stallholders at a tidy profit.

If the al-Shalifi sailed on time, Deacon had to be floating at an exact location 1.8 miles southeast of Suza pier at 05:15. To be on time, Deacon needed to be heading away from his beach cove no later than 04:00.

Garden lights illuminated the last villa. None were aimed directly at the building, pointing instead at the pathway leading to the property or at a fountain in the front garden, but the glow and amount of ambient light made his NVGs redundant. Keeping well clear of the loom from the lights, he circled the building twice, trying to see any slight movement or sign of life within. The building looked attractive and was made from plaster-covered cinder blocks, then painted a terracotta color. The southeast side of the downstairs lounge was one long set of sliding glass doors offering fantastic views across the terrain and sea. He saw a tall tripod with a large set of binoculars mounted on it just inside the windows.

This place looked promising. He now needed to find a way inside without being discovered, so he moved a little closer to some trees.

46

SUDDENLY, all hell broke loose. Whether it was a sunken pressure switch or an invisible beam he accidentally broke, he didn't know. Still, four small but extremely powerful floodlights suddenly lit the entire garden and building up as an alarm wailed. A section of the door to the garage swung open automatically. Deacon heard rather than saw the pounding of feet as two attack dogs ran out, saw him, and charged.

With nowhere to hide or anything to climb to be out of the dog's reach, he chose the only option left.

Gripping his weapon in both hands to steady his aim, he sighted on the nearest dog and pulled the trigger.

Twice.

The soft-nose rounds found their mark, and the lead animal went down in a flurry of galloping legs, mouth open, panting and drooling.

The second dog didn't falter. Ignoring what had happened to its mate, it came on at full speed. Leaping over the dying body of its teammate with determination glowing in its shining eyes, it fixed its glare on Deacon's throat and charged on.

With the light from the floodlights shining right in his face and the speed of the dog's movement, Deacon's next shot missed.

As he reeled back, left arm across his chest to protect his throat, two sets of drooling fangs sunk themselves into his left forearm. He couldn't contain a gasp of pain as the jaws clamped tighter. Deacon fell backward under the weight of the animal's persistent attack, dragged down with the animal still attached to his arm. The weight of the powerful animal was enough to trap Deacon on the ground. He could feel the dog's teeth grinding his arm bones as he jammed the muzzle of his gun into the side of the animal's chest and fired.

The dog's jaw relaxed slightly, but still, the animal held on. Whether it was in pain or its adrenaline was so powerful it was masking it, the dog began to shake its head from side to side.

The pain in his arm was unimaginable. He could feel the dog's teeth grating his bones. Close to passing out, all Deacon could do was fire again and again. Finally, after five bullets into its chest, the light in the animal's eyes dimmed, then finally extinguished, and the pressure on Deacon's arm eased. Prising the jaws open, Deacon staggered to his feet just as the front door opened and two men armed with MP5 submachine guns rushed out.

The lights worked in Deacon's favor. He could see the red burn marks on one of the men's faces from the hot chili powder. It was simple.

Kill or be killed.

Steadying his aim by leaning against a tree, he pumped two rounds directly into his assailant's chest, who went down without a sound. The second guy raised his weapon and fired blindly in Deacon's direction as he leaped back in through the doorway, slamming it shut behind him.

Deacon had dived left as soon as he'd seen the second guy raise his weapon. The shots went wild, peppering the tree behind him and to his right. Splinters of tree bark and leaves showered him, but none of the rounds came close to hitting him.

Deacon staggered back to his feet, the pain in his arm pulsing agonizingly. He fired at the closed door, but his rounds failed to penetrate. He tried to kick the door open, but the lock held. Picking up the dead guard's submachine gun, he fired a burst at the glass sliding doors shattering the first three before the hammer clicked on an empty chamber. A quick frisk of the dead guard's body found a spare magazine. He'd ejected the spent clip and loaded a replacement in less than a second. Slipping the carry strap over his shoulder, he entered the house stepping over the broken glass while also slipping a fresh clip into his handgun.

With the alarm still sounding, he knew the gatepost guards would be radioing for assistance but would likely be on the scene within minutes. He needed to end this quickly.

He heard shouting from upstairs and footsteps. Carefully scaling the staircase, weapon poised and ready for action, he'd gotten almost to the landing when he heard a downstairs door slam.

Cursing, he realized whoever had been up there was escaping down a second staircase. Turning, he ran back down as he heard an automatic garage door opening and an engine turning over and starting. As he cleared into the kitchen, he saw Saif being bundled out through the door into the waiting SUV by the second guard with a laptop bag over his shoulder. A third guard, as yet unknown, was in the driving seat.

Deacon fired, his first shot smashing the door window. His second and third thudded into the door and internal upholstery. His fourth hit Saif high in the shoulder, causing him to jerk upright.

Taking a deep breath, Deacon lined the front tritium painted sight of his Sig P226 squarely on the center mass of the rear of Saif's head and gently pulled the trigger.

The hammer fell, and the primer exploded, igniting the propellant. The expanding gases rapidly pushed the soft-nosed lead bullet out of the muzzle. Unfortunately, the second guy had chosen that exact moment to dive on Saif and push him into the vehicle.

Instead of burying itself in the brain tissue of Saif's head, the bullet hit the second guard in the center of his neck, shattering his spine and causing instant death.

As Saif laid across the rear seat with a dead guard on his back, half in and half out of the car, the driver slammed it into drive and sped away, the legs of the dead guard dragging grotesquely along the road. Twenty meters along the drive, the guard's legs still dangling out of the vehicle snagged on some undergrowth, and the body was dragged out. The driver of the SUV didn't hesitate. He floored the gas pedal as the vehicle accelerated away.

Deacon knew he had maybe two or three minutes before the gatepost guards would arrive. Still holding the machine gun the first guard had dropped, he rushed after the SUV. The second guard was lying at a grotesque angle, legs bent under him. Deacon didn't bother to check for a pulse - his head was only attached to his shoulders by a large flap of skin hinting at his demise. Snatching the laptop bag from the body, Deacon quickly returned to the house. It only took him seconds to confirm he was the only one there.

Yanking off his backpack, he grabbed the roll of duct tape and quickly strapped it around his damaged arm. It stopped most of the bleeding and would hold it partially immobile. With it taped, the pain lessened slightly.

The lounge and kitchen contained nothing of particular interest. A flashing yellow light connected to an alarm system confirmed his suspicion that he'd triggered a hidden sensor when he'd been outside.

Running upstairs, he found four bedrooms. Three were obviously set up for the guards as the furnishings were spartan. The fourth was quite luxurious. A duplicate yellow light was in the area at the top of the stairs, and an audible warning buzzer sounded. Glancing out the large window, he could see the gate post guards' jeep pull up and three men in uniform spilled out.

Reversing the weapon, he used the metal stock to smash the bedroom window before taking careful aim and pulling the trigger. The first burst took out both front tires, the radiator, and the windshield but missed bodies. Two of the three guards ducked down behind the wrecked vehicle while the third, possibly the leader, ran toward the house, weapons blazing. Deacon fired again, and the lone attacker went down as a row of three holes appeared neatly in the center of his chest. Losing the will to fight, the other two guards ran away, chased by a burst or two in the dirt behind them.

Deacon quickly headed to the main bedroom. Two cell phones were on the nightstand. Both went straight into Deacon's backpack and a diary on a nearby desk.

He knew he wouldn't get many more details without a complete house search, especially checking for anything such as a hidden safe.

And reinforcements were arriving. The low throbs of truck engines could be heard over the alarm. Checking, Deacon could see the first truck had already passed the gatepost and was lumbering up the hill. It would be at the house within minutes. Two more trucks could be seen in the distance on their way.

Rushing back downstairs, he found the main fusebox in the garage. He closed the garage door and fired the last few rounds from the MP5 into the electrics. All the lights went out with a flurry of sparks, and the entire area reverted to darkness and silence.

Surprised at how quickly the alarm had been raised and reinforcements were arriving, Deacon rushed out through the main sliding doors while refitting his NVGs and ran. He knew he'd be pursued but hoped they'd lose him in the darkness and be slowed by the terrain. However, the entire area would be swarming with guards within minutes.

The green display showed every rock and boulder, allowing him to travel almost as fast as during daylight. Glancing at his watch, he saw it was already 03:54.

The pain in his arm was agony. Either the Ulna or the Radius was broken, possibly both. The dog's teeth had badly punctured the skin and torn the muscles as it had fiercely bit down. He had no strength in his left hand even to hold anything. He slung the laptop bag over his shoulder. Trying to run while holding his injured arm in close was hampering him.

Reaching the sandy inlet, he immediately started to fit the wet suit on. Again, his left arm was slowing him down, especially when pulling on the leggings and trying to slide his arm into the jacket. The movement made the splintered bones grate together, forcing the bite marks to re-open and start bleeding again. But he knew he needed the wet suit's thermal protection if he was to survive the cold water temperature.

04:05.

The next problem he had was his waterproof backpack. The laptop wouldn't easily fit, but he couldn't afford to leave it. Under attack, the only item Saif had grabbed was his laptop. Whatever was on it was worth dying for. He quickly came up with the solution. Using his knife, it took him just two minutes to prise open the laptop's plastic case and remove the hard drive. He tossed the remainder of the electronics into the ocean, hoping they wouldn't be seen. Then he stashed the hard drive along with everything else into the waterproof inner of the backpack, grabbed his mask and fins, and waded out into the water four minutes before the first of the pursuing soldiers reached the small cliff overlooking the inlet.

Those four minutes saved his life. He managed to swim almost two hundred meters out into the sea and was lost to view from the shore before his pursuers arrived. Although the soldiers had torches, their beams couldn't reach that far.

04:16.

He was now in a race against time. The game was up, and the place was crawling with soldiers. The cove was north of Suza pier. He had to make a two-and-a-half-mile swim in less than an hour. If he missed his pickup, he was sunk. He could either try swimming the thirty-plus miles across one of the busiest and most congested shipping routes in the world or head back to shore and risk capture and prison by the IRGCN. This would result in torture and execution by PAVA – the Iranian secret police, or he could float in the water until he was either run down by a passing vessel or eaten by sharks. None of the options were inviting, he thought.

He swam using the Combat Side Stroke – a technique taught to Navy SEALs for water-based missions when swimming below the surface isn't an option. A combination of breaststroke, freestyle, and sidestroke allows a swimmer to swim more efficiently and reduces the body's profile in the water to be less visible when surface swimming is required.

An hour-long swim of almost two miles in the open sea is tiring for anyone. Deacon knew the risk of trying to swim a lot quicker would merely tire him sooner. The secret was for long, slow, but powerful strokes. While fitting his oversized fins, he calculated just a fraction increase in speed wouldn't affect tiredness noticeably, but it should trim up to eight minutes off the duration.

However, that would mean he'd still miss the pickup by at least four minutes.

He realized his only option was to increase speed and absorb the fatigue. He waited until he was four hundred meters offshore where he wouldn't be seen, and started front-crawl swimming. However, he found he couldn't travel in a straight line as he was unable to put as much effort through his injured left arm as his right.

He began mentally saying it to himself, *Forget the pain. Left arm swim. Right arm swim. Forget the pain.* Over and over until it became a mantra while keeping as close to the required course as he could.

04:25. *Forget the pain. Left arm swim. Right arm swim. Forget the pain.*

04:45. *Forget the pain. Left arm swim. Right arm swim. Forget the pain.*

05:00. *Forget the pain. Left arm swim. Right arm swim. Forget the pain.*

Finally, at 05:15, his GPS beeped to show he was at his target point. 1.8 miles southeast of Suza pier at exactly 05:15.

But no al-Shalifi and no Captain Yusef.

47

HIS heart rate slowed, and his breathing became less labored as he floated. Floating in the sea with his head just a few inches out of the water, his field of view was less than a half-mile in any direction, but al-Shalifi's navigation lights would show at many times that distance. Having completed a 360-degree look around and seeing nothing, he double-checked his GPS, verifying the position was exactly as agreed with Captain Yusef.

The simple truth was that she wasn't there.

Then the sound of machine gun fire echoed over the waves.

Looking along the al-Shalifi's expected direction of travel, he saw the faint loom of a searchlight against the clouds. The source of that light was at least three miles away, but it still brought a shiver to Deacon. The guards had called in the Iran Navy to search for him. Perhaps Yusef had changed his mind, or even worse, he thought.

Then he realized. If Yusef had sold him out, the Navy would be waiting for him at the pick-up point, not wasting their time trying to find him.

Or was the gunfire aimed at the dhow, the al-Shalifi?

The only question remains: Had the al-Shalifi already come and gone, or was she still coming?

The agony in his arm had increased in his effort to fit his wet suit and again when the salt water hit it, but now it had faded to a dull, heavy pulsing ache. However, the swimming and water had loosened the tape, and his arm was bleeding again. With each swim stroke, the broken bones grated against each other, with more blood leaking into the sea.

With nothing to gain or lose, he decided to remain peacefully floating. It took minimum effort, and it wouldn't get really dangerous for another hour when the sky would begin to brighten.

Twenty minutes later, things heated up. The searchlight loom came closer to within three hundred yards. Deacon's black wetsuit hood blended in perfectly with the black sea making him invisible, and he'd removed his mask to minimize any possibility of reflection, but the worry was they might come closer and discover him. As he bobbed up and down on the waves, he could see the patrol boat. It was about thirty feet long with two powerful outboard engines mounted on the transom at the rear. There was a helmsman's position with a searchlight mounted on its roof, and near the bow was a powerful mounted machine gun. He could see five crew; one steering, one operating the searchlight, one machine gunner, and two lookouts. The machine gunner seemed to be firing randomly. As soon as a small wave crested, he'd shoot at it, convinced it was who they were chasing.

Then Deacon had an idea. He quickly removed his backpack. Keeping the opening above water, he managed to remove his Sig handgun before reclosing and refitting the bag. He kept the weapon out of the water as he watched the patrol boat.

If it came closer and saw him, he would offer to surrender. Then, when he was alongside the patrol boat, he would shoot the machine gunner, then the helmsman. His gun was silenced so they wouldn't hear him shoot in the noise and turmoil. He would kill the others in the following confusion and commandeer the craft. Or he'd die trying. He had no intention of being captured alive by the Iranians.

He began to relax when he saw the patrol boat move away north, its searchlight probing the dark waters ahead, its gunner still churning up every wave. Then he saw it. The navigation lights of the al-Shalifi as it barreled toward him to the exact pickup point. Two hundred yards away, it slowed to around four knots. Deacon shouted and flashed a torch. Captain Yusef changed course fractionally, and the two crew rushed forward to the port side.

As the al-Shalifi drew level with Deacon, one crewman threw a knotted rope out wide. Deacon grabbed it with both hands, dropping his weapon, which quickly sank, and wincing and gasping at the sudden pain in his left arm as he was jerked forward. The rope began to slide through his hands, but the knots caught on his clenched fists. As the rope pulled taut, the movement of the al-Shalifi dragged Deacon the last yard into the vessel's side. The impact winded him, and he almost let go as his head collided with the al-Shalifi's solid wooden hull splitting the skin on his forehead, but the second crewman was quick off the mark and had a boathook ready.

With a twist of his wrist, the crewman expertly slotted the hook between Deacon's back and backpack, and the hook secured itself on the webbing straps.

Half unconscious from the swim effort and the battering coming alongside, he didn't feel himself being lifted and placed on the deck. Nor did he feel eager hands stripping his wet suit off and removing the blood-soaked tape. The crew washed and set his arm as best they could, temporarily rebandaging it heavily to stop any movement. Strapping it to his chest, it needed better medical care than they could provide.

But he missed it all.

EUROPE

48

PATRICK wasn't the sort of person to just sit around wasting time. On his second complete day of leave, he drove down to the New Forest to visit the country house and the scene of his godson's accident. The gates were closed and padlocked with a sign indicating a telephone number for inquiries. Following Google Maps, he drove down various lanes until he met part of the wall surrounding the garden in a much quieter area. He stopped here, parked under a tree, climbed up on the wall, and dropped over the other side.

Keeping an eye open for gardeners and workers, he walked through the lush gardens and approached the house from the rear. As expected, the house was locked, but he could see in through various windows. After an hour of looking, he realized there was nothing to be seen. The incident had happened too many weeks ago for any evidence to be hanging around, and anyway, the accident with the ambulance and Peter had occurred almost eleven miles away.

Heading back to his car, an older man and a boy approached him, shouting, 'Hey, you. You can't be here. This is private property. How did you get in?'

Offering a handshake and a smile, Patrick said, 'I'm sorry. I'm considering hiring this place for my wedding anniversary and wanted to look around. The gate was open, so I just walked in.'

Not in a position to argue as his young helper had left the gate open on numerous occasions, the old guy shook Patrick's hand and said, 'I'm Bill. Chief gardener. This here is Jimmy. He's always forgetful, the young bugger. You shouldn't really be here, but since you are, can I help you with anything?'

Over the next fifteen minutes, Patrick gently quizzed him about the sort of parties held here. Weekday events were usually business related, such as company training courses or conferences, over one- two- or three days. Weekends were mostly engagements or weddings, or sometimes just birthdays. Patrick then asked if there was ever any trouble at any of the gatherings.

In his strong country accent, Bill said, 'No, we don't have any fights if that's what you mean. Some people have too much to drink, which can get rowdy. Even found a few of our guests asleep in the gardens at times. They usually blame the food, though. Never admit they've had one or two too many,' he laughed.

Smiling, Patrick said, 'Didn't something happen about three and a half months back? I remember reading something about an ambulance crashing on its way to the hospital. Was that to do with a party here?'

'Yeah, I remember. Well, I'm not one to gossip, mind you, but that were a bit of a strange evening, that one. Young Jimmy had already gone home, but I'd knocked over some stuff in the shed, so I stayed late to tidy up and put everything away. Took me ages, it did. Cars started arriving about half seven, but guards were checking people's passes on the gate. So I thought we might have someone like a film star or music star. You know, someone famous. So I had a quick nose around. Wanted to tell the wife who I'd seen. But it were all men arriving. I thought it might be footballers. Posh lot, as well. Fancy cars, mind you. Foreign makes. German and some

Eyetalien sporty ones. Some were chauffeur driven. But these men were mostly too old. Older than me. Then I looked in a window at the rear and saw all the women. Well, girls, really. All dolled up. Cracking bodies and skimpy clothes. Not an ugly one in sight. Made me wish I was twenty years younger,' Bill said, laughing. 'There must have been some families though 'cus I heard some kids crying. Never saw 'em, though. What was strange was the ladies serving drinks were all wearing face masks across their eyes. You know, just black ones like cartoon bank robbers, but these posh birds weren't. As to the male guests, I couldn't recognize any of 'em. All had full face masks on. Like those that rich folk wear at parties or charity balls. Very strange. Then I think someone was ill. An ambulance was called and took someone away on a stretcher. They're the poor buggers that crashed heading to Southampton,' he continued.

Patrick thought for a second or two before saying, ' So did you speak with anyone there that night, Bill?'

'Yes, to tell you the truth, I did. Some foreign women. She wasn't a guest. I think she was one of the organizers. She saw me when the ambulance left and told me to go home in no uncertain terms.'

'What did she look like, Bill? Can you remember?'

'Yeah. About 5-2, maybe 5-3. Brownish hair to her shoulders. Quite pretty, but not a match against them other women.'

'Last question, Bill. You said she was foreign. What makes you think that?'

'I heard her on her phone. She weren't talking English. Maybe German or summit, but it definitely weren't English.'

<><><>

After thanking Bill for his time, Patrick headed toward the gates before doubling back to where his car was parked. He kept a careful eye out not to bump into Bill again. He drove to the scene of the accident, but the only evidence anything had happened was the fading skid marks on the embankment and the damage to the tree. An SUV traveling at speed had missed a corner turn and slammed into the ambulance, forcing it off the road and into a tree. The driver fled the scene, and the SUV was reported stolen. No one had ever been identified or arrested as the driver of the SUV. With no new leads, the case was still open and unresolved.

Having left the New Forest, Patrick headed to Peter's rental apartment on the outskirts of Southampton. Peter was still off work due to his injuries, although he was healing fast and hoped to be back working within another week or so. The two of them spoke for over an hour. Peter's story now was the same as when Patrick had visited him in hospital just a few days after the accident had occurred.

Patrick hit the phone lines after arriving home. First, he contacted the commercial company advertising the house rental as shown on the gate billboard, but to no avail. Either the rental that weekend had not been through them, or they were deliberately refusing to answer. Next, he tried the local council, but they said private rentals were nothing to do with them. As a last resort, he tried Hampshire Constabulary. They were called to the accident scene, and he asked if the detectives had visited the country house and spoken to the party organizers as part of the investigation. After being given the runaround and passed from one person to the next, the lead detective eventually called him back and confirmed they hadn't visited the party as they hadn't found any connection between the two events.

The only information Patrick did discover was the name of the patient in the ambulance who died. He was Sir Eugene Prendercast, Earl of Strathmorgan, aged 82.

Patrick spent the following morning trying to make contact with Prendercast's next of kin to ask about the party but was stonewalled at every turn.

In the afternoon, Captain Youngman called, 'Patrick, I've received confirmation of the content of those vials. Let's meet for a beer after work.'

<><><>

At 18:35, Patrick walked in through the doorway and saw Chris sitting in an empty booth. He stopped at the bar to pick up two beers and then headed over and sat down.

Keeping his voice low, Patrick said, 'You first, pal. What do they contain?'

'You were partly correct. Nothing deadly. They were both the same. Small amounts of a standard antibiotic, trace amounts of potassium and sodium, and minute amounts of parvovirus.'

'Parvovirus? I've heard of that. Isn't that something—'

'For dogs! Yeah? For dogs. Why the fuck are you getting me to check a vaccine for a dog? It wouldn't work anyway. It is too weak a mixture. Do you know what an awkward position this puts me in using our medical facility for this? What's going on, Patrick?' he said, the underlying anger in his voice coming to the surface.

'Ssshhhhh! Keep it down. We found these in a warehouse. Someone was trying to sell them as the current vaccine against Covid,' Patrick said while trying to limit giving away too much information.

'What? Well, they're useless.'

'What if it was given to humans? Would it harm them?'

'Only if they had distemper, chasing cars or drooling at the mouth. C'mon, spill. What the hell are you into this time?' he said, relaxing a little.

With that, Patrick had little option but to tell some of his story. Not all, but enough.

'You do what you want with the information, Patrick, but I'm going to warn people. I know quite a lot of doctors in Europe and in the Center for Disease Control in Atlanta. I also know a number of African doctors. You need to realize many of us meet at conferences. I intend to warn them that a load of counterfeit Covid vaccines is hitting the market. It won't kill anyone given it by mistake but it will make them feel ill for a day or two. Ok?'

'Yeah, you got to save lives, doc.'

Smiling, he said, 'Yeah, it won't kill them. But it might stop them pissing against lampposts or chasing cats,' he laughed.

49

ARRIVING back at his London apartment, Patrick booted his laptop and logged on to his account set up by Melissa. There were dozens of files she had forwarded on after removing any passwords or encryption. She had also translated them from German to English. The FBI, along with many other three-letter organizations working for the US Government, has access to some of the most advanced automated language translation tools in the world, far superior to those available commercially.

Pouring himself a large William Heavenhill 5th Edition bourbon, he settled down for a long read. His eyes were tired, but he'd read some key information that he would add to his previous report and forward to Ronaldson. By 03:00 the following morning, he called it quits for that session. One folder he'd marked to read later was titled *Party Dates and Venues.* Like most of the folders and files, had Melissa not removed the password protection and encryption, they would have been unable to be accessed.

Later that same morning, he was ready to continue. After showering, shaving, breakfasting, and with a mug of black coffee on hand, he quickly rechecked his notes from the previous evening and added some key data. Govorov had kept full details of total numbers of illegals being transported, dates, which vehicles and drop-off points were used, and monies paid. This information alone was enough to ensure a conviction if Europol ever chose to arrest and charge him, Patrick thought.

Then he came to the folder he'd identified the previous evening - *Party Dates and Venues.* This was a diary and calendar of past and future planned pedophile party meetings in Europe. He only read half the first page before the bile began to rise in his throat. The list was broken down alphabetically by European country. There were meetings in most of the countries. The UK was by far the most regular, with Germany a very close second. Italy, France, and the Netherlands were next in line, but a long way down the list, and Spain and Portugal were the lowest.

Looking through the details shown under the UK heading, he scrolled through until he found the date of his godson's accident. There, printed in black and white, was a reference to Rocklands Country House in the New Forest, the cost of hiring the venue, the names of all the invitees, and the host's initials: SP. Svetlana Petrovich.

Govorov's name wasn't shown, only Svetlana's, but here was proof that she was involved in running at least one illegal pedophile sex party in the UK, possibly many others.

He murmured quietly, 'Yeah, this ain't over by a long shot.'

<><><>

Later that same day, around late afternoon, Patrick's phone rang. As he picked up the receiver, before he could speak, he heard, 'Patrick. It's John. Hey pal, have I got news for you.'

Half laughing, he said, 'Hiya pal. OK shoot. What's new?'

'I'm still in Dubai, about to board the late flight to London. I get in at 23:30. Can you pick me up at Heathrow Terminal 5 and I crash at your place tonight?'

'Yeah, of course. What's happened?'

'Tell you when I see you,' and the phone went dead.

<><><>

The flight landed a little ahead of schedule, and by 23:50, they were in Patrick's X5 heading into London. On seeing Deacon's arm in plaster, Patrick's first comments were, 'What the hell happened to you? You only left me less than a week ago?'

By the time they arrived at Patrick's apartment, Deacon had managed to tell most of his story. The crew had dressed his broken arm as best they could. The al-Shalifi had docked back in Dubai at lunchtime Dubai time, and Deacon was ushered directly to the hospital, where his arm was set and plastered after the jagged bite marks were cleaned and stitched. He received a hefty dose of antibiotics and the first of several rabies shots.

Ignoring advice to stay in bed for a day or two, he booked the late London flight, and now here he was. He connected his laptop to Patrick's wifi and plugged in the stolen hard drive from Qeshm before calling Melissa with the IP address.

Thirty seconds later, the hard drive started whining as Melissa sucked the data off the disks as fast as she could.

As the data was received by Melissa, she ran a specialist program that would hammer break any files with passwords. The software would also translate any spelling within each document into American English before making a duplicate, English language, non-password version.

Melissa called back, and Patrick put her on speaker.

'Melissa, you're in work late,' Patrick said, knowing Washington was five hours behind London time.

'Hmmm, I've had trouble sleeping lately after seeing the data from Govorov's computers. So I spent some more time looking at other stuff on their hard drive. 'There's something I don't understand. Some old dated documents have the name Morozov on them, but that stops in late 1994. Everything then refers to the name Govorov. Does the name Morozov mean anything to you?'

Hythe went silent for a minute, causing Melissa to ask, 'Patrick, are you still there?'

'Yeah, yeah, sorry. Just thinking. No, it doesn't mean anything, but thanks anyway. Dinner's on me next time I'm in Washington,' he said, sitting there totally stunned. The room seemed to darken as years of nightmare dreams suddenly made sense, along with all the pain from when he was just a boy.

Deacon had overheard both sides of the telephone conversation and was surprised to see how his friend reacted. He was sitting on the edge of the chair, eyes open but unfocused, staring. In his mind, he was miles away, almost trance-like. Deacon left him like that for a few minutes before approaching him.

'Hey, pal. You ok?' he said.

Receiving no reply, he tried again louder, 'Patrick! Pal, are you ok?'

This time it worked. Patrick shook his head slightly as if to clear it, smiled, and said, 'Yeah, yeah, sorry. Deep in thought. Miles and years away, but I'm fine. There's a loose end I need to clear up. If this bastard Govorov was just shipping illegal immigrants and getting rich off it, I could live with that and allow the authorities to arrest and charge him. But to find out he's also supplying a number of pedophile rings in Europe and especially the UK with kids, and that he's a 'phile himself and that he will be killing hundreds if not thousands of people by supplying fake Covid vaccines is too much—'

'We're not sure about the vaccines. It's only guesswork.' Deacon said, interrupting.

'Yeah, good point, although someone's shipping counterfeit Covid drugs. If not Govorov, then who? As to Govorov, I was sure I'd come across him before but couldn't work out where. He was called General Morozov back in the nineties, and I was convinced he was dead. I should have killed him when we saw him the other day. I will this time.'

Looking at Patrick questioningly, Deacon merely raised an eyebrow.

Patrick eventually answered, 'He killed somebody I loved, and yes, I want revenge. I'll tell you about it sometime.'

50

TEN hours later, Melissa called Deacon and Hythe again. 'Boys, we've been decrypting the data from the Qeshm Island hard drive overnight. You've hit the motherlode. They're linked,' she exclaimed breathlessly.

'What do you mean, *linked?*' Deacon said, grateful to Hythe for letting him stay last evening.

'One of the documents is a letter, a proposal, all in Farsi, from Saif Mohammed Khan. Other documents show it's the Arabic name Steve Caan assumed when he converted to Islam. It is addressed to Ali Khamenei, the Iranian Supreme Leader, and dated over four years ago. It suggests an ongoing method of deploying sleeper agents in both the UK and the USA to destabilize their governments. It proposes using Hezbollah, al-Qaeda, and even ISIS-trained terrorists and insurgents as fifth columnists within both countries to promote civil unrest and terrorism. It suggests these people should be trained in the culture and ways of the West. In the case of the USA, they should mix with genuine asylum seekers heading from South America through Mexico, having been supplied with false documents showing citizenship from various South American countries. For the UK, false documentation showing refugees escaping persecution from countries around the Persian Gulf and Horn of Africa is suggested. Countries such as Ethiopia, Eritrea, Sudan, Iraq, Syria, Yemen, and Iran are listed. The document goes on to remind or suggest to the Supreme Leader how the Ministry of Intelligence of the Islamic

Republic of Iran's documents department is set up to make perfect copies of every western country's passports and identification documents, including Israel.

'It then proposes sending these people to the UK through the people trafficking networks in Europe through Calais and suggests the large refugee camps in Turkey would be an ideal starting point. It even details how these new arrivals can liaise with UK underground networks. The largest has been set up by Al-Qaeda and ISIS through a longtime Iranian undercover agent based in Reading, UK, using the cover name of Mr. Green.'

'Does it give his real name?' Patrick asked.

'No, unfortunately not,' Melissa said, 'Just his cover name, and there wasn't any contact information either.'

'How certain are you that you hit Saif?' Patrick asked.

'Positive. Got him in the shoulder three inches to the left of his neck. Four, four and half years and so damned close.' It'll be a complicated recovery, but it wasn't a kill shot. It was a snapshot, and his guard was covering him for the second.'

'Maybe you'll strike lucky and find him again?'

'Yeah, maybe. And you?'

'You need to head on back to DC and get yourself fixed up. Me? I've got a date with Mozorov, Govorov, or whatever the fuck he calls himself now.'

51

PATRICK caught an afternoon crossing via Eurotunnel. Officially on leave, he was careful to take only minimum equipment with him in case of questioning by customs. He packed a snow camouflage outfit he could explain for hunting, but the only weapon he carried was an old Makarov pistol he'd taken off a dead Iraqi captain in Iraq years before. He split this into parts and hid them in the spare wheel compartment of his X5. The eleven-hundred-kilometer journey via the A4 and the A8 from Calais to the Fortress would take almost twelve hours of continuous driving, so Patrick stopped overnight at Reims.

He was back on the road by 07:30. The weather varied from rain showers, sleet, heavy snow storms, and strong gusty winds, but the roads were open, and the traffic was light. He arrived in Walchsee, a small village ten kilometers from the Fortress, by mid-afternoon and waited. As the daylight faded, he headed off toward his target, parking hidden in the trees over a kilometer away.

Staying undercover, he approached the edge of the forest where he could observe the building. He lay down in the snow behind a large bush. He was completely invisible to anyone looking in his direction, but he could see clearly through the gaps between the branches and leaves. He didn't know why but things seemed different this trip. Maybe it was because he knew what the outcome would be. He first noticed the lack of guards patrolling the outer walls. He waited almost an hour, but there was no one. It took over thirty minutes to move back into the forest and change position so he could see the other side of the property, and this also reconfirmed a lack of guards. The rubble from the explosion through the outer wall was still where it had fallen.

The place looked deserted, but Patrick could see light glowing from a ground floor window. He climbed down from the tree embankment and jogged across the unbroken snow until he was close to the outer wall. He stayed there a few minutes, watching, but nothing moved. Any footprints from guards patrolling were gone, covered by recent snowfalls. Careful not to dislodge any loose rubble, he climbed in through the gap and quickly moved among the trees.

As he approached the walls of the building, he could hear faint voices. Armed only with the Makarov pistol, he didn't want to storm in and find himself heavily outnumbered, so he waited and listened. Two years ago, Patrick had modified a SIG's suppressor to fit the weapon. It wasn't a perfect fit, but it did the job and worked pretty well. It was the perfect weapon for clandestine work, as any investigation would show it as Russian-made. He silently entered through the side door, crept along the hallway, and waited. Two voices casually talking, both male.

The door was slightly ajar. Patrick stepped back three feet and then rushed to the door, slamming it open and dashing in.

Surprise is always a good weapon. It provides a shock delay. The slam of the door almost off its hinges stunned into inaction the two men sitting at a table playing cards. One of the men, trying to react, knocked over a half-empty mug of coffee as he tried to stand. Still in shock, he didn't see the butt of the raised Makarov swinging down to strike him.

Within a second of Patrick slamming the door open, one guy was slipping into unconsciousness as he slumped in his chair, blood dripping from his head. The other guy's reaction time was slower, and he hadn't moved. He now found himself staring at the black muzzle of a weapon aimed at his face.

Many people find that the 9mm muzzle of a weapon looks far larger when it is just a few inches in front of your eyes and pointing directly at you. Especially when held by a man wearing white camouflaged battledress with a blackened face.

'Where's Govorov?' he growled in perfect German.

Stuttering from fright, the guy managed to answer, 'G..G..G…Gone,' as he dropped his playing cards.

'Don't fuck with me. Gone where?'

When the guard didn't answer, Patrick tried again. 'I said gone where?'

Counting to three, he changed his aim slightly and fired, taking the guard's ear lobe off. The soft *kerthuk* of the silenced round wouldn't have been heard outside the room, even if anyone had been there to hear it.

The guard started to scream and clasped his hand to the side of his head.

'Next shot is between your eyes. Then I'll wake your colleague up and ask him.'

'T … To his other home in S … S … Slovakia, up near the P … Polish border,' the guard half stuttered.

Firing again, this time at one of the playing cards on the table, he said, 'Where exactly? And what are you doing here?'

'W … We are just guarding the building. Everyone has g … gone. Someone attacked the compound and blew up the wall. M … M … Major Govorov moved everyone to his estate in Slovakia.'

After obtaining the full address of the estate outside Nová Sedlica, Patrick tied them both up. The one he'd hit was groggy but otherwise unharmed, although he might experience severe headaches for a week or two. His colleague's bleeding ear had congealed. Neither guard was armed apart from carrying torches and nightsticks. Patrick removed both their IDs and made a note of names and addresses before dropping the ID cards back on the table.

After rechecking their bindings, Patrick quickly searched the remainder of the property. Apart from a few discarded items broken on the floor, the place was barren. The only piece of furniture remaining was the long table in the dining room. Taking a rough guess at its length, Patrick reasoned it might have been too long to fit in the removal trucks.

He headed back to the room before leaving and spoke to his captives. 'I'm leaving now. The heating's still on, and I'm sure you can manage to undo yourselves in an hour or two. You have a choice. Either keep quiet about what has happened tonight – I won't say anything, but I'd imagine Govorov doesn't accept failure easily. Or call him when you're free. Your choice. Option one leaves you both embarrassed but alive and healthy, whereas option two's outcome depends on Govorov's mood. However, you will also have me to contend with if you choose wrongly.'

With that, Patrick jogged back to his car and drove back down the valley before heading toward Salzburg.

52

HE'D taken the rest of the afternoon and evening the day before to prepare. First, he spent a couple of hours using his computer to examine the area in great detail around Govorov's new location before heading out. He'd also found photos of the compound from an old property website.

Secondly, after locating a large hardware store, he purchased a shovel, three standard-sized crowbars, two rolls of heavy-duty duct tape, three meters of foam pipe insulation, and eight meters of 20mm rope. He also bought a thermos flask, which he subsequently filled with coffee. In addition, he also purchased sandwiches, a dozen high-energy food bars, and some sugary drinks.

The weather forecast predicted heavy snow everywhere for the next few days, especially the further east he traveled. He parked his X5 in a covered parking garage close to a car rental bureau. Fifteen minutes later, having hired a four-wheel drive SUV using a fake driving license and passport, he pulled up alongside his X5 to transfer his purchases. He'd chosen to hire a vehicle for two reasons. First, his X5 had UK license plates and was easily identifiable; secondly, his rental came with snow chains.

Due mainly to the inclement weather, the planned nine-hour journey via Vienna and Bratislava eventually took nearer to thirteen, with him arriving a couple of hours before dawn the following morning.

Fortress Two was located in a low-population, wild and semi-mountainous region of eastern Slovakia, less than twenty kilometers from the Polish and Ukrainian borders. The drive from Salzburg had been long and arduous. The roads themselves through Austria and the first part of Slovakia had been relatively free of snow due to the number of snowplows in use. However, as he neared Kosice, the gritting and plowing had ceased reducing progress to one lane and a much lower speed.

The closer he got to Nová Sedlica, the worse the weather and roads became. He had trouble driving the last dozen kilometers up narrow tracks toward the estate's rear, even with snow chains fitted. The forest here was extremely dense. Parts had been felled and new trees replanted in lines, ready for easy felling in the future, but this area was overgrown and wild. It meant access through the forest would not be straightforward, but a direct approach along the main access road was out of the question. It would likely be guarded as it was a private road. Even if not, it would at least have CCTV monitoring.

Finding a small access track with a chain and padlock barring entry, Patrick gently edged his vehicle against the chain until it snapped. Before stopping, he drove another six hundred meters through the trees until he was totally hidden from view. His GPS estimated he was within two kilometers through the forest to his target. He put the heater on full for five minutes, drank some coffee, pulled a blanket and winter clothing over himself, cracked open a window slightly for airflow, and switched everything off. He was asleep within minutes.

<><><>

He awoke a few hours later just as the sky was beginning to lighten, although he couldn't tell as the car was covered in over a foot of new snow. After fitting a heavy-duty pair of gloves, he pushed the passenger side door open against the weight of the snow. Stepping out, he quickly cleared all the windows and used the shovel to clear the wheels to ensure he had traction.

Standing under the opened door of the tailgate, he placed all three crowbars together back-to-back at 120 degrees from each other. He then bound them together along with one end of the eight-meter rope, along the straight shafts with masses of duct tape. Next, he slid the foam pipe insulation over the entirety, taping it into position, leaving just each bent metal end with the sharp nail wrench exposed. Finally, he looped and securely tied the rope around the crowbars' bottom. He then knotted its remainder every fifteen inches to make climbing easier.

It was improvised, homebuilt, and would never win any design awards. But he had a rough and ready grappling hook complete with sound deadening - ideal for scaling walls in quiet places.

Dressed in his winter white camouflaged battledress, he headed through the trees. Although it was less than two kilometers away, the journey took him over an hour because of the thick ground-level foliage. The snow had both benefits and drawbacks. An advantage was that it was deathly quiet, and the sound of small twigs breaking under his feet was totally masked by the thick covering. A drawback was this also worked for the bad guys. It would be easy to bump into someone patrolling or guarding the place accidentally.

He got to the treeline border and could see the buildings clearly in front of him, or at least as clearly as the falling snow would allow. Setting up an observation point was simple. As before, he found a location heavy with ground foliage where he would remain invisible even if someone was looking directly at him, but he could see through the gaps.

Fortress Two consisted of a compound containing various small outer storage buildings and a three-vehicle garage. The primary residence was in the center and contained at least a dozen rooms split over two floors. On first inspection, the overall size seemed almost double that of the other location near Munich and better protected. There appeared to be six guards patrolling, with two inside the twelve-foot-high walled perimeter and four outside, each covering a quadrant. Watching their routine, it seemed to be similar to the other location. Each guard or set of guards was responsible for their wall section from one end to the other. Guards came together at the ends of each wall, turned, and repeated back along the same section. There was a hefty solid wooden gate access for vehicles into the compound. It seemed to be the only way in or out.

It took the guards approximately seventy-five seconds to patrol the length of each wall. Having understood their routine, he moved around the entire area, studying the compound, walls, and buildings from all aspects while staying hidden safely within the thick treeline. As expected, all four quadrants looked to be guarded in the same way. It confirmed his plan of approach, the only way in would be over the wall. After watching for almost an hour, Patrick determined the maximum time available to gain entry unobserved was approximately fifty seconds before the guard turned and started to return.

He watched them hour after hour. Although twice an older woman brought out a tray with drinks and food, possibly sandwiches, this basic routine never varied. After six hours, the guards were replaced. It seemed to

Patrick their routine was six hours on, six hours off, twice per twenty-four-hour day.

By mid-afternoon, he'd seen enough. He moved further back within the treeline and slept. He considered the chances of being disturbed almost zero, but he needed to catch up a few hours to be sharp and on his game. He knew that over the years, many soldiers have died or been injured due to overtiredness and losing concentration.

Awaking after seven hours of sleep, he stood and brushed fresh snow off himself. After eating a couple of high-energy food bars washed down with a mug of slightly stewed strong black coffee, he felt energized and refreshed. Carefully moving back into position, he resumed his vigil. It didn't take him long to confirm nothing had changed with the guards or their routine.

His plan was to commence his incursion into the compound at around 02:50, as the early morning hours between 03:00 and 04:00 are when most people are the least alert and less observant. They are usually cold and tired, and their reaction times are also at their slowest. As he'd expected, the only way to gain access undisturbed was by climbing over the wall.

Reaching the treeline directly opposite the single gate entrance, he remained hidden while observing. This was the only section where he could get across the twenty meters without being seen or leaving tracks. His footprints would be masked by heading along the access track to the main gate, where the snow was already badly churned up.

Timing is everything. Before moving, he double-checked his workings. Slightly slower now due to fatigue, they still took seventy-five to eighty seconds to walk each quadrant. Silently running across the access track, he reached the corner of the nearest wall. Looping the rope and splitting it between his hands, he swung the hook assembly up and over the wall. The homemade grappling hook sailed almost two feet higher than the top of the wall before arcing over, out of sight. The foam covering and fallen snow minimized any noise as it fell against the far side of the stone. Gently pulling on his end of the rope, the hook clawed back up the far side of the wall, its steel tips trying to find purchase before failing and falling back to Hythe's feet. Swiftly snatching it up, he tried again with the same result.

If his third attempt failed, he'd have no choice but to either run and chance being seen, or kill the approaching guard, delaying any detection by a minute or two.

Without even coiling the rope, Patrick picked up the hook, swung it once, and released it, watching it sail over the wall for the third time. As soon as it had dropped to the far side, Patrick started pulling on the free end.

This time the steel claw-hammer ends of the crowbars managed to dig into the stone enough to grip. As Patrick put weight on the rope, the hook slipped once but regained its grip a few inches further on.

Realizing if it wasn't for the falling snow, he'd already be in view, Patrick scaled the wall faster than he ever thought possible. Swinging his legs over, he dropped down the inner side, pulling the dangling rope with him just as the guard approaching on the outside could be seen through the snowflakes.

Crouching there, deep in shadow, he waited, weapon in hand, until his raging heartbeat began to slow. He stayed behind a bush watching for the further guards patrolling around within the compound, but they were not in sight.

Another benefit of the snow was silence when walking or running. Glancing around to confirm he was alone, he sprinted toward the house with his Makarov in his hand. The garage was close to the main building, so he entered it first. One rule drilled into him in training was whenever you enter into an unknown situation, always plan an escape route. The chance of a quiet escape back through the garden and over the wall was unlikely if the alarm was raised. Last time he and Deacon had used the explosive charge on the outer wall as a diversion tactic. However, this time he was alone and didn't have access to the same equipment.

The lock pick gun took seconds to open the solid wooden side entrance door. No alarm. All quiet. Stepping into the darkness, he closed and locked the door behind him. His torch lens was covered in black tape, leaving a small section uncovered and producing the narrowest of beams. The garage was spacious, with tools and various items along one wall, including a dozen or so jerricans filled with gasoline. Vehicle access was through two tall wooden entrance doors attached to the walls with large iron hinges. The doors were secured with a simple key lock and had a removable wooden beam across them; however, they moved slightly when Patrick pressed gently on them. The wood of the doors themselves looked old and had seen better days. Looking around, he could see three vehicles were parked; a four-wheel-drive quad bike, a dark-colored saloon car, and a long-wheelbase silver-grey Mercedes SUV with darkened windows. Examining all three, all had keys in their ignitions. An idea began to form in his mind.

First, he took the keys and slashed the tires of the quad bike and saloon car. He grabbed two full jerry cans and placed them flat on the rear seat of the SUV. He then placed two shovels against the wall next to the side door before unlocking the door and stepping outside.

Twelve feet away was another wooden outer door. It took only seconds to unlock it and step in. He was in what appeared to be the laundry room. He grabbed a towel and wiped his boots and clothes free of loose snow. The room had another door leading into a long hallway into the central part of the house.

He could hear the snoring of the next watch of guards sleeping, so he headed away from their room. The wide staircase was to his right. Polished wood and over twelve feet wide, gradually getting narrower near the top. Glad that the dry boots were not leaving a trail, he carefully climbed the stairs, fearful of a creak or noise to awaken anyone.

The second set of stairs was covered in carpet leading up to the main bedrooms. As he silently reached the last few steps, he could see a long corridor in front. There were six doors, three on each side leading to rooms, but these were single doors. At the far end of the hall was a set of double doors.

Govorov's bedroom.

Careful to step as close to the wall as possible to minimize any floor creaks, it took him half a minute to reach the double doors. The corridor continued to the left, and he saw a second staircase down to the floor below.

He gently tested the right side handle of the double doors.

It was unlocked.

Gently pressing the handle down, opened the door the barest minimum so the hinges wouldn't squeak, and stepped in.

53

PATRICK stood and listened with the door closed behind him, and his weapon leveled and ready. There was the faint sound of breathing. Just one person. Switching on the torch after shielding the already small beam, Patrick could see a large king-sized bed with Govorov asleep. Turning, he saw the left door of the two had a top and bottom sliding lock, and the right door had a key. Reaching up, he made sure the sliders were engaged and locked the other door with the key.

Whether it was a sixth sense or the sound of the near-silent lock engaging, Govorov stirred and partly sat up. Sensing someone else was in the room Govorov immediately reached for a weapon under the adjacent pillow with his hand. The *'phutt'* of Patrick's silenced handgun sounded loud in the bedroom as the pillow exploded, and Govorov gasped.

'Make a noise, and you're dead,' Hythe said quietly, moving over toward the bed, the barrel of his gun pointing directly at Govorov's face. Patrick saw a silver handgun lying on the mattress next to a bloody finger as the remains of the pillow tumbled to the floor. Slipping the fallen weapon into his pocket, he glanced at Govorov's bloody hand with its middle finger missing. His other fingers were blooded from when the round had hit the butt of his handgun and fractured. His palm was also split from small fragments embedded in the flesh and was bleeding.

'No middle finger? That'll make it awkward to say fuck you in America,' he said, smiling. 'Make any sudden moves or sounds, and I'll shoot that off as well,' as he lowered the barrel of his weapon to point at Govorov's crotch.

'You're going to die for this, Johnson, if that's your real name,' Govorov hissed through teeth clenched in pain.

'Maybe. Maybe not. Now shut your fucking mouth until I tell you to speak.'

Flicking on the light after making sure the drapes were closed, Patrick checked the bedside cabinet for other weapons while keeping his gun pointing directly at Govorov's face. He also ripped the phone connection from the wall. Satisfied, he turned a desk chair around and straddled it, his weapon still aimed at Govorov.

'Now we talk very quietly. Any sudden noise and I shoot you,' he said.

'This is the second time you have me at a disadvantage,' Govorov said. 'But this time, you will die here. You will not get away again, so I will tell you. Since we last met, I have decided to cease operations in your British Channel. It is getting too busy, and the Albanians and Serbians want to compete there. They are not nice people to work with, so you can go tell your masters in London that you have won, and I am stopping.'

'Feodor, if I may call you that? That's good news for the UK, and I'm sure they will be pleased, but are you really worried about a little competition?'

'They are animals. Four of my men are in hospital; one will never walk again. Street wars are not good for any of us.'

'Feodor, now you're not telling me everything, are you? Come on, what else?'

Govorov hesitated for a few moments before saying, 'Well, in trying to act tough, your Home Secretary will be announcing plans in the next couple of weeks that anyone crossing the Channel illegally from France will be shipped off to someplace in Africa.'

The statement, although informative, left Patrick unclear. He said, 'How do you know this?'

'People tell me many things,' Govorov smirked.

After pausing and thinking for a couple of moments, Hythe said, 'So why does the Home Secretary's planned announcement affect you?'

As if explaining to a child, Govorov said, 'It means our customers crossing will insist we aren't just dropping them off on the beaches in Kent to be arrested and sent to Africa. They will want guarantees we will get them ashore safely. It will mean more effort, and I can't be bothered.'

'Why?' Patrick said.

'There are richer pickings closer to home. I plan to move operations to the Polish border – lots of women and children are starting to be displaced because of the Russian - Ukraine war. Why go hunting for fish in the middle of the ocean when they are already swimming near the beach,' he said, smiling.

Sighing, Patrick murmured, 'You're a sick fuck.'

Refusing to answer, Govorov just raised an eyebrow, still smiling.

'And you're telling me this why?'

'You have a choice, Mister Johnson. You can join me, or we will kill you. You will never leave this place alive – you must know that. But you are resilient, resourceful, and determined. I could forgive you and make use of someone with skills like yours. You could become my second in command.'

'Even after I have ruined your hand?'

'Well, I may seek some revenge, but I have suffered worse.'

'I thought your trafficking and smuggling into the UK was going well?'

'It was. Even better since Brexit. Numbers are up, profits are up, and things have become easier. The UK was meant to take control of its borders, but hardly anything is being checked. Currently, there are very few issues in the UK ports. UK customs just waive everything through. Your Prime Minister said only recently that implementation of checks will be delayed again for the fourth time, in a desperate measure to keep shelves stocked.'

'So if every day brings milk and honey, why are you changing?'

'Milk and honey? I don't understand.'

'If everything is so good and you are making lots of money, why would you consider changing?' Patrick said. 'If you move away from Turkey, you won't be able to ship terrorists into the UK, and the Iranian Government will stop paying you. I can't see Saif Khan being too happy about that, can you? Or perhaps you know him by his original American name, Steve Caan.'

Seeing the look of surprise in Govorov's eyes, Patrick continued, 'So you plan to change your business structure, eh? Hoping smuggling counterfeit Covid vaccines to third world countries will pay the bills instead?'

After a moment of silence, Govorov's voice turned a little harsher as he said, 'My, my. We have been doing our homework. I think I may have underestimated you?'

'Well, you won't be able to supply any vaccines for now, will you? 'Cus your factory in Bastuny exploded and burned down, didn't it?'

'YOU! You did this! You're a fucking maniac?' he spluttered.

'Sshhh! Keep it down, pal,' Patrick said before continuing. 'I don't want to have to kill you yet. So you think the Polish border with the refugees will save you? But let's be honest. It's the women and children you're after, isn't it? Well, the children, actually. Younger the better, eh?'

With his voice much lower both in volume and tone, Govorov answered, 'What do you mean?'

'I know you have a predilection or fondness for girls under a certain age. Maybe for boys too?'

'I don't know what you are talking about,' Govorov said uncomfortably.

Having made himself comfortable, Patrick said, 'Oh, I think you do. You're a pedophile. You run at least one group and supply kids into the UK by drugging them and hiding them in containers. And how do you know about this planned announcement from the Home Secretary? You told me before you knew there was a spy in the last lot of refugees. How?'

'How do you think? I told you before I have many friends. How do I know all these things? Simple. The British government is helping me. Not all of them, but a few. Like I said. People tell me things. What is that English saying? *It pays to have friends in high places.*'

'And the pedophile rings? Do they know about those? Do you organize these so-called *parties* for them? One was in a large country house in the New Forest a couple of months ago when an ambulance had to be called. Someone had a heart attack. Was that one you arranged?'

Govorov, looking proud and almost smirking, merely nodded before adding, 'Svetlana and I arranged it.'

'And then one of your people arranged for the ambulance workers to have an accident because they saw something they shouldn't have. They saw the kids, so they had to be kept quiet. You are both sick perverts.'

With a low voice, almost a growl, Govorov spat as he answered, 'That was Sveta, not me. I wasn't even there. You, my friend, are as good as dead.'

54

ADJUSTING his position in his chair to make himself comfier, Patrick said, 'Apart from recently, you might not recognize me, but we've met before. On the evening of Tuesday 27th September 1994 to be precise. You were known as Captain Morozov then. Do you remember? I was a lot younger. I was just ten.'

Clutching his injured hand, Govorov/Morozov remained silent, but a look of worry briefly flashed across his face as he tried to recall.

'I don't remember. I can't even remember what I had for breakfast last week, let alone some random date almost thirty years ago,' he said unconvincingly. But Patrick was looking him straight in the eyes and could see a flicker of recognition flash across with maybe a twinge of panic.

Patrick continued, 'Let me remind you. The ferry MS Estonia, carrying 989 passengers between Tallinn and Stockholm, sank in the Baltic Sea at 01:50 on the morning of Wednesday 28th. 852 people died that morning. Men, women, and children. All completely innocent. Some died of hypothermia in the sea, it was very cold and stormy, but most died trapped within the ship. They drowned, trying to escape, fighting for their lives as the ship capsized extremely quickly and sank. The official reason given for its sinking was the drastic failure of the bow doors in very heavy weather, causing the ship to take on hundreds of tons of water, quickly lose stability, and sink,' Patrick said.

'Does that jog your memory? It was all hushed up very quickly. First, it was declared that the ship would be raised as she was only in about 250 feet of water, but suddenly, after just 94 bodies were recovered from the wreckage, it was decided that would be too expensive. So instead of allowing each body to be buried with honor, the ship was entombed with thousands of tons of sand and pebbles.'

'Mmmm, I do remember vaguely. A terrible accident. I was stationed in Moscow then, but I remember something about this on the news.'

'Official records show only 137 people survived, or now it seems 138 survived,' Patrick said.

'I think you have made a mistake. I have no idea what you are referring to.'

'Is that right? Mind you, in those days, you were using your birth name of Morozov. Governments hushed up the truth, but not quickly enough or in as much detail as needed.

'There were various theories about why the door had fallen off. That Estonia had hit something floating, a container maybe, or even bumped into a Russian submarine known to be operating in that area at the time. Then, just a year later, the entire area was declared an official burial ground. So many countries wanted to hide any investigation. Didn't want the truth to come out. Too embarrassing. But you know why the bow door failed, don't you? And so do I. Because I was there and I saw you, pal, I was there.'

Pausing to move around the room and line up the forward sight from his handgun onto Govorov's chest, Patrick continued. 'I've found out since but didn't know at the time, as I was only 10 years old, that MI6 in the UK, along with the CIA, was buying equipment. Some of the latest Russian weapons and defense systems had been abandoned after the fall of the Berlin wall. The collapse had happened so quickly that Russia hadn't managed to remove them first. And the West bought loads, didn't they? All from Estonian military and government people eager for western money. All to the worry of the Kremlin. They'd warned the Estonian Government twice to stop selling what Russia considered their property, or something bad would happen, hadn't they? Back in 1993 and again in '94. But the call of western money was too great. This was the last planned shipment and included some of Russia's latest and most advanced radar systems, didn't it?'

'If you say so, Johnson, but I don't know what you are talking about,' Govorov said.

'Oh, I think you do. Russia couldn't allow this advanced technology to fall into western hands. Russia's warnings had been ignored, so you were on board to stop the ship at any cost. At the time, my father was in the British Army. Along with a team of eight, he was ordered to bring those items to the UK via Stockholm. They were all dressed in civilian clothes to make the operation less noticeable. It was even suggested those with children take them on the ferry. It was deemed perfectly safe and would add to the image. Remembering now, pal?

'My sister, Annie, and I flew with our father to Tallinn - the first time either of us kids had flown. I was just ten, and she was fourteen. My father wanted to keep us close, so we stayed down on the lower car deck with them while they looked after the eight big trucks parked at the stern carrying the gear. We played hide-and-seek amongst the cars because the ship rolling in the gale wasn't as bad down there. Do you remember now?'

Receiving a slow nod from Govorov, Patrick continued, 'I saw you creep past one of the cars carrying a rucksack. I couldn't find Annie 'cus she was hiding and then I heard her scream a few minutes later. She was in one of the side compartments, and someone was holding her down. You! I saw the tattoo on your wrist and your deformed ear. I didn't know what you were doing at the time, but your trousers were down, and her skirt was pushed up. All I knew was you were hurting her. Do you remember?'

Seeing the look in his eyes, Hythe knew he was remembering. 'I tried to stop you, and you punched me. I tried again, and you slapped me even harder. Annie screamed at me to run and get Dad, so I tried. Then there was an enormous explosion, water started pouring in, and the ship started listing to port. I couldn't get to my father because many of the vehicles had moved as the ship was listing. I shouted for help, but the noise of the cars banging about and the alarms blaring was so loud. So I ran for the stairs up to the decks, but everyone was trying to get away, and no one would listen or help. Finally, someone grabbed me and passed me to others, and the next thing I knew I was outside in the cold and rain and dropped into the freezing sea before I was pulled into a life raft. Do you remember? Do you remember what you did to my sister, you sick fuck?'

'Yeah, I'm sorry.'

'Sorry? Is that all you've got to say? Fucking sorry?'

'Yeah, I'm sorry. Sorry I didn't bend you over and fuck you as well,' he laughed.

'Listen, you piece of shit. My father survived along with four of his men, but Annie died. No one believed my story; even my father thought I'd run away from Annie to save myself. It wasn't until I was older that I realized what I'd actually seen. Years later, I tracked you from your tattoo and discovered your name as Morozov. You were listed as dead. That's what I knew you as, Morozov – Captain Morozov of the KGB before you became Major

Gorovov. But in the end, you're just a murdering kiddy fiddler, aren't you? Just a sick fuck kiddy fiddler?'

Govorov didn't even look ashamed. He used his good hand to lever himself up a little, gripping the top of the bed frame headboard. As he moved his injured hand, he groaned in pain. His groan wasn't loud, but it was enough to mask the near-silent click as he turned the wooden shape on top.

He said, 'The fusing was wrong. I set it for sixty minutes and planned on being up on deck when it exploded, but it went off prematurely after just six minutes. I was trapped down there as well.'

'What are you trying to say? My sister was just collateral damage? You're lying, you piece of shit. Maybe not about the fusing. Perhaps it was set for an hour and went off sooner, but you attacked my sister after you'd planted the bomb and before it detonated. You weren't trapped then when you attacked her - you thought you had time to rape her and get away before the bomb exploded.'

There was a slight movement of the bedsheets. Leaning forward, with his gun still pointing at Govorov's face, Patrick snatched back the sheets with his left hand. In doing so, he made the mistake of turning slightly until his back was toward the entrance doors.

Half smiling, he continued, 'You know I was going to let Europol arrest you for the trafficking and smuggling. That's what my orders are. They could have even had you for setting up the pedophile network. But you cold-bloodily murdered almost 900 people, and the courts won't be allowed to reopen that can of worms. You raped and left my sister to die and call her collateral damage. For that alone, you deserve to die. But you lie there now without a shred of regret and have even got a hard-on thinking about what you did to my sister. Now there can only be one outcome. It's just a shame I can't make you suffer more for all the pain you've given others.'

With that, Govorov tried to reach for another weapon, but his injured hand slowed him. Hythe shot him straight in the groin, before twice in the chest and then a final through his forehead, just as the door behind him received a heavy kick and flew open.

55

AS he began to turn back, he could see Svetlana standing in the doorway, dressed in a t-shirt and shorts, with an assault rifle in her hands aimed directly at him.

'Don't move.'

She took a step into the room and said, 'I thought I heard voices before he buzzed me. So you know Feodor's secret? He preferred children. Fourteen years old was about his limit. But now he's full of holes. Oh dear,' she giggled. 'How did you guess?'

'It was you, Svetlana. It got me thinking when you said you were too old for him. Then I discovered his real name of Morozov, which clinched it,' he replied while very slowly bringing his weapon around to face her.

'So what happens now?'

'I'm going to have to take you in. The UK authorities want you for murdering Adam Paisley and Adnan. The Czech Republic for killing Petr, and who knows how many others you've despatched over the years.'

'And what if I don't wa—,' she said as she opened fire on automatic just as Hythe dived sideways from where he was standing and returned fire.

Hythe had been staring into her eyes while talking. He'd seen the barely perceptible movement of her eyelids just as she pulled the trigger. It gave him a fraction of a second notice of what was coming. Already tensed, his muscles reacted instantly, and he started to dive to his right. As her rounds sprayed within the bedroom, one of them hit Hythe in his left bicep as the staccato noise of the gunfire echoed around the building. His suppressed weapon was much quieter, but his aim was better. She staggered back with an injury to her flank. Glancing down, her T-shirt was already turning scarlet on her side. On its own, it wasn't a kill shot, but she would need urgent medical attention to stop from bleeding out. Reeling back through the doorway, she dropped her rifle and began to half run, shouting as she did so as a piercing alarm started sounding throughout the compound.

<><><>

Hythe didn't think her bullet had hit bone, but he had trouble moving the fingers in his left hand. And it hurt like hell. It was also bleeding a lot. With the alarm raised, he knew he had to get out of there quickly. The six guards outside would be on the ball but had to get into the building, four of them from outside the wall through the main gateway.

The guards off duty were asleep, so they would take longer to react. Heading out into the corridor, he picked up the fallen rifle, turned the other way, and ran for the other set of stairs. He clutched his left arm to try and stem the bleeding from leaving his trail. It was a fifty-fifty chance which entrance the two inside garden guards would use to enter, front or rear. Seconds later, they crashed in through the front doorway as Hythe carefully exited the rear. He had no compunction in killing the guards if they stood in his way; however, he also wouldn't take someone's life just for the sake of it. The main gate was still closed but began to open as the four armed guards, assault rifles at the ready, ran in. They headed toward the house as the gates started closing automatically.

Reaching the side door to the garage, he dove inside, grateful he'd not relocked it earlier. Pushing it shut, he locked it before jamming the blades of the two shovels under the door's lip. It wouldn't hold for long but should give a few extra seconds if needed.

Moving the wooden beam away from the doors, he climbed into the SUV, leaned into the rear, and flicked open the caps of the jerrycans. He put the rifle on the passenger seat, grabbed a few bits of paper from the glovebox, pushed in the cigarette lighter, counted to ten, and turned the ignition key. As the engine caught, he jammed the gearstick into drive, hit the headlight switch, and floored the accelerator.

The tires spun, gripped, and the next moment, Patrick was careering toward the wooden doors faster and faster. The powerful engine accelerated the vehicle quickly, and in the few seconds it took to cover the forty feet to the doors, it was traveling at almost thirty miles an hour.

The old doors were stout. Built over a hundred years ago and reinforced with diagonal wooden cross beams, they could take quite a battering. However, against an accelerating mass of metal weighing almost three tons, they didn't stand a chance. Under the weight of the SUV, they exploded outwards, shards and pieces of wood flying everywhere.

Unfortunately for them, two guards from outside the wall were close by the doors when Patrick started the engine. Its sudden roar into life made them stop and look.

A large section of one door nearly decapitated one of them, its impact killing him immediately. The second guard was struck by the wing of the vehicle, smashing his legs, pelvis, and ribs. Unconscious from the impact, he died a few minutes later.

Another guard, quicker in his response than the others, swung his weapon up and opened fire. Over a dozen rounds struck the side of the SUV as Patrick tried to steer it toward the main gate. Both offside windows exploded under the assault, showering Patrick with glass. Grabbing the rifle, Patrick aimed single-handedly out of the smashed window and returned fire. Although none hit the guard, it caused him to dive for cover.

Holding tightly onto the steering wheel, Patrick kept his foot down hard. The heavy vehicle bucked and bounced across the courtyard and garden before Patrick straightened up the steering.

Aiming for the dead center of the gates, he wrapped his damaged arm as tightly as he could around the seatbelt hanging down, shut his eyes, and prayed.

The impact, when it came, was far heavier than he'd imagined. The front of the vehicle flattened so much it became almost unrecognizable. The windshield shattered and half fell away. The gates, however, held. Built of hardened oak and reinforced with iron bands, even the SUV couldn't destroy them. But they did come off their hinges and jam partly open. They also trapped the Mercedes totally. Dazed from the impact and the airbag deployment, it took Patrick a second or two to realize he had to move.

Grabbing the rifle from the floor where it had fallen, he grabbed the cigarette lighter from its holder and levered himself up and out through the remains of the windshield onto the vehicle's hood just as some of the other guards began firing at the car. The rear footwells were awash with spilled gasoline, so leaning back in, he pressed some of the paper against the glowing ring of the cigarette lighter. As soon as it caught, he dropped it into the cab and slid off the hood before squeezing through the gap in the broken gates.

The gasoline caught with an explosive *whumf* as Patrick stood and fired through the windshield aperture toward the buildings.

As the guards ducked and dived for cover, Patrick ran at ninety degrees from the gate along the outside of the wall. From the position of the burning car and the jammed gates, the only firing angle from within the compound was directly through the vehicle and along the access road. By moving away at an angle, he was safe.

With stealth no longer needed, he ran across the open approach and was hidden amongst the trees moments later. Stopping long enough to grab two handfuls of snow, he pressed it against his wounded arm. He then lay down in the snow, took careful aim, and waited. As expected, he saw somebody's head trying to squeeze between the burning car and the gate. Patrick waited until he could see him clearly before opening fire.

One shot straight through the forehead.

Knowing this would stop anyone else adventurous from trying for a while, at least, he began jogging as fast as he could back toward his rental car.

Thirty minutes later, he arrived back at his hidden vehicle and stripped off his jacket and shirt. As with most car rental cars, his carried a basic first-aid kit. The cold of the snow had reduced the bleeding and numbed it a little. Gently feeling around, Patrick probed his arm. Svetlana's bullet hadn't penetrated through his bicep; it merely gouged a valley through the skin and muscle. It hurt like hell, and bled a lot. It also would need stitches and likely heal with a noticeable dent from where the flesh had gone. But all in all, he thought he'd gotten off pretty lightly. Cleaning the wound with fresh snow and disinfectant helped as the cold slowed the bleeding. After applying an antiseptic salve, he bandaged the arm before cleaning his hands of blood in the snow.

Satisfied, he changed into clean clothes from his luggage.

Daylight was just breaking as he maneuvered the car back down the track and retraced his route back to Salzburg.

He disposed of the bloodied clothes and food remnants at a service station. As to the weapons, he broke them down into smaller parts, wiped them clean of fingerprints, and dropped them in multiple bins en route.

Fourteen hours after leaving Fortress Two, he picked up his X5 and found a hotel to sleep overnight. The following morning he attended a local hospital. His injury didn't match a bullet wound, so his explanation of falling into a tree while jogging was accepted. He was free to go after twelve stitches and a large tetanus shot.

56

FOUR days later, he arrived at SAS HQ, London. He'd kept a low profile since the incident at Fortress Two and had a mass of data to review. Melissa had read and translated virtually everything from Govorov's servers and Saif's hard drive. She'd then reduced it down to items relevant to what Deacon and Hythe were investigating. All the other data would take longer to analyze and would also be made available to the NSA and GCHQ.

Maj.Gen Ronaldson was waiting for him. After shaking hands, Ronaldson said, 'So much for three weeks' leave, eh? You were meant to be taking things easy before heading back to Wiltshire. Well, you've done an excellent job, Patrick, excellent. But unfortunately, as you know, your time with the SAS is now well and truly passed. Have you decided what you plan to do?'

Before Patrick could answer, the door slammed open, and a very angry Sir Rupert Wainwright stormed in.

Wainwright barreled straight up to Hythe and half-shouted in his face, 'What the fuck have you been doing?' spittle flying in all directions and tiny patches of white foam on his lips.

Staring him straight in the face, noses just inches apart, Patrick said, 'Move back or lose your teeth,' in a voice more like a growl.

Ignoring Patrick, Wainwright continued, 'You were expressly instructed not to injure Major Gorovov or even arrest him. You disobeyed orders and murdered him in cold blood. You're a loose cannon. You'll hang for this.'

Not moving an inch, Patrick shouted straight into Wainwright's face, 'I said move back or lose your fucking teeth.'

This time it worked. Unused to being disobeyed or ignored, Wainwright suddenly realized he was pushing it too far. He continued, moving back over a foot, 'He wasn't even armed when you shot him down like a dog. For that, you have to answer for your decisions, Hythe. You will be dishonorably discharged from Her Majesty's Service, extradited to Slovakia, and charged there for the premeditated murder of Feodor Govorov,' he said, his voice lowering to a more acceptable level.

Patrick smiled and said, 'Excellent. I want my day in court. First, here is the remainder of the information I gleaned working on this case. The people smuggling is only the tip of the iceberg. There is enough information and target names for Europol and Interpol, working with various countries' police forces to close the smuggling and trafficking rings completely,' he said, passing a folder of paperwork over. 'Secondly, this company in Belarus was blatantly manufacturing counterfeit Covid vaccines and selling them to third-world countries. Govorov was involved in distribution. He was only a small fish in a big pond, but there will be many others. Either the FDA or the European Medicines Agency needs to get this company closed down immediately. Third, here is a list of pedophile rings in Europe, with the largest one in the UK. You have two weeks to address all of this and make it public; otherwise, I go to the media.'

Wainwright's eyebrows raised so high Patrick thought they'd disappear into his hairline. 'Why the fuck do you think they would believe you, a disgraced murderer?' he sneered.

'When I release the names and addresses of all the sick bastards who are members of these rings, they will. Here look at some of the names … .'

With that, Hythe showed a portion of the list. 'Here are some of the UK's top business people … bastions of society, I think they're called … and some sports people ... Oh, and some well-known tv people. Look at least a dozen current politicians, some well-known ex-ones, and quite a few civil servants. Oh, and here's your colleague, Lockwood. He was the bastard informing on me to Govorov. He was also at a party recently in the New Forest. He arranged for an accident to happen to the ambulance responders. I thought first it had been Svetlana, she's certainly malicious enough, but no, it was him who ordered it. One responder died, and my godson, the second responder, was injured. I want the bastard arrested today. Finally, look at this name,' he said, pointing.

Both Wainwright and Ronaldson saw the name Hythe was indicating. It was Ronaldson who muttered, 'My god, even royalt—'

'ENOUGH,' shouted Wainwright, looking pale. 'Stay here,' as he went out of the room to make a phone call. Thirty minutes later, looking red-faced and extremely flushed, Wainwright came back into the room.

Coughing slightly to clear his throat, he said to Ronaldson, 'I have taken advice on this. Major Patrick Hythe will receive a full honorable discharge with an associated pension. No further action or arrest against him over this matter will continue on the proviso he doesn't publish the lists of names in part or full.'

After receiving Hythe's verbal assurances, Wainwright phoned Whitehall to speak with the Attorney General for the second time in as many minutes while waiting for the pre-signed written confirmation paperwork to be emailed over. He finally received the email and printed two copies, muttering under his breath that exposing some of those names would make the UK Government collapse.

Patrick read the wording carefully, but happy with it, both he and Wainwright signed, with Maj.Gen Ronaldson signing as a witness.

'You realize you have the tiger by the tail with your threats?' Wainwright said.

As a final parting shot, Patrick looked Wainwright straight in the eye and said, 'I mean what I said about the two weeks to publicly close down the pedo clubs and inform the WHO, the FDA, and the European Medicines Agency as to the contents of the vials. I couldn't imagine any of the countries spending millions on vaccines will be very happy with our government if you delay. As to your comment about tiger by the tail, let me say one last thing you should be aware of. All of this paperwork, including all the names of every member, will be released electronically to multiple media outlets if anything strange should happen to me or I should suddenly die unexpectedly.'

With that, he shook hands with Ronaldson and walked out.

<><><>

Three days later, Patrick was sitting in Business Class on BA 217 bound for Washington. There he would meet Gina, and they would head off to St Lucia for a week or two.

He had choices to make. The day before, he'd been sitting in a Starbucks on Oxford Street drinking an Americano black coffee, trying to decide what to do next. Army life had played such a major part in his day-to-day activities since he was barely seventeen. He wasn't quite sure what to do next.

He'd just taken a second mouthful when his cell phone rang. As he'd answered it, he'd heard Deacon's voice. 'Hiya pal. Gina told me what's happened to you. How are you? Let's get together for a beer or two when you land. I've got a question. I've been waiting to get confirmation back from my lawyers and accountant, but Phylax is doing really well over there in Europe. I'm planning on opening a Phylax UK office there in London. Do you want to head it?'

Decisions, decisions. But for now, he could sit back and relax for the next eight hours.

Reclining his seat, he picked up the first of the journals, opened the cover, and read:

"Diary of the Jedburgh Giants. Diary Number One of Sergeant Thomas Jenkins, 1946.

In September 1943, I was with the 3rd Royal Tank Regiment, which was part of the 7th Armoured Division. after serving in North Africa and El Alamein..."

Epilogue

THREE days after Patrick Hythe walked out of Ronaldson's office, the media was informed six agents of the Security Service (MI5), working in conjunction with the UK's Office for Security and Counter-Terrorism and with police officers from the National Counter Terrorism Security Office (NaCTSO) shot dead a suspected terrorist. He'd taken four members of the public hostage at a coffee shop in Regent's St.

<><><>

Two days prior, Maj.Gen Ronaldson had received a detailed voice message from Major Patrick Hythe. When played, it said, *'One other name for you to investigate is a Mr. Green. That is his cover name. Born in Iraq, his full name was Wissam Abed Hamoodi, but he's anglicized it to William Hammond. He is the main UK contact for terrorists entering the UK, either Al-Qaeda, Islamic State, or any others. He was the main organizer of the VX agent attacks on the UK four years ago. Using Saif's email address I've fooled him and arranged a meeting with him Monday at 14:00 at Coffee World on Regent's Street. He thinks he will be meeting a new recruit sent directly from Saif in Iran. He will be carrying this month's edition of Time magazine in his left hand.'*

Fact File

The UK government classifies people crossing the English Chanel from in and around Calais to beaches in Kent in small boats as illegal immigrants. The numbers crossing each year have been rising consistently. Successive UK politicians and Home Secretaries have committed to reducing and curbing these figures; however, they have systematically failed to do so. Government figures show 299 in 2018, 1,843 in 2019, 8,466 in 2020, and 28,526 in 2021. It is expected the figure for 2022 could be as high as 60,000. 75% of all arrivals are single males of fighting age, aged 18 to 39, many from Syria and Afghanistan, both war-torn countries.

<><><>

Operation Jedburgh was a clandestine operation during World War II in which three-man teams of operatives were dropped by parachute into occupied France, the Netherlands, and Belgium. The objectives of the Jedburgh teams were to assist allied forces who invaded France on 6 June 1944 with sabotage and guerrilla warfare by leading local resistance forces in actions against the Germans.

<><><>

The MS Estonia ferry sank on Wednesday, 28 September 1994, between about 00:50 and 01:50 as the ship was crossing the Baltic Sea en route from Tallinn, Estonia, to Stockholm, Sweden. The sinking was one of the worst maritime disasters of the 20th century, with the loss of 852 lives.

A 1997 investigation found that the ship's bow door locks had failed in a storm, but new underwater footage appears to show a previously unrecorded four-meter (13ft) hole in the ship's hull.
Conspiracy theories exist about the cause of the sinking, including a collision with a submarine and an explosion inside the ship. Laboratory tests on debris recovered illegally from Estonia's bow yielded trace evidence of a deliberate explosion, which they allege was concealed by the Swedish, British, and Russian governments to cover up an intelligence operation smuggling military hardware via the civilian ferry.

The incident was hushed up very quickly. After declaring that the ship would be raised as she was only in about 250 feet of water, suddenly, after just 94 bodies were recovered from the wreckage, it was claimed any further removal of bodies would be too expensive. So instead of allowing each body to be buried with honor, the ship was entombed with thousands of tons of sand and pebbles.

Then, a year after the sinking, a treaty called the Estonia Agreement 1995 between Estonia, Sweden, Finland, Latvia, Poland, Denmark, Russia, and the United Kingdom was signed, prohibiting all citizens from even approaching the wreck, declaring it an official burial ground – highly unusual for an accident unless the vessel was carrying dangerous or highly sensitive material.

About the Author

I am the author of the John Deacon and Patrick Hythe series of action thriller novels. I make my online home at www.mikeboshier.com. You can connect with me on Twitter at Twitter, on Facebook at Facebook and you can send me an email at mike@mikeboshier.com if the mood strikes you.

I love hearing from my readers so please drop me an email. I try to reply to every one.

If you liked reading this book, please leave feedback.

www.mikeboshier.com

Books & Further Details

High Seas Hijack - Short Story

Follow newly promoted US Navy SEAL John Deacon as he leads his team on preventing pirates attacking and seizing ships in and around the Horn of Africa in 2010. When a tanker carrying explosive gases is hijacked even Deacon and his team are pushed to the limit.

The Jaws of Revenge

The fate of America lies in the hands of one team of US SEALs. The US mainland is under threat as never before. Osama bin Laden is dead, and the world can relax. Or can they? Remaining leaders of Al-Qaeda want revenge, and they want it against the USA. When good fortune smiles on them and the opportunity presents itself to use stolen weapons of mass destruction, it's Game On!

Al-Qaeda leaders devise a plan so audacious if it succeeds it will destroy the USA for good. With help from Iran and from a US Navy traitor, it can't fail.

One team of US SEALs stand in their way. One team of US SEALs can save America and the West. However, time is running out. **Will they be too late?**

Terror of the Innocent

As the Iraqi Forces build up for the liberation of Mosul, ISIS wants revenge.

The UK and USA are in their sights ...
In a daring rescue mission to release aid workers held hostage by ISIS, US Navy SEAL John Deacon stumbles across an ISIS revenge plot using deadly weapons stolen from Saddam's regime.
Masterminded by Deacon's old adversary, Saif the Palestinian, and too late to save the UK, Deacon and the world can only watch in horror as thousands suffer a terrible fate.
Determined to stop the same outcome in the US, it's a race against time.
Using all the resources he can muster including his friends in the Pentagon, Deacon must find and stop Saif before the lives of hundreds of thousands of Americans are ruined forever.

Crossing a Line

Once a respected US Navy SEAL, now shunned by friends and colleagues and wanted by the police, John Deacon has gone rogue ...
Recruited by a fanatical religious cult intent on returning the USA to the ways of God, and headed by a man known as The General, Deacon's weapons skills and combat knowledge are put to treacherous use ...
Deacon has crossed a line ... But has he gone too far? Can he ever cross back?

The Price of Deceit

In a world violated by terror, the once black and white terms of engagement have become gray.
One man is determined to stop World War Three.

Now a civilian, to the public ex-US Navy SEAL John Deacon is a businessman running his own security company offering personal protection to VIPs and dignitaries.
Only a few very senior people under the President know the truth ...
Funded with 'black' money from secret funds, Deacon is the guy the President calls on when certain dilemmas or complications need resolving. Dilemmas and complications the President can later deny.
From helping rescue hostages taken by Boko Haram to the delicate discussions with a would-be defector - the daughter of a senior Chinese official - Deacon handles it all.
But when an enemy submarine starts attacking shipping and China plans to impose passage taxes in the South China Sea, and the US and China move closer and closer to all-out war, Deacon takes on his biggest and most dangerous mission yet.
Deep behind enemy lines and with the odds stacked heavily against him, capture will mean certain death.
Success or failure is a mere hairsbreadth apart ...

RED ICE

Bright lights over the Arctic.
A mysterious new super-weapon.
The inexplicable disappearance of an international Arctic weather monitoring station, along with its staff.
Is there a connection?
Russia has developed a secret new weapon able to shoot down missiles, aircraft, and satellites, making the USA's and the West's entire defense strategy redundant overnight.
With relationships already at breaking point, the U.S. cannot be seen to respond militarily.

The President's hands are tied.
With nowhere else to turn, he calls on the one person he can trust to get the job done.
John Deacon answers the President's call and rises to the challenge. This time, he takes along an old friend.
From the heat and humidity of South America to the icy wilderness of the Arctic Plains, from Washington to Moscow, and beyond . . .
As always, Deacon will go to whatever lengths necessary to keep the world safe.
But with a target on his head, and the Grim Reaper nipping at his heels, how much longer can Deacon's luck hold out?

The Project

The daughter of a close friend dies after taking an ecstasy tablet laced with carfentanil ...
A friend and head of the US Drug Enforcement Agency is kidnapped on a trip to Mexico ...
When asked to help in both situations, Deacon cannot say no.
His mission takes him from New York's backstreets to the forests of Mexico and on to deepest, darkest Africa.
With a price on his head, Deacon is determined to avenge his friends and make a difference ...

Check out my web page http://www.mikeboshier.com for details of latest books, offers and free stuff.

VIP Reader's Mailing List

To join our VIP Readers Mailing List and receive updates about new books and freebies, please go to my web page and join my mailing list.

www.mikeboshier.com

I value your trust. Your email address will stay safe and you will never receive spam from me. You can unsubscribe at any time.
Thank you.

Printed in Great Britain
by Amazon

21355437R00171